SKYMASTER

ISBN: 978-1-83557-008-1

Cover Art: Aleksandar Sortirovski

Cover Design: Fringe Element

Editor: KB Spangler

for Henry

SKYMASTER

THE GUILDMASTER SAGA

BOOK III

C.E. MURPHY

a miz kit production

The thick-frozen harbor had kept the *Wafiya* locked in place for days. A pool of dark water surrounded the ship itself, thanks to the crew's efforts, but the ice formed and thickened only a few feet away. Water witchery barely worked on ice, so until it thawed, the sea witches were stuck in a frozen northern harbor.

Rasim had come to the parapets above the harbor every day to stare down at the water and wonder how they were going to escape the North before spring. They had to; something dangerous was building, threatening both his southerly home city of Ilyara and the northern town of Hongrunn, where they were currently trapped. Rasim felt certain the threat was actually even bigger than that, reaching across the whole continent, but the adults around him thought he was being dramatic.

They thought he was being dramatic a lot of the time, and the fact that he kept being right didn't seem to make much difference. If he was lucky, someone would listen soon, and they could deal with the spreading threat, but Rasim was increasingly sure that he would end up being that someone. Again.

"Could you thaw it?"

Rasim startled as Kisia, taller and browner than he, stepped out of a palace door. She picked her way across the slippery stone floor to lean against the parapet beside him, her hands dangled over its edge as she peered down. "Well, could you?"

"Guildmaster Isidri barely survived thawing a *half* frozen harbor, and she knew what she was doing."

"You're ninety years younger than Isidri."

"And I don't know what I'm doing." Rasim extended a hand toward the thick ice, like he could feel its weight and texture from the distance. He couldn't, though he *could* feel the dark, patient water beneath. It slopped against the harbor walls, shifting the ice a few feet this way or that. Its edges broke into ragged shards where it stuck to the sheer mountain walls that plummeted straight into the water.

A month ago, he wouldn't have felt that, not from this high up. A month ago, Rasim had been the least of their guild. He'd been given a position on the Ilyaran flagship, the *Wafiya* because he thought quickly and spoke faster, rather than thanks to any special gift of magic. But two weeks ago, he and Kisia had been thrown into the open ocean, and Siliaria, the sea goddess herself, had saved them and granted Rasim the power he'd always dreamed of. Or at least, that's what Rasim thought. Kisia believed the goddess had only *acknowledged* his power. She thought it had been there all along, and that Siliaria's kiss had just given Rasim the confidence he'd lacked.

Rasim doubted that, but arguing with Kisia never got him anywhere. Besides, whether she was right or he was, after Siliaria had kissed him, the goddess had named Rasim 'Seamaster', the title of greatest power that his guild had. Now he felt the ocean's pull as strongly as any of his guild. Maybe more strongly.

But not enough to thaw ice. The old guildmaster, Isidri, really was at least ninety years older than Rasim, and she was the only Seamaster who could make or thaw ice at will. Ice was *made* of water, but it *wasn't* water, and Ilyaran magic was pure and simple stuff. Sea, sky, sun and stone: those were the elements they could wield. Even Milu, a powerful Stonemaster journeyman, couldn't work the dirt, though stone and dirt didn't seem that different to Rasim's water-witch mind.

"I've tried," Rasim admitted morosely. "But I can't make it respond, and I don't know..."

"You don't know if it's you, or the ice, or Northern witches hiding somewhere and keeping it in place." Kisia lifted her chin and gave the whole of the Northern city a fierce look, as if the blocky grey buildings, rising out of the mountains like rough-hewn cliffs, would spill their secrets if she glared hard enough.

Rasim hid a grin. If anybody could glare secrets out of a city, it was Kisia. She had already broken with all tradition by leaving the merchant's life she'd been born to and joining the Seamasters' Guild at age fourteen.

She'd risen to the rank of journeyman almost overnight, even though everybody thought only very young children could be taught witchery at all. Then she had left their hot delta homeland with Rasim, and was now thousands of miles from home in the frozen north, wearing a heavy coat and a furry hat that settled over her ears. If she thought she could scare Hongrunn's secrets out of it, Rasim believed her. Still hiding his smile, he leaned forward to study the icy water and the sole Ilyaran ship bobbing in it. "I never felt any witchery being worked to freeze the harbor, though, never mind keep it frozen."

Kisia snapped her attention back to Rasim. "First off, there's no reason to think Northern magic feels like ours. Second, none of us really even looked at the harbor until after we'd finished with the lake and—" Her ferocity faded, and a stab of pain shot through Rasim's chest.

"And the memorials," he finished quietly. The *Wafiya* had come north to cleanse Hongrunn's salt-poisoned water supply. They'd succeeded, but at great cost. Almost twenty of their crew and a handful of others had died when fixing the water supply set off an explosive trap. By the time they'd mourned, the harbor had frozen solid.

"Right." Kisia straightened her shoulders. "So we were really busy and using a lot of magic ourselves that week. If someone did use witchery to freeze it, it's no surprise we didn't feel the magic being worked. And once it's in place..." She shrugged. "It's ice. We can't do much with it. Now come on." She pushed off the parapet. "You've been up here brooding all week, when you promised we'd explore the whole city. Let's go."

"I haven't been brooding *all* week," Rasim replied, stung. "A lot of the time I've been arguing with Inga."

Kisia's laugh bounced bright and sharp off the cold grey walls. Snow slid over a pointed roof and scattered on them as if loosened by the sound of her voice. Rasim, mildly offended, brushed himself clean and stared at Kisia.

"Oh, come on. 'I haven't been brooding, I've been arguing with a princess!'" Snow piled on her hat's upper brim and threatened to fall into her face. Rasim pressed his lips together and watched, wide-eyed, without warning her. Kisia thought he was making fun of her and stomped her foot. The snow cascaded down her face. Rasim laughed too, just as loudly as she had.

Howling with outrage, Kisia snatched up a handful of snow and flung it at him. Rasim ducked, still laughing, and for a few moments they were embroiled in a fight, pelting handsful of snow at one another as they slid precariously across the ice-slick roof. Finally, Kisia's feet went out from under her and she landed in a drift, pink-cheeked with laughter and waving for mercy. "But it *was* funny," she informed Rasim as he flung himself into the snow beside her.

"So was the snow falling all over you. And I *have* been arguing with her. She says neither she nor Queen Janna has the power to forbid the other nobles to keep generational debt-slaves. I don't understand how she can think that way. Janna is the ruler of the whole Northlands, right? So if she allows her subjects to run debt slaves for generations, it's no wonder the continental slavers come here for fresh stock."

"They don't come to Ilyara."

"They don't dare." Rasim got up and offered Kisia a hand, pulling her to her feet. "Not as long as we have magic and they don't. Ilyaran witchery is why we don't *have* slaves."

"So that makes us what, better?" A boy's voice broke between its youthful soprano and its oncoming adult baritone as Desimi came through the door behind them. "You two knocked half the snow off the roofs with all that shrieking."

"And you couldn't stand the idea of us having fun without you." Kisia scooped up another handful of snow and threw it at Desimi, who knocked it away easily. Although only thirteen like Rasim, Desimi was already as big as some men, and had always commanded an impressive talent for sea witchery. He had a foul temper to go along with his size, too, and had taken it out on Rasim, until Rasim's misadventures had dragged Desimi to their king's attention. Desimi had rightfully won royal approval for his heroic efforts in keeping King Taishm safe, and the boys had since come to a bickering peace. Rasim thought the bickering was part of what kept the peace.

As long as it didn't involve him getting kicked or punched, Rasim was happy to argue. He was good at that, but he'd always been small, and better at running away than fighting. He threw a lazy handful of snow at Desimi, too. "I guess it makes us…luckier, or more privileged or something. I guess I don't know if we'd be any better if we didn't have magic to use instead of slaves, but we do, and even if we didn't, slavery is awful. Having your life depend on doing what other people tell you to do isn't right. Being unable to make choices of your own all the time isn't right. Being afraid that if the crops die or you lose your flock you'll end up in chains is wrong. People can't live that way."

Desimi shrugged. "People live that way all the time."

"And look at what being afraid and angry did to Missio," Rasim said unhappily. Missio was another sea witch, a handful of years older than Rasim. She'd despised him for being half-Northern, and had tried killing him before disappearing into Hongrunn. "No one should have to live that way. And I don't understand why Inga can't *see* that. Maybe it's because she's never even been threatened by it—"

"You were a slave for about five days, Rasim," Desimi said. "It's not like you know very much about it yourself."

Rasim's stomach clenched. "I know that the first thing I heard when I was separated from the fleet was *'How much is he worth,'* and it scared me. I never had to think about slaves before, because I'm lucky to be Ilyaran—"

"And the princess is lucky, too. She doesn't have to think about it either, and she doesn't want you to make her think about it. Know what's worse than being nagged to death about something like that?"

Rasim cast a look at Kisia, who pulled her mouth into an admission of ignorance. When they both looked back at Desimi, a triumphant light gleamed in his eyes. "What's worse is knowing somebody's right and having them *stop* nagging you about it. It gets under your skin and it bothers you until you have to do something. So shut up about it for a while, Sunburn, and your princess will come around with the tide."

"She's not my princess."

"No," Kisia said under her breath, grinning. "She's Hassin's princess, and I just can't wait to see if they choose the sea or the throne."

For a few seconds both boys stopped to gawk at Kisia, whose eyebrows rose. "What?"

"Hassin's going to captain the *Wafiya* someday," Rasim said. "He can't—he couldn't—he wouldn't!"

"Give it up for a throne? Why not? Would you expect a princess to give her throne up for a common sailor?"

"Well, no, but—"

"She's joking," Desimi growled. "Hassin would never give up the sea." Even he sounded like his ship had hit a sudden trough and dropped his stomach through his feet.

"People do all kinds of strange things for the people they love," Kisia said. "What about that Islands girl of yours, Rasim?"

"What? Who? Adele?" Heat scored Rasim's cheeks, scalding against the cold winter air. "She's not mine any more than Inga is. And besides, I hardly know her. And..." She was very pretty, he had to admit that. But so was Kisia, or Sesin, the journeyman who had just begun studying healing with Seamaster Usia. Still hot-faced, Rasim struggled for a change of topic, and remembered what had started the conversation. "You really think if I leave Inga alone about slavery she'll start to think about it my way?"

Desimi, sourly, said, "Trust me. I should know."

"How—oh." The answer presented itself just fast enough to save Desimi having to respond. As it was, he scowled and stomped to look over the roof's edge at the *Wafiya* while Rasim rearranged his thoughts. He'd argued with Desimi a lot over the years. It had never occurred to him that he'd ever changed Desimi's mind, much less by letting him sit and think on a topic for a while. He knew Desimi wasn't dumb. The bigger boy just didn't think as fast as Rasim did. But then, mostly, neither did anybody else. It had been Rasim's only advantage, growing up small and not very magical in a guild full of witches, but it had landed him in hot water as often as it got him out.

"Where did you sneak in?" Desimi leaned over the edge, searching the shoreline. "The first time you came to Hongrunn, you snuck in through the sewers. Where'd you come in?"

"Um." Rasim joined the other two at the parapet, wishing Kisia wouldn't lean *quite* so far over it. After a moment he located the divot of land where the underwater spillage tunnel was carved, and pointed. "Down there, between the streets—the house with the yellow wood door, do you see it? Just under there. Why?"

Desimi shifted his shoulders slyly, and Rasim snorted. "You want to see if you can get through it more easily than I did? Of course you can. You've got a lot more magic than I do. Did. But if you're going to try, somebody should go warn Gontor that there's going to be a big splash in there when you blow the drop-hole cover off."

A slow grin started over Desimi's face. "Let's see who can get there first. Me through the tunnels or you through the palace."

"You have to start by *getting* to the tunn—Desimi! Desimi, no, what are you—you can't just jump in, the harbor's frozen over!"

"Not right next to the *Wafiya*, it's not." Desimi was already halfway up the parapets. He grinned down at Rasim and began shedding his winter clothes.

Kisia curled her fingers against her mouth, her eyes wild and laughing above them. "Desimi, it's only a few feet around the ship. What if you miss? You'll be killed. Or broken to bits and the healers will kill you!"

Desimi moved forward until his toes were at the parapet's edge and extended his hands. "I can't thaw it, but I can break up the thin stuff around the ship."

The weight of sea witchery pounded the air as water slopped, then burst, upward, shattering ice around the ship below them. The *Wafiya* rocked dramatically, sending its skeleton crew to the railings. Their shouts rose toward Desimi as Kisia shrieked and scrambled up on the parapet with him. "Can you do that for the whole harbor?"

"Nah. It gets too thick away from shore. Coming with me?" Desimi's grin lit even brighter as Rasim saw the thrill of challenge awaken in Kisia's eyes.

"Kees—you can't—you'll—it's—you can't!"

"Of course I can." Kisia wiggled out of her own

winter coat and boots, then, shivering and grinning hugely, pointed at Desimi. "You better keep me dry when we hit the water. I don't know if I can do it myself, and I don't want to freeze before we hit the tunnels!"

"You two—you can't—you—oh, you did." Rasim clapped his hands over his face, then leaned forward to peer through his fingers as Kisia and Desimi, howling with glee, plummeted toward the icy harbor.

CHAPTER TWO

A hole opened in the water before they hit. It closed again instantly, trapping air and two hysterically laughing journeymen beneath the water's surface. The *Wafiya*'s crew pressed against the ship's railing, looking back and forth from the lone journeyman on the parapets to the ones who had disappeared under the harbor ice.

Rasim stayed where he was for a few seconds, hardly able to believe they'd jumped. Then he shoved away from the cold stone and ran for the door, through the halls, and toward a distant room under constant guard. As far as Rasim could tell, the city's sewer tunnels all led either straight to the guarded room or to the harbor, which made them useless for sneaking into the city. He'd found that out the hard way months ago. The memory gave him a breathless little grin as he pelted through corridors. Gontor, the giant of a man who had stood guard over the sewer entrance when Rasim tried to sneak through it, was bigger than

Desimi would ever dream of being. He'd happily drag Kisia and Desimi to the throne room as troublemakers if Rasim didn't get there to warn him first.

Rasim almost tripped over his own feet at the thought. Their appearance would give Gontor a start, but the idea of Desimi getting dragged into the throne room was delightful. Catching his breath, he found another of the palace guards and spoke carefully in his limited Northern. "Could you have a message sent to Gontor that he's about to have visitors, and he should treat them like he treated me? Rasim?"

The guard, amused, cuffed Rasim's shoulder. "I know who you are, Ilyaran. We all do." She unsheathed a dagger from her hip and banged the hilt against the wall in a quick rhythm.

Rasim tipped his head, curious, then looked down the hall in surprise as people fell silent in response to the tapping. The guard banged her dagger several more times, and someone farther down the hall picked up the pattern and repeated it. The normal noises of palace life began to filter back in around them as the guard put her dagger away again. "Quicker than runners," she said to Rasim's questioning look. "That first pattern meant *quiet and listen.* Everybody knows that and the last one, which is *message ends.* The rest gets passed through the palace, even the whole citadel if we need, within a few minutes. Gontor will be waiting for your friends."

"That's brilliant! I saw something like that used in the mines. Can you show me some?"

The amused guard smacked her fist against her

palm in a simple pattern. "That's *message begins*', and the end code is just the opposite. The two most important phrases are friend and enemy, and then words like earth or sea, high, low, and swords, arrows, catapults...." She beat out the patterns for each word as she spoke.

Rasim repeated them, trying to commit them to memory as he nodded in understanding. "We use similar signals with torches or mirrors on the sea, so we can communicate with distant ships. I never thought of using it on shore."

"I bet your Stonemaster friends have." The guard smacked a handful of signals against her palm, then lifted her eyebrows. "That's what I sent to Gontor. What did I say?"

"Friends below," Rasim said promptly, but shook his head. "I don't know the other words. What are they?"

The guard broke into a grin as she repeated the gestures. "That means *scare them*."

Rasim laughed. "Perfect. Thank you. What's your name?"

"Elmra."

"I'll come back and learn more, if you'll teach me, Elmra."

"I would like that, Ilyaran." The guard thumped her shoulder in the Northern salute as Rasim, still chortling with delight, ran off toward the throne room to await Desimi and Kisia's ignominious arrival.

The door itself was barred, suggesting an important council meeting going on within. Rasim sagged in fleeting disappointment, then recovered. Gontor would give them a good scare even if they didn't get dragged into the throne room and cast at Inga's feet.

A thin man appeared down the corridor, hands folded behind his back and shoulders hunched in the uncomfortable pose of worry. He never looked up from his feet as he paced toward Rasim, then turned to shuffle back down the hall. Rasim cleared his throat. "Lars?"

The former debt slave startled and looked around. His beard and hair had been trimmed since he'd come to Hongrunn, but he still had the pale, scarred look of a man only half able to believe in his own freedom. He and a number of others had pledged themselves in Rasim's service, but Rasim hoped they were having second thoughts now that they were coming to grips with being free "Lars, what's going on? What are you doing here? You look awful."

"They're in there deciding what to do about the debt slaves." Lars spoke in a low, tense tone. "About my friends, and about everybody else who has been indentured."

Rasim closed his mouth fast enough to make a popping sound and glanced sharply toward the doors. "Really?"

A smile twisted the corner of Lars's mouth. "It seems we've had an excellent advocate. And your efforts haven't hurt. Thank you, Rasim."

The pride swelling in Rasim's chest deflated. "Oh. Who else has been talking to Inga?"

The doors flew open as he asked and a blast of warmth rolled from the council room. A harried-looking courtier came out with the heat and stopped dead on seeing Rasim. Without a word, she seized Rasim and Lars both by the collars and hauled them inside the council room, thrusting them forward as if they were barriers ensuring her own safety.

Sunmaster Endat, an Ilyaran diplomat, was on his feet beneath the room's extraordinary murals, speaking passionately to a large gathering of nobles. He stopped as Lars and Rasim were shooed forward, and Inga, the tall, pale-haired crown princess of the Northlands, turned her attention to the newcomers. "Rasim. There you are. We wanted you earlier, to speak to the council. Where have you been?"

Guilt surged in Rasim. "Playing on the roof with Kisia and Desimi."

Inga smiled sympathetically. "I forget you're only a boy who never meant to tangle with diplomats and politics. It doesn't matter. You should know it has been fully agreed that unless we discover direct evidence that the slaves you freed were part of the conspiracy against Hongrunn and Ilyara, they are free to go."

Rasim let out a shout of joy before remembering he was in a council of noble and important people. Inga smiled at his outburst, though, and turned that same, gentle smile on Lars. "I'm sorry for what you've suffered. We have not yet determined how to offer reparations, but please know that it's a topic we're discussing."

Lars, stunned into silence, only nodded as Sunmaster Endat picked up the speech they'd inter-rupted. "We've been asking ourselves who could have studied and taught witchery underneath the noses of Northern leadership, but I believe we've been looking in the wrong places, your highness. I believe these new Northern witches have chosen only the most desperate as students. There's no visible conspiracy within your great cities because they have gone to the outliers, to the mines and wretched sea communities, to instigate rebellion from there."

Shock settled in Rasim's belly. He shot a look at Lars, whose expression was hang-dog guilty. "You knew about this?" Rasim hissed. "Did Northern debt slaves offer to study magic with someone?"

"All I heard was rumors," Lars whispered unhappily. "That other mines or trawler ships had been cleared out by slavers promising freedom to those who could learn Ilyaran magic. I didn't believe it was true, and then when I heard what had happened to your city I..." He faltered. "I was afraid if I told you what I suspected, you'd..."

"What, stop being your friend? Tell Inga to send you back to the mines? I wouldn't do that, Lars."

"I know that now." Lars was in his thirties, but his heartbroken expression made him seem half that age. He had, Rasim reminded himself, spent most of his life in captivity. He had been able to take command in the mines when their freedom was on the line, but outside, with that freedom perhaps threatened again, Rasim couldn't quite blame him for keeping quiet.

He put a hand on Lars's shoulder. "It's all right. I understand."

"Your highness, I don't know *what* these witches

are." Endat's voice broke over their quiet conversation, leaving Rasim trying to catch up with what the nobility had been discussing. "They froze our harbor, which our sea witches could not do. They set a trap beneath your lake, which is not a skill our Stonemasters have—"

"That's not necessarily true."

Dozens of pairs of eyes turned toward Rasim, who sighed. Someday he would learn not to let his thoughts leap instantly to his lips. "Before she died, Stonemaster Lusa said she didn't know how it had been done, not that she couldn't do it. And I know Milu has been trying to replicate it. He says the tricky thing is that there are so many kinds of rock in place, and some metal. Journeyman Milu is very good," Rasim explained to Inga, "but even he has a difficult time working with metal. It's like ice to sea witches. Almost but not exactly something we can work with. The point is, a Stonemaster might be able to do it, or at least think of it, and if the Northern witches have...have a...a middle magic, something that falls between ours and..."

He fell silent a moment, trying to imagine what could be opposite of the elements Ilyaran witches worked with. "A long time ago Northerners had magic too, right? What *kinds* of magic?"

Inga looked to at a woman old enough to rival Guildmaster Isidri's years, but considerably more sour-faced and angry. "Rekka?"

The old woman's pinched face tightened further. "My grandmother's grandmother's stories were of masters of ice and metal. The crown your own mother wears is said to have been shaped, not forged, Inga. The rest of their magic was the stuff of living things. Crops and beasts, to keep them through the hard winters. That's what my grandmother's grandmother said, anyway."

"Ice and metal are practical for the hard winters, too," Rasim said into the thoughtful silence that followed. "Witches who could shape and shift the snow and ice makes sense for survival in the Northlands. And metal to shape weapons for raids on warmer, easier cities."

Endat, fascinated, said, "Are you suggesting our own magics are shaped by our place in the world, Rasim?"

Rasim shrugged "We live on a delta in the desert, Sunmaster. Your guild mitigates the heat. Mine works the sea, where we get more than half our food. The Stonemasters *built* Ilyara with their magic. And the Skymasters protect us from the sandstorms in a way nobody else could. Doesn't it make sense that our magic is born from what we need?"

Endat's expression made Rasim sigh. "I guess nobody's ever thought about it that way before."

"Perhaps they have," Endat replied, almost gently. "But not for a long time, Rasim. Not since before the Sunmasters came to power within the Ilyaran palace."

Rasim shot a look toward Rekka, whose grumpy eyebrows rose in question. "It's just that the Sunmasters have been in power in Ilyara for a hundred years or so," Rasim said. "I just wondered how far back your grandmother's grandmother's memories stretched."

To his surprise, a thin smile pulled at the old woman's mouth. "Older than your Sunmasters' reign, boy. The women in my family live on and on. Closer to three hundred years than not."

Even Inga exhaled softly at that. "Witchery in the north is the stuff of long-ago stories, but perhaps those who put more stock in stories than I did have made an effort to rediscover it. But, Master Endat, your people do not rely on slavery. How, then, has treachery slipped inside Ilyara's walls?"

Rasim blurted, "Resentment. Like Captain Nasira. She left the Guild to have a family, and when we leave we're supposed to forswear our magic. Imagine—" A shuffle occurred down the table and Rasim's face turned molten as Captain Nasira leaned forward far enough for him to finally see her. Wishing he could disappear, Rasim mumbled, "Imagine you left, but didn't want to give up witchery, or that you'd been raised in the guilds but never really wanted that life. If you managed to escape—"

"*Escape*? Are the guilds so like indentured slavery, then?" Inga demanded.

Rasim sighed. "Not exactly. I know Des—I know some people chafe at the idea of it being the only choice they have. But it's not like the guildmasters would talk about it much if people slipped away, is it? So if there are witches who snuck off, they might want to break down the system that they escaped from."

Master Endat's face fell into neutral lines as he studied Rasim, then spoke to the room at large. "It's true, of course, that sometimes guild members disappear or are thought to have died when they perhaps haven't. Rasim, you have a devious mind."

It didn't sound like a compliment. Just the opposite, in fact. It sounded as if Rasim was causing trouble just by thinking, which wasn't quite fair. He couldn't help thinking.

"All of this is precisely why the *Wafiya* should sail at the earliest possible moment." Captain Nasira spoke for the first time, drawing the attention of all. "There are certainly spies in this palace, just as there are in Ilyara. These witch-making slavers probably already know we're here. The longer we wait to move, the more prepared they'll be. Whether it's through witchery or by walking out on the ice and breaking it before her prow, we need to get the *Wafiya* underway, and fast."

An eruption of debate rose up so swiftly it was clear to Rasim that Nasira had proposed this before. The idea of walking out onto the ice worried the Northerners, though the seamasters had very little to fear from doing so. Even if the ice shattered beneath their feet and sent them into the freezing harbor, it was hard to drown a sea witch.

"But the unmaking of ice is difficult, isn't it?" Lorens, Inga's younger brother and prince of the Northlands, stood to speak. "Your own guildmaster nearly died fighting the frozen harbor in Ilyara."

"It's well nigh impossible." Nasira didn't look at Rasim as she muttered, "But Desimi al Ilialio alone has nearly the strength to do it, and *that* one," she said, managing to point at Rasim with her voice alone, "has been blessed by Siliaria herself. Together, they may be able to rough up the seas enough to break the ice, and the rest of us can keep the *Wafiya* afloat in their wake."

Rasim clamped his mouth shut and tried not to let his eyes bug too much. Not in a hundred years would he have expected Nasira to champion him. As quickly as astonishment came, so did a burst of pride, until he was so confused with emotion that he didn't know where to look.

Lorens cast Rasim a thoughtful glance that turned amused, suggesting Rasim had less control over his expression than he was trying for. But the Northern prince let him off the hook, speaking as if Rasim wasn't agog. "Then I think it's time we throw caution away, Inga. Counsilors, the Ilyarans have done what they came to do, and have mourned their losses in the aftermath of that great effort. They only lose time now, and time may be critical to those who might have been taken captive half a year ago, just before Rasim found his way to us the first time. We are indebted to them, and shouldn't delay the captain's mission any longer."

Nasira clapped her hands together, a sharp ringing sound that emphasized her satisfaction. "I'll waste no more time in the Northlands. We sail on the tide."

"Wait." Rasim's voice was weak with the weariness of calling attention to himself yet again. But yet again, he couldn't stand by and say nothing, not when there was something important to be said. "Wait. We can't all go after the slavers if we get free of the ice. Someone has to warn the horse clans that trouble is heading for them, too."

CHAPTER THREE

Captain Nasira's stare, bearing down on Rasim, weighed more than any sea witchery. He lifted his chin, holding his ground even as his shoulders slumped with dejection. All he wanted was to avoid infuriating his captain again, but apparently that would never happen.

"I suppose your little Captain Kisia will take you and your slopped-out Northern boat to do that?" Nasira's sarcasm was as sharp as the clap she'd made. "I may not like you, Rasim, but you're my crew and you'll go where I say."

Rasim bristled on Kisia's behalf. His impossible wish to be a captain was no secret, but Kisia was so new to the guild that she'd be ruthlessly hazed for daring to dream of such things.

Inga, misreading Rasim's scowl, said, "Perhaps we can send a ship, Rasim. At the very least, I think you're right that we need to make contact with the horse clans and learn whether they too have been beset with catastrophe these past thirteen years."

"I'm sure of it." Rasim dug his toes against the stone floor as if doing so would help him stand fast against questioning. "Kisia and I mapped it out, Ing—uh, your highness. Ilyara, Hongrunn, the Islands—they're compass points on a map, all the same distance from the center. And the center is Moran, the biggest slaver city of them all. I'm sure all of this is coming out of there, and we're all going to have to work together to end it."

"The Shenryalan clans are nomads, Rasim. Even their upcoming clan gathering allows very few outsiders to attend. We may not be able to work with them," said Inga.

Rasim gave Endat a ferocious glare and the rotund Sunmaster smiled. "We can but try. Your highness, if you send one of your own ships to the west in search of the Shenryalan, I will sail with it as the Ilyaran representative to this cause. Certainly building stronger bonds between nations is never a bad thing."

"Shenryal isn't a nation," someone muttered. "Just a bunch of savages living in tents and riding on horses."

"They no doubt consider our heavy stone walls and sailing ships to be equally savage," Endat replied evenly. "The world would be a dull place if we were all alike."

"Someone wouldn't be trying to poison our water supplies if we were all alike!"

"Someone," Inga said in a cool voice, "has failed in that attempt, Counsilor Kif. Failed badly, since we are now united with the Ilyarans in our attempt to discover who is behind it, and why. It's been a long time since you went west to meet the Shenryalans for my father. They may have changed."

Kif, who looked to be only a little younger than Rekka, gestured at the rough scar that cut across his nose and spliced his beard. "Anyone who does this to a man doesn't change."

Endat's eyebrows flickered up as his gaze came to land the heavy blade Kif wore at his hip. "An assumption that comes from experience, perhaps?"

Kif faltered, then flushed with anger as poorly muffled laughter rushed around the room. Lorens, still on his feet, flashed a wide grin at the older man. "We laugh with you, Kif, not at you. Your caution is noted," he said more solemnly, giving Kif a nod that acknowledged his age and wisdom. "I think Sunmaster Endat would do well to have you with him when he sails west. You spent time with the Shenryalan tribes, and may still have friends there."

Kif nodded slowly, and settled back more graciously than Rasim expected. For a man who'd just called the horse tribes savages, Kif didn't seem dismayed at the idea of visiting them again. Rasim wondered how he had come to visit in the first place, and how much time he'd spent in the west. He didn't look like a man who would answer a curious boy's questions, though. Maybe Lorens could tell Rasim the story, and maybe Rasim could learn something important about the Shenryalans by listening. His ears pricked at the idea, like he was already trying to hear and learn. Instead of stories, he caught a sharp uncomfortable sound, like stone cracking. His hands went cold and he held his breath, trying to hear more clearly, but the chatter in the chamber made it hard.

"Stop!" Rasim climbed onto the table, hands spread wide to bring the sound down. People stared at him, but he didn't care, his attention focused on the walls. Confused silence fell amongst the councilors as a broken pattern became audible.

Words. Words communicated in a secret language, a language that Rasim had only just learned a little of from the palace guard. They rattled out across the room, gaining speed and urgency:

Enemies by sea.

Rasim's stomach turned to a lump of ice, and he couldn't push his voice past a whisper. "The harbor's under attack. The crew is down there."

The words didn't carry, but they didn't need to. Most of the Northerners understood the tapped-out message. Some were already on their feet, loosening swords in their sheathes and striding—almost running —for the enormous double doors. Lorens vaulted onto the table, gripping Rasim's shoulder. "Can you fight?"

Memories of shipboard sword-fighting lessons swept Rasim in a sudden wave of heat. He looked at his hands, searching for callouses from the mock sword he'd learned with and finding the rough lines of ship work instead. "If not with a sword, then with witchery."

His own voice sounded strange to him: grim and suddenly older somehow. Lorens, eyes bright with approval, squeezed Rasim's shoulder again before leaping off the table and joining the others as they swept from the room.

Nasira caught Rasim's arm as he followed Lorens. "What's happening, journeyman?"

"The harbor's under attack," Rasim said again, knowing Nasira hadn't been able to hear him the first time. "Our crew is in danger."

"And you know of the attack how...?" Endat joined them, which sent Rasim into a dance of impatience. He wanted to act, not explain!

Getting around Sunmaster Endat was like trying to circumvent a small mountain, though, so Rasim ground his teeth and answered him. "Because a guard just taught me some of the drumming language the Northerners use to communicate over distances. It's like our ship signals," he blurted to Nasira, hoping it would clarify what he didn't have time to say.

The captain's expression cleared at once, then darkened again. "The crew can take care of itself. Anyone foolish enough to attack sea witches next to a harbor deserves what they get. The city will be fine, with us to protect it."

Rasim reeled back, staring at Nasira. Pieces fell into place in his mind like water drops falling into the sea, becoming a part of a whole. "You're right. Nobody would do that. Which means they're not after the city, Captain. They're after the crew. After all of the Ilyaran witches who are here right now. I'd bet my journeyman's braids on it."

"Slavers?" Nasira's face was pale. "But who told them we were here?"

"We sailed to the Northlands with a certain amount of fanfare, Captain," Endat replied. "Our presence here is hardly a secret. After the Seamasters' cleansing of the water supply, there was little else spoken of in the city. And Rasim has just ably demonstrated that speech and ships are far from the only way to send messages across great distances."

"Most of us are quartered near the docks." Rasim pulled out of Nasira's grip again. "We have to get down there. We have to—"

"No one can subdue a barracks full of Seamasters, Rasim. They don't know what they're dealing with."

"Of course they do!" Anger flashed through Rasim again, but he didn't turn back. All that kept him from running was an awareness of Endat's slower pace, but his feet itched and he didn't know how long he could keep himself to a walk. "If they're the same people who've taken your old ship's crew, of *course* they know how to deal with Seamasters. They'll have drugged them with mindkiller in their food or drink, and they'll command them not to use their magic and—" He burst into a run, leaving the adults behind. "Go find Inga and tell her what's going on!" he shouted over his shoulder. "I'll get the crew!"

EVERYONE at the palace was running. Soldiers, servants, nobility—people from every rank carried weapons and shields, or wore hastily-donned armor, as they flooded through the tall grey halls and toward the city streets. Others swept children inside, toward safety, while others still prepared for the inevitable injuries that came with battle. Very few of them seemed afraid. Mostly they looked angry or determined. Rasim raced with the outgoing tide of people, for once glad for his small stature. It made it easier to duck under elbows and squeeze through narrow spaces between hurrying bodies. Someone shouted his name, but he ignored it.

The courtyard, when he broke through the palace's sweeping doors, was startlingly empty: warriors racing for the harbor wasted no time there. From the palace's vantage, the city looked as if it had grown out of the rocks and mountains that made up the Northlands' shorelines. Grey blocks rose squat and square with white-capped roofs, just like the mountains above them. And like the mountains, they revealed surprising depth of color and shadow when sunlight fell on them, dazzling snow rich with blue highlights and cobbled streets thrown into sharp relief. Rasim caught his breath at its beauty even as he skidded across the courtyard and raced, half-falling, down the steep roads toward the harbor.

The streets were full of people, but their movements surged and roiled, a moving battle instead of the camaraderie of a market day. Rasim skidded through them, stopping on a corner to decide where should go, then bolted toward the inn that Sesin and Seamaster Usia were staying at. As healers, they might be able to shake off the effects of the mindkiller drug, which forced those who had taken it to use magic as they were commanded, rather than as they wished. He ducked fights, squirming between bodies and trying hard not to see who stood between himself and his goal. If he looked, if he saw faces he knew embroiled in battle, he would never be able to keep going. He needed reinforcements, but aside from himself and Captain Nasira, the only other sea witches who had been staying at the palace were mucking about in the sewer tunnels beneath the palace. Rasim could have killed Desimi and Kisia for deciding to play their stupid game. Without them, his only hope was the healers.

The inn was shockingly dark after the snow-reflected sunshine, but even through the dimness Rasim saw that the common room's tables and chairs were overturned and splintered. The bar counter was broken into pieces, too, with flagons spilled and ale dripping on the floor or across plates half-filled with cooling food. An open stairway, barely more than a black hole in the dimness, led up. Rasim raced across the room toward it, then smashed hard into an unseen door as it opened unexpectedly beside the stairwell.

Sesin, wide-eyed with laughter and apology, appeared from inside the door, a basket of dry clothes on her hip. "Rasim! Are you all right? What—" Her gaze went beyond him to the ransacked common room and her question turned to a gasp. "What's going on?"

"Sesin!" Rasim grabbed her hand and pulled her up the stairs, desperate to find safety somewhere. "Where were you? Didn't you hear the fighting? Thank Siliaria that you didn't," he added, quiet but heartfelt.

"I was washing clothes. They've got a clever system to pump the water—" Sesin broke off again, realizing it wasn't important. "It's all stone and oak down there. Quietest place in the building. What's going on?"

"We're under attack and they're using the mind-killer drug. Probably nobody who's been at the palace has been drugged, but out of the rest of the crew, I'm hoping you healers might be immune."

"Mindkiller," Sesin echoed. "The drug that means you can't use your magic without being told to?"

"Right. I'm going to try to make you do something. Make yourself sneeze."

Sesin's nose turned red and an explosive sneeze erupted as they ran into the room that had become the Seamasters' infirmary. She stopped, astonished, and pressed her fingers against her face. "What was that?"

"You're drugged," Rasim said grimly. "We need to find something to block your ears so you can't take orders while we figure out if you can clear it from your system." He shot a glance out the window, watching fights meet in the street. "And unless you can do it right now—clear the drug from your system, Sesin!" he said hopefully, but then went on, "then we should probably get out of here. Do you know where Usia is?"

"Here, Journeyman." The door banged open, Usia's thick frame filling it. "Clever lad, coming for the healers. I wish you hadn't, though." His spoke through his teeth, straining as if he pulled the weight of a ship behind him. "Run, Rasim. Run!"

Panic seized Rasim's breath. "Master Usia, wait—"

Usia lifted one hand, made a fist, and crushed the strength from Rasim's heart.

CHAPTER FOUR

The shock was almost worse than the pain. Rasim's breath went out of him as stars danced behind his eyes. It hurt, hurt worse than even diving deep with the sea serpent had. His knees gave out and he dropped, hand still over his heart. He had to respond. That was obvious, but gathering his thoughts enough to try seemed impossible. Dimly, through a roaring in his ears, he heard Sesin cry out, and Usia say, "Sesin, come here to me."

She did, at a run, her hands lifted to pummel the older healer. Usia caught her easily, then gave a frustrated snarl as Rasim felt, faintly, the weight of Sesin's magic come into play. For the space of a blink her magic alleviated the pain in Rasim's chest, but Usia whispered, "Siliaria forgive me. Stop using witchery, Sesin," and to Rasim's horror, she did.

She said something Rasim couldn't hear above the pounding in his ears. Usia's face twisted with pain and he spoke again, inaudibly, before pushing Sesin out the door behind him. Rasim clawed his fingers against the stone floor, trying desperately to concentrate, but the sound of the sea in his head drowned out almost all possibility of thinking. He managed a thin breath around the pain and used it to whisper, "Siliaria."

The heart-wrenching agony stopped so fast Rasim fell face-first onto the floor, unable to believe the relief. After a ragged gasp or two, he flung himself onto his back, staring wet-eyed and exhausted at the door. It wouldn't have surprised him, he thought, if Siliaria herself had stood there, somehow punishing one sea witch for harming another.

Instead, Sesin stood above Usia's prone form with a stubby, smoking length of wood gripped in her hands. Her eyes were huge and dismayed, but her grip on the doused torch was certain. "I had to," she said to Rasim, or maybe to the room at large. "I tried to use my witchery and I couldn't, but there were torches along the wall outside. I had to," she said again. Then she dropped the torch and ran for Rasim. She fell to her knees beside him, hands dancing across his chest in light, useless gestures.

"Heal me," Rasim suggested, then shut his eyes to hide the way the room danced and spun. "If you can," he added. "Don't hurt yourself trying."

The torn, beaten feeling inside his chest lessened almost immediately, as Sesin's power soothed the damage done by the master healer. When he could breathe more easily, Rasim dared open his eyes. "Thanks. What should we do about him?" He nodded toward Usia.

Sesin followed his gaze. "He said he was sorry, just before he threw me out of the room. Well, I'm sorry too, but we have to leave him there and run."

"Run *where?*" Even as he asked, the fighting outside surged and crashed against the inn's front door. Rasim flinched to his feet, eyeing the windows. They were big enough to fit through down here, in the main room, but there was no point in climbing out them straight into the fight. "Is there a back way in?"

"At the other end of the hall upstairs, yes." Sesin got up too, then stalked to a nearby table where candles dripped wax. She balled some of it up, tucking it into her ears, then looked defiant. "There. I can still kind of hear, but that should help."

Rasim curled a smile. "And I thought I was supposed to be the clever one. Can you hear me?"

"Sort of. I can tell what you're saying if I look at your lips. And you *are* clever. How are we going to get out of here?" She offered her hand, and they ran up the stairs together, Rasim discovering that his whole body ached. He felt wobbly and had the worst headache he could remember, but at least his heart was beating properly.

A long hall lined with doors stretched back from the stairs. They raced for the other end, clattering down the second set of stairs to a back door barred from the inside. After exchanging glances, they lifted the bar, and Sesin opened the door a little.

Almost immediately, somebody slammed into it, knocking it father open. The person outside scrambled against the door, trying to get in. Rasim and Sesin threw their weight against it and barred it shut again, then leaned against it, panting and staring at one another. "The rooms have windows, right?"

Sesin's expression went dubious. "Yeah, but they're narrow. I don't think we'll fit."

The inn, like virtually all of Hongrunn's buildings, was made of stone. Rasim could use witchery on the windows, if necessary. "We'll have to. I'll go first, because nobody can catch me off-guard and command my witchery. I can protect you that way."

"The idea of you being able to protect anybody, Rasim..." Sesin smiled and shook her head, obviously pleased through her astonishment. "All right. You go."

They ran back upstairs, testing the doors as they went. The second one opened, and Rasim raced to the window, dragging the window's single shutter open. Cold winter wind blasted him in the face. It tasted of snow and salt, and for the space of a breath Rasim wished for nothing more than to be back in Ilyara, where nothing ever tasted of snow or cold, and the salt water scent came on warm breezes.

He muttered, "Only way to get home is through that window," and clambered out.

It was a tight squeeze, and he was small. Sesin wasn't much bigger, but a little bit in any direction might be too much. He exhaled and pressed at the stone with witchery, all too aware of Sesin's eyes on him. So far only Kisia suspected he could use more than one magic. Rasim had become all too aware that despite the Ilyaran king hoping that young witches could learn to do just this, the reality of it could unsettle the whole Ilyaran social structure. He wasn't looking forward to trying to explain himself, later.

Of course, if he and Sesin didn't fit through the window, there wouldn't be much of a later. The stone gave slightly, making the shutter creak and shift. Rasim could take a full breath now, and figured that would give Sesin room to squish through. He slithered out, peering up and down the street.

Now that he was willing to look, he could see it was full of brown-skinned sea witches fighting against big pale Northerners, and against others whose clothes suggested they came from the Islands. There were some he didn't recognize by coloring or clothing, but they, too, fought his crewmates. But the important thing was the fights were *physical*: fists and feet, elbows and knees. Not one of the Ilyarans used the witchery they were known for. Instead, the others leapt on the Ilyarans one by one, subduing and chaining them, then rising up to move on to the next.

The noise was amazing, like flocks of gulls screeching over choice bits of fish guts. No one was looking up, though, or paying much attention to anything beyond the battle surging down the street. Rasim squirmed out, hung by his fingertips, and then dropped a hideously long distance to the stones below. He hit with a thud and fell onto his back, narrowly avoiding cracking his head on the street. Someone nearly stepped on him and he leaped up, plastering himself against the inn wall, and peeked toward Sesin.

Her face was pale as she looked down at him. Belatedly, Rasim recalled that it had only been a few weeks since she'd had the bad fall off the *Wafiya*'s crow's nest, and that heights had bothered her ever since. He crooked his fingers encouragingly. Her mouth set with determination and she gave one quick nod before thrusting herself out the window with a little too much force. Rasim hopped back a step and didn't so much catch her as provide a softer landing place. Their heads bashed together, and Rasim's also bounced off the stone street as Sesin's weight took them both to the ground. He saw stars and tasted blood as Sesin pulled him up, her expression apologetic. Rasim gave her a wavering smile and they slipped down the street, still clutching each other's hands.

The weight of witchery chased them, icy harbor water rising beyond the seawall and clawing at their feet. Rasim pushed it away, but using magic made his head hurt more. A rough, almost-silent laugh escaped him. It would be stupid to get caught now, just because of a bump on the head, but he didn't want to waste time being healed. He pushed Sesin along and turned, shouting, "Ilyarans! Fight back with your magic!"

His voice boomed down the streets and across the water with far more strength than he expected. Dizziness swept him again. Sesin grabbed his upper arm, hauling him away as some of the *Wafiya*'s crew begin to do as he commanded. The fight turned in their favor, then almost as quickly, turned again as other voices shouted counter-commands.

Rasim cursed helplessly. He couldn't stand there all day shouting countermands. Even if he could, his own experience with mindkiller told him that it worked most effectively when orders were given by someone in a position of authority. His booming shout had given him that air, but his was a boy's voice, and the drugged witches would be less able to heed him than those who had drugged them.

A surge broke through the nearest edge of fighting. Whip-slim warriors in light padded armor left the crew members behind and sprang toward Rasim and Sesin. Sesin shrieked and pulled Rasim into a run. Halfway up the street, she leaped toward an inn window, swarming up rough-cut stone walls like they were a ship's rigging. Rasim followed less gracefully, his head still aching too much for him to move fast. Sesin dug her fingers into a narrow gutter and heaved. Then she was over the edge of the roof, lying on her belly and offering Rasim help.

He caught one quick glimpse of the warriors behind them as he seized her hand. They were armed with slender swords and short, powerful bows that they nocked without slowing their run. Panic turned Rasim's blurred vision to sharp focus, and he grunted as Sesin pulled him onto the roof. They fumbled upward on the stone-tiled slant, both of them cursing.

Northern roofs were all angled. It made sense: snow would slide off the roofs instead of bearing down and breaking them under its weight. But trying to climb tilted, ice-slicked tiles made Rasim wish for flat Ilyaran roofs. Safety was on the far side of the roof's crest, but neither he nor Sesin could get a decent grip on the slick surface. Rasim's shoulder blades itched with the knowledge that archers stood below him. He didn't know why they hadn't fired yet. He and Sesin should be full of holes. They were easy targets, barely moving and in the open. But they were also Ilyaran witches. Maybe they were too valuable to shoot down like birds. Rasim smashed his palm against the frozen stone, fear and frustration heating his whole body.

Frozen *stone*. He was an idiot, not clever after all. He would never think to use stonemastery as naturally as sea witchery. He sent magic outward, let it flow into the patient tiles, and was somehow still surprised when divots appeared in them, giving the two journeymen a chance to grip the roof and scramble upward.

Sesin didn't seem to notice that the divots were new. She only gasped in relief and dug her fingers in, pulling herself upward. Rasim twisted on the rooftop, hanging on by the fingertips of one hand, and spread the fingers of the other toward the stone tiles and gutters beneath him. It wouldn't take much of a shield to protect them from the arrows, if only he'd thought of it soon enough.

He didn't *like* working with stone, he decided half a breath later. Water let him know it was responding, but stone remained inert until suddenly it wasn't. He had no sense of the roof tiles accepting his witchery; they were just flat, and then they were a thin wall climbing upward. The archers below vanished from view, but their voices rose up in anger and surprise.

A hail of arrows finally battered his shield. Cracks appeared in it, the arrows' force much greater than Rasim had expected, but they only needed a few seconds to get away. He flipped on his belly again, looking up the roof.

Sesin lay pinned to the tiles, an arrow through her shoulder.

The chill of the roof tiles suddenly ate through his stomach, making him empty and cold all the way through. He pulled himself to Sesin's side and lodged his feet against a broken tile so he wouldn't slide away again. "Sesi..."

"Go." Sesin's cheek was pressed against the icy tiles, her brown skin nearly white from pain and cold and pressure. Blood leaked from her shoulder, though not nearly as much as Rasim expected. Swallowing nervously, he reached for the arrow. Sesin barked, "Goddess, no! Pull it back out and the arrowhead will tear me up."

"Well, then, he—heal yourself if you can! You can do that, you can—" Rasim broke off, unable to give any more orders to his injured crewmate.

Sesin drew a ragged breath, tears spilling over her nose and melting the ice under her cheek. "Go, Rasim, you've got to get out of here. If they catch you then no one will be able to rescue us."

Rasim whispered, "That's crazy," as more arrows fell around them. He swatted at the air, knowing it was stupid, then clenched his teeth and began to rise. She couldn't hear him, but he made a promise anyway: "I'll get you out of here, Sesin."

"Rasim!" Sesin's fist scraped against the roof like she was trying to pull him down again. "Just *go*! Tell the captain what's happened, tell her I sent you away if she gets mad, but go. Go so you can come save us. *Go!*"

Rasim grabbed her fist and put his mouth by her ear, speaking as clearly as he could. "No."

Then he stood, calling magic.

CHAPTER FIVE

First he pulled more stone into place, hiding Sesin under a dome instead of just behind a low wall. He would never be able to talk his way out of that, but it didn't matter anymore. Not if he could keep Sesin safe from the slavers below.

With falling arrows clattering off her dome shelter, Rasim turned his attention to the nearby harbor. Ice locked it surface, but he used witchery to find the weak places: at the sea walls, and around the *Wafiya*. Black, cold water surged in response to his power, slopping through narrow crevasses to run quick and clear over the frozen surface. It slithered up the walls, the stone popping as its temperature changed, and it picked up speed as it rushed through the streets to seize the slavers' feet.

He heard cries of outrage and confusion, and then the satisfying crash of bodies hitting the ground. Armor clanked as they were pulled away from the fight by magic-filled water. More slavers fell, not drowning, but removed. If he could split his concentration and use two magics at once, perhaps he could cage them as well as pull them away.

The idea made him woozy. He swayed and put a hand on his stone shield to keep himself upright. Maybe just washing the slavers away would be enough for now. The trick was getting to them and leaving the seamasters standing. It was easy enough on the edges of the fight, where slavers were mostly running toward the fight, but as they waded deeper into battle, it became impossible to tell who was who. It *should* have been easy: the seamasters *should* have been able to use their own magic. Rasim would be able to feel it then, but instead—

Shouts rolled through the crowd, and suddenly he *could* feel their magic. He felt it as slavers commanded mindkiller-numbed witches to find and attack the source of unknown sea witchery. The water he'd pulled into the streets was wrenched away from him as dozens of sailors brought their talent to the fight—

—and turned it against him.

Rasim staggered under the onslaught, his control of the rising tide torn to tatters. He drove his shoulder against the inside of his stone shield, bracing himself and struggling to reach through a wall of oncoming witchery determined to drown his power. It felt impossible. Harder, even, than a lifetime of trying to be good enough with a witchery that could hardly keep his shoes dry. Back then, the guild hadn't turned against him, only pitied him. Some had tried to make things easier for him, even if others definitely hadn't.

This was different. This was a ship's worth of seamasters uniting against a single witch. No one could withstand that.

A blush crashed over Rasim's cheeks as he remembered, with shocking clarity, the press of Siliaria's cool, salty lips against his own. She hadn't laughed at him then, but he thought he heard laughter now, light as the lapping waves and mocking as an errant breeze, as if to say, *Seamaster? Not this one, and more fool I to think so.*

Not that Siliaria would call herself a fool, and not that Rasim dared to either. But she *had* named him Seamaster, and if he couldn't figure a way to save himself from a boatload of angry witches, he didn't deserve the name. Or the reputation for being clever, either. He peeked around his shield, horrified to see that most of the fighting had stopped and *everyone* in the streets was focused on his rooftop.

For an instant he was grateful Kisia wasn't among the witches below. When only barely trained in sea witchery, she had thought to use magic to squeeze a man's heart, the way Usia had just done to Rasim. If any of the crew in the streets were that creative, Rasim would be dead.

Well, he could be creative too. He slithered down his shield, huddling in on himself, and closed his eyes. The weight of sea witchery was impressive, with all those sailors lifting water from under the ice and working it toward him. Lucky for him Desimi wasn't there. He'd remember how they'd wove water and flown it through the air to stop the fire in Ilyara. Or maybe the crew *did* remember that, and were doing their best to not be quite that efficient. He could hope.

Rasim shook off the feeling of their magic and concentrated on his semi-secret stonemastery. If he could make stone shields, he could also grow stone boots from the streets and capture the slavers in place. It wasn't an exciting way to fight, but anything *more* exciting would leave Sesin alone and pinned to a rooftop. He just wished he could feel stonemastery working the way he could water witchery. He didn't want to keep peeking around his shield to see if his magics were working.

"Seamasters, *fight!* Fight the slavers! Fight with the magic you command!" Nasira's voice rang out, impossibly loud as it bounced and echoed off rooftops. Rasim shot to his feet, trying to find her. She stood in the distant *Wafiya*'s crow's nest. Beside her was Skymaster Arrat, whose magic lifted her shouts until they drowned out all other sound.

Pride rose in Rasim so fast it felt like fury. Captain Nasira wasn't the sort to think of working with other guilds, but she'd done it now, to the benefit of them all. With a fierce grin stretching his face, he turned back to his own part of the fight. The strength of the *Wafiya*'s crew was working with him now, fighting the slavers. As Nasira's counter-commands came ceaselessly, Rasim focused harder on his stonemastery, now concentrating solely on the slavers. They needed to be held in place, preventing them from kidnapping his friends and, should they see that the tide had turned, keeping them from fleeing. And now it was easy to tell who were slavers and who were Ilyaran witches, because the crew were using magic. None of the slavers were watching him now, instead paying attention to the water witches around them. Rasim concentrated on one, then another, watching as magic flowed through stone and encased the enemy in rocky boots. Those he'd captured lost their balance or swore, and some began hacking at the stone boots, trying to free themselves.

A momentary break in Nasira's voice made Rasim look her direction again. Skymaster Arrat had batted away an arrow–a whole *sheaf* of arrows–with the wave of one hand and a look of parental exasperation. Admiration surged in Rasim. The guilds weren't warriors by nature, but together they proved why Ilyara had been a proud, undefeated city for so long.

And they proved why outsiders saw them as so potentially dangerous. Rasim shivered, returning his gaze to the streets, and went still.

A wall of water swept toward them, grey and implacable. It came fast and silent, with no weight of water witchery heralding its arrival. If he hadn't looked up, he would never have known it was coming.

Neither did the sea witches. The oncoming tide slammed into them, knocking them asunder, while somehow twisting and leaping to avoid the armor-clad slavers. The last thing Rasim heard clearly was Nasira's fear-ridden bellow: "Seamasters! Save yourselves!"

Then the water was upon them all, suddenly roaring in Rasim's ears like a tidal wave. He cast magic around himself, keeping the sea spray from wetting him as the ocean ripped through the streets below. Chunks of ice, carried by the onslaught, smashed into houses and people, breaking both. Seamasters were swept away, though Nasira's desperate command saved lives: Rasim saw dry, if terrified, faces as his crewmates were flung through the water. Kisia had saved him from the rising water in the mines the same way, by ordering him to preserve his own life. The mindkiller's limitations would allow that, at least, and for that, Rasim was grateful.

He scrambled out from behind his shield and climbed on top of Sesin's, trying to gain just a little more height to see the chaos. It wasn't natural, it *couldn't* be natural, even if he felt no witchery behind it. But someone was doing it, whether a sea witch or some unknown Northern magic.

Either way, it could be fought. It *had* to be fought, if Rasim's crewmates were to survive. From his perch, he could see the water rose from the very center of the harbor itself, where a new hole had been punched through the ice. The sea water there ran deep and cold, and arched upward like a fountain, then crashed to the harbor's icy surface. From there, it careened wildly toward shore. It was a massive undertaking of magic, as tremendous a display of power as Isidri had used when she thawed the Ilyaran harbor. But the Guild-master wasn't here, and even if she had been, she was no longer strong enough to do this kind of working. Someone else was behind the torrents of water, but no other Ilyaran that Rasim knew of had the raw ability.

Not even Desimi. Not even Rasim, now that the goddess had blessed him.

But thinking of Isidri gave him an idea. She'd never waste time fighting the magic if she could find the witch wielding it. There were too many places to hide in Hongrunn's streets: Rasim would have to draw his opponent out. And the best way to do that—

The middle of the harbor seemed a terrible distance away, but *someone* was hauling water from there to the shore. If someone else could do it, so could a goddess-blessed Seamaster. And Rasim didn't have to drag the water out of its bed. He just had to cut it off. He stretched his hands toward it, almost able to feel the sea running through his fingers. His fingers closed convulsively, like he was throttling the upward rush of water, and threw power into the gesture.

Halfway across the harbor, the rising sea guttered and fell. Rasim sat down abruptly, shocked at the amount of energy necessary to cut the ocean's flow. But it wasn't done: he had to keep his enemy from starting it up again. Isidri might have re-frozen the harbor over the broken hole, but Rasim didn't know how. More, his opponent had already broken it open once already. Refreezing wouldn't be enough of a deterrent. Instead he imagined weight pressing down on the water's surface, preventing it from rising.

But water was forgiving, and slipped around the edges of his pressure. It rose a little with displacement, then fell again in a salty sprinkle across the ice. Rasim, breathing hard puffs of steam into the air, leaned into the magic, pressing his own hands flat against the top of Sesin's shelter, as if he could contain the water that way. His arms trembled with the effort, even though cutting off the fountain of rising sea hadn't been exactly physical.

There didn't seem to be any resistance to the cap he held in place. Shaking, hardly able to lift his head, Rasim stared out at the black hole in the icy harbor and wondered why his adversary wasn't fighting back.

Well, water was heavy. Lifting that much to begin with, even for someone with huge power, was exhausting. He knew that from experience. He'd slept for over a day, after freeing Lars and the other slaves from the mines. He wouldn't have been able to do it again immediately, either.

Which meant he didn't have to keep the pressure on. Instead, he slid off Sesin's shelter and leaned on it, then shook himself and began peeling the stone away with stone witchery. Sesin's eyes were clenched shut. Before light or cold air touched her to tell her that the shelter was melting away, Rasim saw what she had done and lost his breath in shocked admiration.

It must have been terribly painful. The arrow shaft was broken, no longer pinning her down. She had lifted herself off it, and now lay curled around the shaft, clenching it in both hands. As cold air washed over her, her eyes opened in, first wary, then astonished. She sat up, clutching her shoulder, which, though blood-stained and raw-looking, had healed. Her color was still bad, yellow under her dark skin tones, but she still looked much better than she had before. "Rasim." His name was only a whisper. "Rasim, did you shield me with...."

"You healed yourself." Rasim spoke quickly and quietly, not wanting to face the question even though they both knew the answer. Something flashed in Sesin's eyes, but after a few seconds she nodded as Rasim gestured toward her shoulder in awed respect. "Sesi, you did it."

She hesitated a moment longer, but he saw her choose not to pursue the question of the stone shelter. Not right now, at least. For now, her mouth twisted ruefully. "You told me to do it, if I could, and I could, so I had to. It's all right," she said hastily. "I'm not sure I would have been brave enough to try without orders. But Rasim?"

"Yes?"

"Try not to get me in any more trouble, please."

A quick laugh escaped him. "I'll try. No more high places for you and me."

Sesin smiled. "Oh good. How do we get down?"

"I don't know if we can right n—!"

"Look out!" Sesin lunged forward, knocking Rasim sideways as another weight flung itself at him from behind. It hit them both, Rasim squashing Sesin as someone on top of them screamed and kicked ferociously. A knife glinted, shockingly bright in the sunlight. Rasim rolled off Sesin and dug his feet against the roof as he tried to capture flailing hands without endangering himself.

The knife stuck between roof tiles just as the arrow head had. Rasim seized luck and his assailant's wrist at the same time, then flipped himself over to pin his attacker down with his weight.

Familiar features contorted with rage as the woman tried slamming her head against his. Rasim reared back, gaping, then lurched forward to pin her again as he blurted, "*Missio?*"

CHAPTER SIX

Missio looked awful. Worse by far than the last time Rasim had seen her as a captive in the *Wafiya*'s brig. Then she'd been angry and defiant, but healthy, with good color and a shine to the journeyman's braid she wore her hair in. Now that braid was frazzled loose, her hair dull and coarse, and her skin looked like someone had scraped the color away with a ragged seashell. Yellow circles haunted her eyes and fiery red blotches burned her cheekbones. Worse than that, though, her whole face was drawn and hollow-looking, like someone had knocked her teeth out. Her shoulders and chest heaved under the lightweight cloak and shirt she wore, and sweat slid into her unnaturally bright eyes. She was too skinny, even for a naturally long-boned, thin woman.

It was ridiculous to be concerned. She'd been trying to kill him just now, and had tried at least once before. Rasim's fear and anger still sluiced away into a worried frown. "Missio, are you all right?"

"She's not all right. She's sick," Sesin said. "Hold her still, Rasim, maybe I can help her. Where have you been, Missio?"

"Hold her—!" Rasim nearly laughed in despair as Missio bucked, trying to throw his weight off. She had dreadful strength for someone as thin as she was, and he was smaller than she. "I'd need a rope to hold her!"

Sesin spoke in the superior tone of an older sibling. "Use stone."

Rasim snapped his gaze to her, half amazed and half horrified. Sesin arched an eyebrow with cool expectation. He swallowed and ducked his eyes from that look, only to meet Missio's enraged eyes. She flung herself upward again, trying to knock him away. Rasim gritted his teeth and did as Sesin had ordered, calling stone witchery to make loops around Missio's wrists and ankles, and then, as she pitched her body upward again, over her hips as well. He looked once at Sesin, whose expression was carefully blank. She would make a good Sunmasters' apprentice, Rasim thought, and looked away again.

Before he finished, Missio had realized what he was doing. Her struggles ceased and her eyes narrowed in enraged cunning. "How'd you do it, Rasim? How'd you command a second magic? If you can teach me that, you might get out of here alive."

A ball of worry knotted Rasim's belly, but at the same time, he smiled a little. "I'm not the one stuck in place, Missio. How did you call so much power?" He glanced at the mess lining the streets, and at sea witches still being snatched up, despite his efforts.

"Sesin, they're taking the crew. We can't—" He hesitated. "We can't leave her here." He was ashamed that it was almost a question, but Sesin's neutral expression tempered into sympathy.

"We can't. She's too sick." She, too, looked at the streets below, and bit her lower lip. "I think I got the mindkiller out when I healed my shoulder. Maybe I can help."

"Drown yourself in your own blood!" Missio shouted. Rasim and Sesin both startled, then stared at their captive in horror. Her lip curled, then peeled back to bare all her teeth and display gums that were too red as Sesin put a hand to her throat and gave a nervous laugh.

"That's not how I would have tested it, but at least now we know. Thank you, Missio." She knelt, mouth tightening with determination. "Captain Nasira and half the Northern army are out there, Rasim. The slavers are never going to be able to escape with our crewmates, and we're the only ones with Missio. I can't —" Sesin took a deep breath. "She's half mad. I don't even know where to start with a sickness like this, Rasim. We need Seamaster Usia."

Rasim cast a glance toward the room they'd left behind. "If we're really lucky, he's still unconscious and in half an hour he'll be here to help. What do we do if we're not lucky, though?"

"We get her somewhere warm and safe, and find a Northern doctor."

"The palace is the only place I'm sure is safe. There must be doctors there."

"Then we need to get her there."

"No!" Missio threw herself into more violent thrashing, banging her head against the roof and slamming her shoulders.

Astonished, Rasim leaned forward to put his weight on her shoulders, trying to keep her from injuring herself. "What's wrong with the palace?"

"Full of Northmen," Missio hissed. "Full of traitors."

A chill curled around Rasim's heart. "Traitors? Who? Who are you working with, or who's betrayed you? Where do these people think they were going to take our crewmates?"

Missio spat. "If Nasira still calls you crew, I'm no mate of theirs."

Rasim flinched, wiping spit from his cheek, then stared at the captured journeyman. "What did I *do* to you, Missio? I know the captain doesn't like me because I'm part Northerner and she blames all of them for the fire, and I know you followed her lead, but...she got over it. Kind of, anyway. What's your problem with me?"

"My brother should have had your place on the *Wafiya*."

That made no sense at all. Guild members were orphans, and rarely had siblings; that was why Kisia leaving her family to join the guild had been unprecedented. Rasim blinked in confusion before a face came to mind: a boy of his own age, quiet, careful, and devoted to Missio. They weren't blood-related, but they'd seemed like family to each other, even more tightly connected than the guild members were in general. And he had died during the sea serpent attack. "You mean Trisk? I—"

He broke off, following Missio's logic through to the end. Trisk had been a far better witch than Rasim, and she was right. Rasim taking a place as one of the *Wafiya*'s journeymen meant someone else had been placed elsewhere. Rasim had never thought of it that way. There was no telling if Trisk had really been intended for the *Wafiya*, but Missio clearly thought so...and all of the *Wafiya*'s crew had survived the serpent's attack.

Of course, they'd survived because Rasim had been on board, but that didn't stop the sick twist of sorrow that slumped Rasim's shoulders. "You might be right. I never thought of that. I'm sorry, Missio. I'm really sorry. Trisk was nice."

"He was my *brother*!" Missio howled and flung her torso forward like she could escape her bonds and strike Rasim down. Instead, foam flew from her lips and her teeth started chattering uncontrollably.

Rasim leaped forward, releasing the stone bonds that had pinned her. He felt a prick of regret: he might have talked Sesin into keeping quiet about his second witching gift, but Missio would never stay silent. "We have to get you to the palace."

The Ilyaran journeyman went limp. Dread seized Rasim's throat, but Missio was only unconscious. Rasim bared his teeth, then flopped around until she hung crookedly across his shoulders. Sesin stepped forward to help and went white again as weight settled on her barely-healed shoulder. "No, don't," Rasim muttered. "We'll make do."

"She's taller and weighs more than you..."

"She used to weigh more. I'm not sure she still does." Rasim smiled grimly and worked his way toward the roof's edge. "Sesi, there's no way off this roof except..."

"Everybody already thinks you set the *Wafiya*'s ropes on fire," Sesin said with a shrug. "Nobody's going to be surprised if you're a stone witch, too."

Rasim gaped at her in dismay, then drooped and nodded. "Let's move away from the fighting before we come down, at least. Since we can't be of any help to them." He cast a worried glance into the streets as they stumbled along roof edges, moving from one close-fitted building to another.

Soon there were fewer bodies in the streets below them than there had been closer to the harbor. Fewer slavers and fewer Ilyarans, both. The fight had turned again, with sea witches unable to use their magic. Another bolt of terror shot through Rasim. He searched for the *Wafiya* and Nasira, but ship and captain alike were out of sight now. "We should tell them to fight," Rasim whispered, but Sesin gave him another of her too-calm looks.

"We can't afford to get shot down, Rasim. If Missio's really working with them, she's the only one we've got for sure who might be able to tell us something. She might even know what happened to the captain's old crew. Oh!" She slipped, caught herself, and stood at the roof's edge, looking down as she breathed hard. Then her jaw set. "Someone's down there, Rasim. One of us, I can tell by the color of their skin. They're hurt."

Rasim looked over his shoulder, judging the distance they'd traveled away from the roving fight. "Somebody who crawled away, maybe. Go ahead," he said, suddenly decisive. "Try to help them. I'll get Missio to the palace. Sesin?"

She was already climbing down a gutter, mostly one-handed, but she stopped to look up at him.

"Be careful," Rasim said. "If it seems at all funny, run. Don't get caught."

"I won't." Something in her voice made Rasim believe her. A few weeks ago she'd seemed—not soft, exactly, because no sailor was soft, but gentle. A stream of resolution had grown wide in her, though, and she now seemed like someone who would be difficult to cross. She would make a magnificent master healer someday. Rasim gave her a quick smile, waited until she'd climbed down the gutter, then went on with his burden.

Missio got heavier with every step, and in the end he was thigh-tremblingly grateful that the rooftops he'd chosen eventually sloped downward to meet a cobblestoned road. He was too tired to even think about using magic by then, and hated the idea that he might have to. At least the path to the palace was clear.

Strangely clear, in fact. Rasim faintly remembered children and frail people being hustled aside while the young and strong ran to the docks for the fight. The latter weren't back yet, and maybe the former wouldn't emerge from hiding until they were fetched. A few guards, left behind to protect the palace, nodded at him, but didn't offer to help him with his burden.

Familiar voices rang through the empty halls: Sunmaster Endat, arguing with Prince Lorens. That surprised Rasim. He'd thought Lorens would be out fighting. Maybe the heirs to the throne weren't allowed to do more than supervise, or were expected to stay in the palace for their own safety.

"I don't understand how they could have *escaped*—"

Lorens's protest was lost beneath Endat's booming voice: "With witchery we do not yet understand, my boy. Witchery unlike anything we know."

"But they disappeared in front of me! And no one can take the harbor now! It's ice-ridden!"

"There are mountain passes, are there not?"

"Impassable at this time of year!"

"By the likes of us," Endat agreed, and on that, they swept into the foyer like ships on a racing tide. Both Sunmaster and prince looked harried. Lorens was splashed with blood, his bright pale hair in disarray, and there was an unfamiliar grimness to Endat's usually-pleasant expression.

His face went slack with surprise, though, as Rasim dumped Missio onto a side table in the empty palace hall. Missio's head lolled. Rasim lifted it, afraid her tongue would roll back in her throat and choke her.

She came awake with a shout of hatred and the weight of magic pouring from her. There was no water nearby: the palace stood high in the city, well above the harbor, and it took someone of Desimi's strength to pull ground water up through bedrock and buildings.

Missio had never displayed anything like that kind of power, but deep beneath their feet Rasim felt the sudden rush of water awakening to witchery's call. He let go of her, focusing on pushing the water back down. Missio rolled to her feet and grabbed Rasim, slamming him against a wall to disrupt his concentration. For a moment they were kicking and biting, elbows and knees flying everywhere, but Missio had a madman's strength, and Rasim was small.

Lorens reached into the tangle of their fighting bodies, caught Missio's shirt in one big fist, and cracked the other across her jaw. Her eyes rolled back and she collapsed, all her weight suspended in Lorens's strong grip. He shook his hitting fist, then turned, still holding Missio, to Rasim. "I see you've found our wayward sailor."

Rasim slid down the wall and pressed his head against it, though Lorens's droll tone almost got a laugh from him. "I guess I did. Something's wrong with her."

"*Aside* from trying to kill you?" Lorens was obviously trying to lighten the moment, but Rasim was too weary to respond in kind.

"Yes. She's using too much magic, and she's sick. And she knows what's going on, who's behind this." Rasim closed his eyes to admit defeat. "And I didn't save the crew. I mean, some of them, maybe, but...I got Sesin. She's the only one I know for sure escaped. She stopped to heal someone while I brought Missio back. There were Islanders, Northerners, slavers from the continent...it was a coordinated effort, and Missio's the only one who might know the details." He opened his eyes again in time to see Lorens shoot a triumphant, *I-told-you-so*, look at Endat.

"There are always foreigners in any large city." Endat shrugged. "They could well have been here for weeks or months, even years, and only acting now. They might never have meant any harm to anyone, and might now be being coerced. How they arrived is irrelevant. How they intend to escape is the matter of importance now. Does this girl have that knowledge?" He nodded at Missio, whom Lorens placed gently on the floor.

She all but sank into it, so boneless was she. But even unconscious, she sweated, beads sliding down her temples and disappearing into her hair. Once she trembled, like the seizures of before, but with no resistance from unconscious muscles. "I'm sure she does," Rasim said miserably, "but I don't know what's wrong with her. Seamaster Usia was hurt in the fight on the docks. We need a doctor."

Lorens spun toward a nearby wall, taking his dagger's pommel to the stone in a series of short cracks. Rasim made a sound in his throat, wishing he'd known the code for calling healers, then let it go. There was only so much he could learn in a day.

Endat knelt beside Missio as her quiet inhalations turned to a single huge gasp as she awakened. Rasim startled forward, then thought better of it. He was the last person she wanted to see, and maybe she would talk to Endat if she thought Rasim wasn't there. He skittered behind Lorens and peeked around the big prince's fur cloak. Lorens arched an eyebrow, but otherwise ignored him.

Missio lay still a few seconds, staring blindly at the ceiling above, then surged to sitting. Endat caught her as she began to fall back again, and she seemed aware that couldn't have caught herself. Breathing harshly, she gaped at the Sunmaster, then clutched his arm in white-knuckled fear. "What's wrong with me?"

"You're ill. I've sent for Northern doctors. Do you know me, child?"

"Sunmaster Endat." Missio sounded as if she wanted to spit the words but lacked the energy. "Why would you try to help me?"

"Why would I refuse to help anyone in need? Tell me the symptoms of your illness, quickly, so if you fall unconscious again I can relate them to the doctors."

"I didn't *fall*—" Missio snarled the accusation at Lorens, who took a startled step backward. Rasim stumbled, trying to stay out of sight behind him as Missio visibly lost strength again, looking ever-smaller in Endat's arms.

He held her closer, broad face serious with concern. "Tell me of this illness, Missio."

"He didn't say this would happen." She turned her head against his chest, her eyes closing with the effort. "He said it would make me stronger, and it did." Color flushed her cheeks suddenly, giving her the illusion of health. "I was so strong. I could do things Seamaster Isidri only dreamed of. But then it started hurting. He gave me more, but it got worse and worse."

"More." Endat's conclusions leaped the same place

Rasim's did, and Lorens crept closer to hear his questions and Missio's answers. Rasim hung back, trying to stay out of sight while also trying to see Missio as Endat asked, "A drug, Missio? Who gave it to you? Where is he?"

Missio's eyes flew open, her gaze going around the hall wildly. She launched herself from Endat's arms, screaming and clawing as she threw herself against Lorens. Rasim flinched back, afraid she'd seen him and was attacking, but her rage didn't seem to have a focus. Lorens stumbled, catching her, and held her like a flapping fish as her screams redoubled. She kicked and thrashed, not even seeing Lorens as her attention landed on Rasim. He froze as Lorens caught Missio's arms and tucked them against her torso, then sat without dignity and wrapped his legs around hers. She screamed again, turning her teeth on the big Northern prince, but his heavy fur cloak protected him easily.

"Tsha, tsha." He was barely audible above her shouts, but he gathered her close as she convulsed and twisted in his arms. He kept murmuring, reassurances that Rasim couldn't hear clearly, until Missio went suddenly, terribly limp in his grasp. The echoes of her screams lasted forever in the wake of her collapse. Rasim took one jerky step forward with a sick certainty rising in his belly.

It took a long time for Lorens to look up, his blue eyes wet with sorrow as he shook his head and spoke the words Rasim had been afraid of. "I'm sorry. I'm sorry, Rasim. She's dead."

CHAPTER SEVEN

Time passed in a blur. Missio was taken to a cold room to await funeral rites, but Rasim refused to leave her side. Her body looked all used up, in death. Shrunken and old, for all that she wasn't yet twenty. It didn't matter that she'd tried to hurt him or the guild, not now. She'd had her heart broken, and the least Rasim could do was wait with her a while. He found a scrap of cloth to fold beneath her head, and tidied her clothes. At her belt hung a small pouch. He opened it, fishing around. A small carving of Siliaria, crude but heartfelt, like all apprentices made, met his fingertips, and dust crawled under his nails. He tucked the carving into Missio's hands and re-tied the pouch at her belt.

Doctors finally came to take her cooling blood and taste and sniff at it. With them came Hassin, the *Wafiya*'s first mate. His slim, rangy form was battered and bloodied, but otherwise unhurt. He stood for a long time with his hand on Rasim's shoulder and tears streaking his face, only speaking after the doctors left.

"The slavers escaped somehow. A third of the crew has gone missing."

"A third." Rasim's voice cracked. "With the people we lost at the lake, that's half our crew, Hassin. Can the *Wafiya* even sail at half crew?"

"It can. It must." Hassin sounded grim. "We've found four dead."

"Sesin? Usia?" Rasim hated to ask.

Hassin shook his head once. "Usia's missing. Sesin is with the captain and the dead, at the docks. Nasira will not leave the water again, I think. We'll sail for Moran as soon as we break free of the ice."

"How did they escape?" Rasim remembered Lorens's protest even as he asked: slavers had disappeared in front of him, he'd said, vanishing without a trace. Unknown witchery, Sunmaster Endat had replied. Certainly Missio had managed unknown witchery, or at least witchery far beyond what she used to be able to do. Maybe the slavers were all drugged in some way, letting them use extraordinary magic.

Or maybe, Rasim thought in a flash, maybe *Lorens* had been drugged, too. Losing moments of time to hallucinations made more sense to him than people vanishing into the air.

He stared at Missio's thin hands, their skin grey with death. Siliaria was curled in her fingers, and the dusty leather pouch the goddess icon had been in looked limp and wan without its little carving. Nothing shipboard ever got dusty. It was always too damp.

"No one knows yet. The captain didn't see how they escaped. All we know is it wasn't by sea, because she'd have felt that. She's asking for you and Desimi, Rasim," Hassin said. "You should come. There's nothing we can do here."

Cold drained through Rasim, worse than anything he'd felt all day. He looked up at Hassin: tall, handsome, his neatly braided hair falling over one shoulder. It was easy to forget Hassin was a master, that he was nearly thirty, because he was so easy and familiar with the younger crew. But that was his strength as a mate, and why he'd gone from second to first in a year. He'd have a ship of his own when they got back to Ilyara. If they ever got back to Ilyara. Rasim focused on each of those things with sea-crisp clarity, because somehow he had not thought once of Kisia and Desimi since the attack had come at the docks. "They're not here?"

The words cracked again, though he spoke in no more than a whisper. Hassin tilted his head, eyebrows furling. "Who's not here?"

"Kisia. Desimi. They..." Rasim put his hand over his mouth, afraid to speak. Afraid to think. Hassin, frowning, turned Rasim to face him and put both hands on his shoulders in silent encouragement. Rasim moved his hand enough to wet his lips, but spoke through the muffling comfort of his fingers. "They went into the sewers just before the attack. They were going to see if they could find their way to Gontor's chamber faster than I had. They...hasn't anybody seen them?"

"No."

The simple answer carried all the cold depths of the ocean into Rasim's bones. It drowned every emotion he might have; that was the only way he could borrow

Hassin's belt knife and step to the wall so calmly. He tapped out the only message he knew: *Quiet. Listen. Friends below?* and waited. Someone picked it up, their tapping response audible to him, but the next moments lasted forever, until a new series of taps came back.

No friends below. The message ended, then, like an afterthought, another series of beats echoed through the walls: *No enemies below.* He sank to his knees, one palm against the cold wall, and couldn't make himself speak.

"Rasim?" Hassin crouched beside him, worry creasing deep lines around his mouth and eyes. "Rasim, what did they say?"

"Kisia and Desimi never came out of the sewers."

"Maybe they're hiding."

Rasim gave Hassin a look of pure disgust, so potent that the first mate's mouth twisted. "Remind me not to try offering you false hope again, Journeyman."

"With the amount of sea witchery going on, there's no way Desimi could have missed it. He would have come out fighting if he could, and Kisia never met a fight she was willing to run from. They either got captured or they're dead, Hassin. We need to sweep the sewers."

"I'll do it myself," Hassin offered quietly. "They're vast, but nothing's as quick as witchery to find trouble in the waters."

"I'll help."

Hassin said, "No," and it sounded like an order. Rasim lifted his eyes to find Hassin's face set in resolute lines. The first mate said, "No," again more gently, and this time, Rasim knew why. Hassin didn't want him to be the one who found Kisia and Desimi's bodies, if there were bodies to be found.

His courage failed him and he nodded gratefully. "Then I'll go to the captain." Resolution tightened his stomach, better than the emptiness of fear, and he turned to Missio's body. "I'm bringing her with me. I want her to have a Seamaster's burial."

Hassin was already on the way to the door, but that brought him up short. "After what she's done? After all we've lost?"

"Even so." Tears suddenly burned Rasim's eyes. "She lost everything too, Hassin. She lost Trisk when the sea serpent attacked, and it broke her. Don't tell me Captain Nasira can't understand that, but if she can't, if she won't, then *I'll* sing for Missio, and ask Siliaria to take her back into her arms."

The first mate's throat tightened before he pulled a quick, tense smile of sorrow. "Wait for me before you sing, Rasim. If you can sing for her, I'll join my voice with yours."

Rasim nodded. "Be quick, and pray to Siliaria that we only have five souls to sing into the sea."

Hassin left without answering, which was answer enough. Rasim curled Missio's cold body into his arms and followed after, not meeting anyone's eyes as he walked out of the palace. It wasn't as late in the day as he'd imagined. The early Northern sunset was only just beginning, streaking the sky bitter red and deep purple. The fight that morning seemed like it had been days ago. But he hadn't lost a whole day sitting by

Missio's side. Captain Nasira wouldn't have let that happen.

The journey back to the docks seemed much shorter than the one away had been earlier, although wasn't any less tired. Something drove him now, though: fear, or anger, or both. People moved out of his way, and he wondered what his expression was like, or if it was only that he carried a dead woman in his trembling arms. Maybe both, because when he approached the *Wafiya*, even Captain Nasira paused to frown at him like he'd become someone else. Someone more worthy of respect, maybe.

Or maybe just someone who'd lost his mind. "Endat came to tell me you'd found her. Don't *you* tell me you think she deserves a Seamasters' burial."

"If Siliaria doesn't think so, she can cast her back out onto the shores," Rasim said flatly. The other bodies already lay together under rough canvas at the ship's prow. He made his way there with Missio and laid her with the others, then, lower lip between his teeth, looked to see who they'd lost for certain.

None of them were young: no journeymen, this time. All masters, which was a greater blow to the guild as a whole than Rasim personally. He re-tucked the canvas, then hesitated and took Missio's pouch from her belt, whispering, "You don't need this anymore," before he stood. The bite of cold northern wind felt good against his cheeks. "Is Lorens here? Or Inga?"

"I am." Inga's wheat-blonde hair and pale skin were out of place on an Ilyaran ship, but she climbed out of the hold like a sailor born. "Where's Hassin?"

"Looking for Kisia and Desimi. When he gets back, with or without them, I think the captain wants to sail."

Nasira's mouth pinched, but she nodded. Inga made a soft movement of protest with her hands, but Rasim cut her off. "You need to have a ship ready, Princess. If Sunmaster Endat is going to visit Shenryal, your ships need to launch with ours."

"They're in dry dock—"

"Take some of our witches. They can get a dry ship seaworthy faster than you'd ever be able to do. Just be ready." He was being rude. Possibly disastrously rude, given that Inga was heir to the Northern throne and his own king wanted strong relationships with the North. Rasim felt too hard and cold inside to care. He had an idea. A dark, frightening idea that he couldn't do if he let himself feel anything *besides* the hardness and the coldness. Nasira looked like a puffer fish, holding back her opinion of his behavior, but Inga only regarded him steadily for a few moments, then nodded.

"Captain? May I have use of some of your crew? I know it puts you in a bad spot, but—"

"I'm no worse off another five crew short than I am now," Nasira said shortly. "But it's not going to matter if Hassin can't find Desimi. What's that about, Journeyman?"

"They were playing in the sewers just before the attack and no one's seen them since." Rasim couldn't make that gentle, either.

Nasira's face went slack, then tightened with complicated remorse. "Without Desimi this is all a fool's errand. We've been testing the ice for days, and now we're at barely half strength."

"Just get the ships ready." Rasim turned away from his captain and the Northern princess alike, moving to do his part in just that: preparing the *Wafiya* to sail. It was strangely quiet work, with so few crew members. Those who remained knew their duties, though, and Rasim was grateful he could fall into familiar rhythms that occupied both his body and his mind.

From the position of the stars, it was after midnight when Hassin finally returned to the *Wafiya*. Everyone hesitated a moment when he came on board, waiting without wanting to ask. Nor did they have to: Hassin met Rasim's eyes and shook his head.

No bodies, then. But no Kisia or Desimi, either. They had been captured.

The captain's curse was loud across the quiet night. The crew stayed silent, absorbing the unspoken bad news. Nasira, though, lifted her gaze sharply and found Rasim's. One of her eyebrows arched in challenge. He turned away, finishing the job he'd been doing—tying off ropes—before speaking to whomever could answer him: "Is the Northern ship ready to sail?"

"It is," Hassin replied. "I stopped on my way here to check."

Rasim, nodding, made his way to the prow. "And are we?"

"Except for a harbor full of ice and a fierce wind in front of us," Nasira snapped.

"Skymaster Arrat or his journeymen can help with the wind," Rasim said quietly. His heartbeat was calm and steady and he had no sweat on his palms, no dry mouth, none of the things that usually told him he was about to do something foolish.

Well, not usually, maybe. He didn't generally think things through far enough in advance to worry about them too much. It was mostly afterward that he recognized he'd been rash, and got cold sweats and sick to his stomach. But he'd been thinking about this for hours without scaring himself silly over it, and that was probably awful in its own way.

The *Wafiya*'s figurehead rose high against the horizon. Rasim crawled up behind it, then stood on its struts so he could see the whole of Hongrunn's ice-ridden harbor. With the figurehead vanishing in the lower reaches of his vision, it was almost like standing on air. There were old stories about the most powerful Skymasters being able to do that, but Rasim thought no one really came any closer to it than this.

The ice below was blue with moonlight that cast shadows of deep rich grey. The water beneath was black, hidden from light, and so cold that to touch it, even with sea witchery, sent bumps over Rasim's arms. Sounds carried on the wind: ropes and boards creaking, footsteps on the deck, voices that were little more than murmurs. Normally, casting off was noisy business, with sailors shouting orders and calling farewells to those on shore. Not tonight. Tonight everyone was being quiet, trying to see what Rasim would do, while also attending to their own duties.

No point in drawing out the suspense. Rasim

unfolded the bag he'd taken from Missio's belt and spilled its dusty contents into his palm.

It wasn't much to look at, dull and ashy in the moonlight. No sparkle to it, nothing that gave any hint or promise as to what it did. Even he had thought it was dust at first.

Except no sea witch who still carried Siliaria's figurine would ever let it get so dirty. Only something absurdly precious would be kept with Siliaria. Not even coins went into the goddess's carrying pouch, because they could scratch and damage her. The dust had to be important, and once he realized that, he knew what it was.

Rasim took a deep breath and swallowed a palmful of the drug that had killed Missio.

Power came alight within him.

CHAPTER EIGHT

It was fire under his skin, making him sensitive to every drop of water in the air, to every pulse and wave of the harbor beneath the ship. He felt beads of moisture hanging along the *Wafiya*'s oiled boards, and the steam of breath exhaled from the crew behind him. Some witches, like the healers and Kisia, saw the water in a human body clearly enough to work it. Rasim had never been able to, but now he could. He could stop a heart. He could stop a hundred.

And for the first time, he felt water within the ice. He'd always known it was there. Everyone did. But something changed when it froze, making it nearly impossible for a sea witch to access. Now he could barely imagine what the problem had been. The water was still there. *Thinner*, maybe; stretched out in a way that unfrozen water wasn't, but it was still only water, and any sea witch could master that.

He extended his hands, barely aware the satchel of drug-dust dangling from his fingers. The ice beyond was what mattered. Thin, hard water: it could be broken with a flex of his will. Or not so thin after all; the ice was many inches thick, but even so. Rasim clenched his extended hands into sudden fists.

A boom shattered the quiet Northern night, and then another, dozens of them piling on top of each other until the air was filled with the sound of thunder. Rasim glanced upward, half expecting the stars themselves to be shaking in the sky, or the moon to be breaking into pieces. Neither happened, but in front of him, ice shattered. Lumpy chunks burst upward and fell back into the black sea. Cracks appeared everywhere, leaping left and right as they found the weakest places in the ice. Rasim stood above it all with a wild grin on his face. His heart throbbed with each explosive snap of ice, but even that wasn't enough.

Fingers of water reached up to seize huge floes of ice, dragging them into the depths. They would melt on their own, but not quickly enough. Not when he could force them to fragment into smaller and smaller pieces by driving thin wedges of sea water into fine cracks and widening them until they broke. He let the smaller pieces go again, laughing with delight as they burst back to the surface like breaching ship-fish all over the harbor. Once they were small enough he could even make them melt by pressing the thin-stretched frozen water back against itself. *He* began to feel stretched thin, like there wasn't enough of him to go around the whole harbor, and that was awful. In the beginning he'd felt unstoppable, and he wanted that to go on. There was an easy way to *make* it go on, an easy way to be sure he could finish clearing the harbor of ice.

Very dimly, he recognized that he didn't need to clear the whole harbor. He *wanted* to, because it would be so impressive no one would ever doubt his abilities again. He wanted to because he would look like a hero, and it didn't matter that he'd already decided that being a hero was overrated. But really all they needed was a clear passage, and that already existed.

He still couldn't stop himself from smashing and melting chunks of ice. It should all be destroyed, to show the slavers the true power of Ilyaran sea witchery. They would know not to steal away his friends and family, if he could clear the harbor entirely. All it would take was another dose of the drug.

Even more faintly, Rasim knew taking a second dose of the drug would be stupid, but he couldn't make himself let it go. Just in case he needed it again before he finished. Just in case. He kept whispering that to himself as the heightened power began to drain away. His legs were oddly weak, like Missio's had been. He swayed, suddenly less confident of his perch on the figurehead. Someone's hands caught his ribs and he was lifted off it, then set on the deck with a grunt. A concerned face peered into his. "Rasim?"

"Help." Rasim, trembling, pressed the bag of Missio's drug into Hassin's hands. "Throw this overboard right now. Now, while I can see you. Make sure it sinks deep. I can't do it myself."

Hassin's eyes were black in the moonlight. He accepted the bag gingerly and took a few quick steps away. Water rose to the *Wafiya*'s rail in an elegant spout, tiny shards of ice spinning in it. Hassin shook the pouch over it, emptying it of dust, then dropped the bag as well. The spout folded over itself and dove back into the harbor, streaking away. Rasim felt it dissipate over the distance, spreading the drug into impotency. Only when Hassin released his witchery did Rasim relax at all, and even then he still shook and shivered. "Don't ever let me near that stuff again."

"That good?" Hassin's question was hushed.

"Better. Better than anything I've ever felt. Even better than Siliar—"

Hassin stepped up quickly and laid his fingers across Rasim's lips. Rasim's eyebrows shot up and the first mate's eyes twinkled. "Don't say anything that might offend the goddess, Journeyman. We've got a long voyage ahead of us."

"Right." Rasim smiled thinly and looked into the ice-free harbor water, whispering, "I'm glad I never saw that stuff before she kissed me. All that power. I'd have done anything for it. I almost still would."

"But you won't die for it." Nasira stalked up to them, frowning like she was trying not to look impressed. "You've got your friends to live for, so don't be stupid. You've already got more magic than sense."

Both Rasim and Hassin turned skeptical looks on her, and the captain's mouth twitched as she allowed, "All right, you've got an uncommon amount of wit, I'll grant you that. Skymaster Arrat and his journeymen are on board, and the Northern ship is ready to sail.

Let's cast off." The last words were spoken loud and clear, and awe-stricken sailors hopped to their duties.

"Captain." Rasim's voice was hoarse and he wondered if he'd been shouting at the ice. He felt like he might have been. Nasira arched an eyebrow at him and he cleared his throat. "Captain, Missio was wrong to go to them, however she found them, whoever they were, whyever she did it, but if they gave her that stuff..." He shook his head.

So did Nasira, wearily. "Have you ever met anything you couldn't forgive, Journeyman? You've got us free of the harbor. If you want Missio buried as a Seamaster, she will be. Just don't expect everyone to sing for her." She walked away, attending to her own duties, and after a moment, so did Rasim.

The *Wafiya* was under sail within minutes, canvas cast to catch wind that Skymaster Arrat bent toward the sails. One of the Skymaster journeymen was on the Northern longship, filling its single vast sail as well. The Northern ships had admirably low drafts, though Rasim thought the Ilyarans' many masts and sails were naturally superior.

Usually, launches meant many people on the docks, waving goodbyes. Tonight, when Rasim thought to look back, there was only one: Inga, standing with clenched fists and leaning into the wind like she might leap onto a ship and sail away herself. Reminded of Kisia's comment, Rasim looked for Hassin, and found him unnaturally still at the stern of the ship, watching the Northern princess recede with the shore. When she was no more than imagination, he turned from the rail and caught Rasim watching him. Rasim's face heated, but Hassin smiled like he was glad to not be entirely alone in that moment, and put his hand over his heart before returning to work.

Through luck, they'd caught the last of the outgoing tide after Rasim's witchery. His attention kept going to the brilliant moonlight reflected on black slopping water littered with chunks, not walls, of ice. He didn't exactly feel drained like he had after raising the sea to empty the mines, though he knew his magic must be limited right now. The lingering effects of the dust-drug just made him feel like if he had a little more, he could do amazing witchery again. He was lucky no big magic needed to be done, and luckier still that Hassin had dumped the remaining drug into the harbor.

They weighed anchor just beyond the harbor's mouth, where the sea became choppy and rough with winter winds. All the crew turned out on deck, and it looked strangely, sadly empty with so many sailors missing. Together they lifted the four who had died fighting the slavers and, just as Hassin had done with the drug, they called flutes of water upward to rest the bodies on. Sesin began to sing, her voice pure and sweet and high. Rasim, still a soprano, joined her, as did one or two other journeymen and many of the women. Nasira, whose singing voice was much warmer than Rasim had expected, brought in the next singers, and so on until the very deepest voices finally joined. From surface clarity to the dark depths of the ocean: that was how Seamasters lamented their dead as they gave them back to Siliaria. Only when magic had brought them all deep did Nasira look to Missio's body, and then to Rasim.

He lifted his chin. He would carry her, and sing for her, even if no one else would. Even if his magic was tired now, he had strength enough for that. He would be sure of it. He knelt at Missio's side and made sure her carving of Siliaria was still in her grip before he slid his arms beneath her body to lift her.

To his astonishment, someone else helped too. Rasim looked up to meet Sesin's tear-filled eyes, then nearly staggered with disbelief as first Hassin, then Nasira, came to carry Missio's head and feet. Their witchery came together, too, four weaving strands of water rising to take Missio gently from Seamaster arms. This time, Rasim began the keening song, and Sesin was the one to join in. Hassin drew breath to sing as he had promised, but Nasira, whom Rasim had never expected to see cry, brought her voice in first, and sang as if her heart was broken. Then Hassin's tenor came in more quietly, gaining strength, and for long moments it seemed like they might be the only four to sing. That was too bad, Rasim thought: without the baritones Missio couldn't go so deep, and Siliaria might cast her onto the shores after all. But then a bass rumbled in, and one by one the crew all joined, until, like the others, Missio was brought to the ocean's floor to rest in Siliaria's arms.

CHAPTER NINE

The Northern longship was a slice of darkness against the moonlight, waiting at a respectable distance for the Ilyaran funeral rites. Only when sailors began returning to their posts did the longship come up alongside the *Wafiya* so that Skymaster-assisted conversations could fly back and forth between the two ships. Sunmaster Endat and one of the Skymaster journeyman were already aboard the Northern ship, but Rasim had expected that. He searched for another face and found it: Lars, shadowing Endat, and also far more of Lars's men than Rasim had expected.

Prince Lorens was there, too, and Kif, the grumpy elder, who looked as if it was the last thing he wanted. Rasim pressed his fingers into the corners of his eyes, trying to shunt weariness away. It didn't help much. He sighed and went to Nasira's side.

She glowered at him. "What now?"

"Permission to leave the *Wafiya*, Captain? I want to check on Lars. He's got too many men with him."

Nasira's eyes narrowed. "And will you return, Journeyman?"

Rasim's heart seized, then plummeted into his stomach. His jaw dropped as well. Nasira actually laughed. "What, you didn't think I could see through that one, boy? It was as clear as harbor water."

"I—" Shaken, Rasim put his hands on the rail and stared across the short distance between ships. He hadn't intended to abandon the *Wafiya*. Not consciously, anyway. "I hadn't...thought that far ahead yet. I suppose maybe I...meant to stay. I don't know."

"I believe you," Nasira said after a thoughtful moment. "But the question remains. Will you return?"

"I don't know what to do," Rasim whispered in a desperate burst. "It's Kisia, Captain. She's my best friend. And Desimi, he's..."

Nasira put a hand on Rasim's shoulder, a momentary gentle touch. "Sometimes our closest companions are the ones we clash the hardest with, Rasim. Don't dishonor him by naming him something other than your friend."

"Then my friends are out there somewhere," Rasim said. "They have to be. How can I go west without knowing if they're all right?"

"You can't," Nasira said almost cheerfully. "Captain's orders. I'm already running this ship at half-hands. I've no intention of letting you or anybody else swim off to the horse clans until I've got my crew back."

"But—but, Captain, they're going west because of me. I'm the one who started all this."

Nasira's eyebrows lifted. "Did you. You set the Great

Fire, poisoned Hongrunn's water supply, and set that smooth-voiced warlord Roscord on the Islands throne? All before being tossed into the river in your third month? You *are* remarkable, Rasim al Ilialio."

Sullen, Rasim muttered, "You know that's not what I meant," and felt sulkier yet when Nasira grinned. A month ago he'd have been delighted to make this captain smile. Now she was laughing at him, which wasn't worse, but certainly wasn't what he wanted.

"I know," said Nasira, still cheerfully, though she sobered. "I also know you feel too responsible, lad. Endat's a diplomat. Going west is his duty, and will make the best use of his skills, whereas I need yours on this ship. More than usual," she admitted with a flare of her nostrils. "Most of my upper crew is missing, and what's left doesn't have the strength to stand against a bad storm without an anchor."

"Me?" Rasim asked after a disbelieving moment. "You need *me* on board in case we hit bad weather?"

"I do. So go on to the longship if you must, and say your goodbyes, but if you're not back on the *Wafiya* by the next bell, I'm coming after you myself. And you won't like that, Journeyman. You won't like that at all."

"Aye, Captain." Rasim called a water spout to carry him to the next ship, surprised to be trembling when he set foot on the Northerners' deck. The short journey shouldn't have taken that much energy out of him, he thought. He reached for the ship's rail to steady himself, but Lars stepped away from Endat to offer Rasim a hand, which suited Rasim. "I'm surprised to see you. I didn't think you'd leave Hongrunn."

Lars cast a stealthy glance over his shoulder, taking in both the Sunmaster and the various former slaves who were on deck. "Not one of us trusted that we'd still be free men when you got back. I'd rather be on your ship than this one, truth be told."

"My ship is going straight to Moran." Rasim's lip curled. "Into the heart of slave country. You don't want to be going there at all. Sunmaster Endat won't let anything happen to you."

"You're not coming west, then."

Rasim took his turn at a surreptitious glance toward the *Wafiya*. "I guess not. The captain wants me on board the *Wafiya* and..." He swallowed, blurting, "And I can't just leave them, Lars. I don't want to abandon you, either, I want to make sure you're safe, but my friends—"

"Your friend, your *ligen* captain, Kisia?" Lars made a gesture to describe Kisia's height, much shorter than his own, when Rasim looked uncertain at the word he'd used. "She got us out of the mines as much as you, and she sailed us to Hongrunn in that bucket of holes without one of us getting our feet wet. I wouldn't want you to do anything but find her. Would your captain take us on?"

"Slave country," Rasim reminded him.

Lars shook his head. "Ilyarans don't keep slaves. We're safer with you than with our own people. We'd feel safer," he amended with a shrug. "And we will fight to find your countrymen."

"The captain's probably more interested in whether you'll learn to sail. I can ask." Rasim touched Lars's shoulder in promise, then wobbled to Endat. The water was calm, no noticeable pitch to the ship. He really shouldn't be so weak. Endat offered a hand of support, and Rasim accepted, relieved at the help.

"I'm not sure what's wrong with me."

"Don't you?" Endat looked toward the harbor they'd left behind, then at Rasim, whose shoulders twitched.

"All right, I guess I do. Captain says I'm supposed to go to Moran with her, Sunmaster."

"And are you here to plead her case or your own?"

Rasim hesitated, then slumped. "Hers. I want to go with you, but...it's my guild. My friends."

"And not one of us will think less of you for that, Rasim. Or are you worried about my sincerity in warning the Shenryalans, or in investigating their politics?"

Sudden dryness made Rasim's lips sticky. He tried to swallow and to wet them, but his throat was as parched as the Ilyaran desert. There it was, out in the open where he had to think about it. Where he had to acknowledge that he didn't trust the Sunmaster. He didn't trust *any* Sunmaster, not after hearing how they'd manipulated the Ilyaran royal family into relying on them more heavily than any other guild. Not when he weighed that alongside the Great Fire, which they had been unable to stop.

The moonlight was bright enough that Endat could read every suspicion that flickered across Rasim's face. The Sunmaster lowered his eyes, mouth pursed, then met Rasim's guilty face again. "I see. Who *do* you trust, then, Journeyman?"

Rasim turned again, looking across the water toward the *Wafiya*. Hassin climbed the mast and stepped lightly onto a crossbar, then crouched with lithe grace to check knots and sails. Endat followed his gaze and chuckled. "Your captain is unlikely to let her first mate go, Rasim."

"Sesin, then, but Hassin knows more about what's been going on. I just, I can't—"

"Let us go unsupervised? How, young man, do you suppose we got along without you?"

Anger, as cold as ice, rose in Rasim's breast. He swung back to face Endat, no longer in need of any support. "Badly, Sunmaster. Badly. The Ilyaran palace is under your sail, the Islands are a heartbeat away from internal war, the Northlands are pitted with corruption, and Siliaria only knows what we'll find within the horse clans. I'm only a Seamaster journeyman, and until a few weeks ago not even a very impressive one. I know that. But at least I *see* the problems, and at least I'm trying to do something about them. If you're a good man, and I think you might be, then what's your excuse? You've stood by and let the Sunmasters run our royal family into the sea and enjoyed the benefits of it. *Somebody* has to keep an eye on you. On all of you, because even if I'm only thirteen I can see perfectly well that you're doing a terrible job of it yourselves!"

Across the water, he caught a glimpse of Nasira clapping an exasperated hand over her eyes as his voice rose in pitch. Endat, however, looked amused, not upset, and lifted his palm to stem Rasim's tide of anger. "That may be fair," he allowed. "None-the-less, you are needed on your ship, and I on mine. You will have to trust me, Rasim, because you have no other choice."

Fuming, Rasim turned away to find Lars at his back and looking like he wanted to take up arms against Endat. "What was that about?" he asked, making Rasim realize he'd slipped back into his native tongue.

Rasim replied through his teeth, but in the Northern language. "I need to tell the Shenryalan clans what I've seen and what I suspect, and I don't trust Endat to do it. Not entirely. But I have to go with the *Wafiya*, too. I just—*argh*!" The sound burst out of him and he kicked the air in frustration. After a few more seconds he drew a deep breath, trying to calm himself, and said, "I've never needed to be in two places at once before. Everything's happening too fast now. I don't know what to do."

"You don't trust the Sunmaster," Lars echoed, almost a question.

"I'm afraid he's got plans of his own. I don't think he'll do anything to compromise Ilyara, but I'm not sure he'll do the Shenryalans any good. I want to keep an eye on him, to make sure he does what he's supposed to, and I can't!"

Lars straightened to his full, impressive, height. "Then we'll watch him for you."

Rasim's eyebrows shot toward his hairline. "Are you sure?"

"Do you trust *me*?"

After the escape from the mines, Lars was more loyal than Rasim knew what to do with. He didn't like it, but he trusted it absolutely. He nodded once and the big miner's shoulders seemed to widen even further. "Then we'll be your eyes, Seamas—"

Rasim made another sound, this time alarmed, and Lars broke off in surprise. "Don't call me that," Rasim said with a lopsided smile. "I appreciate the honor intended, but that's a title to earn from my guild. Just...call me Rasim. Nothing more formal than that. Please. I'm just...I'm just like you."

The look in Lars's expression said otherwise, but he nodded. "We'll be your eyes, then. We'll watch for you."

"Thank you." The words were heartfelt. Rasim tried not to look too hard at Endat, who had of course heard and understood every word of the conversation.

So had Prince Lorens, who was obviously amused by it. He moved in, lifting his chin to dismiss Lars. The miner went to the ship's railing, not too far away, but far enough, and Lorens smiled his disarming bright smile at Rasim. "My mother would be wise to give you a title, so those men might call you *liege*."

"I don't want a title," Rasim said fervently. "All I've ever wanted was to sail on the *Wafiya*. I don't know how I keep getting caught up in these messes. And speaking of messes..." He glanced around the ship's deck, searching for Kif, the old man who had spoken out against contacting the Shenryalans, but also hadn't seemed unhappy to join the group sailing west. "What's Kif's story, Lorens? Why does he know anything about the horse clans?"

"Kif served as a guard for merchant ships. His captain once tried to sell to the horse clans. It...didn't go well," Lorens said with a wave of his fingers. "They knew nothing of Shenryalan customs, and offended the wrong people. Most of them died. Kif was spared because one of their young women took a fancy to him, and helped him heal from his injuries. They were wed, I think." Lorens's voice softened at that. "But she died in childbirth and he was blamed. Driven out. He's hated them ever since."

Astonished, Rasim asked, "Then why does he want to go back?"

"Because the child she died bearing was not their first. He's never taken another wife," Lorens said quietly. "I believe his love was all left behind in the Shenryalan steppes."

Rasim put a fist over his heart, trying to ease the ache there. "I'm glad he's getting a chance to go back, then. Be careful out there, Lorens. Inga would kill me if I got you in trouble."

The prince flashed another of his charming smiles. "So she would, and I wish I could say I was going to do as you ask. I've thought about it, though, Rasim. I'm coming with you."

"What?" Rasim's voice broke on the word and he shot Endat a quick glance, then looked back at Lorens.

"You're going to be dealing with the Moranese high council. You can't afford to not have someone with diplomatic practice and high connections on your side, and Sunmaster Endat's language skills are better than mine. He's of more use in Shenryal than I am."

"Does Inga know this?"

"Inga nearly got on this ship to sail west with Endat, because of this. If we could have contacted our mother quickly enough, she would have. She may yet sail in Endat's wake."

"Why didn't you just get on the *Wafiya*, then?" Rasim's head spun with weariness.

"Because you had crew to bury, and you didn't need an outsider there. I wish I had been, though," Lorens said more quietly. "I'd have liked to have seen that show of power up close."

Rasim shuddered. "Well, you won't see it again. I— Sunmaster Endat? Do you know about this?"

"I may even grudgingly approve," the Sunmaster said, now that he'd been invited into the conversation. "I'd like to have an official Northern representative with us when we reach the steppes, but Kif may be of equal value, given his history with the horse clans. I think you'll need Lorens more than we do."

A whistle blasted from the *Wafiya*. Rasim turned that direction, increasingly weary. "All right. I don't know if the captain will be glad of your presence, but she'll probably be glad of your help once we're in Moran. Do you need to get anything?"

"I've my pack here." Lorens lifted a traveling pack from a shadow on the ship's deck, and stepped closer to Rasim, who glanced to Endat and Lars.

"Safe journeys, Sunmaster. Lars." Rasim smiled at the former slave in particular, then called witchery and vaulted back over the railing to carry himself and Lorens to the *Wafiya*.

The sea, so reliable of late, did not rise up to catch him, and he fell.

CHAPTER TEN

Rasim remembered, hazily, the ice-cold ocean bath he'd taken as his witchery failed him. He remembered, vaguely, that Hassin had gotten him aboard the *Wafiya*. He remembered more clearly that Sesin sat at his side a long time after that, soothing Rasim with a magic he both coveted and, in the moment, feared. He wanted more of Missio's drug so he could feel the immense bliss of incredible power. At the same time, he was terrified of *any* magic, afraid it could somehow overwhelm him all by itself. Still, he huddled as near to Sesin's gentleness as he could, even when he was certain it would burn him.

Clarity returned slowly. His head ached, but not with the craving for power. He was thirsty, that was all, and drained a water skin that lay close to hand. Then there were other necessary functions to attend to. He staggered onto the deck, gasping at the strength and chill of fresh-blown air. It carried the scent and sounds of land: distant earthy dryness and the cries of gulls and other near-shore sea birds. Someone offered him smoked whitefish and more water. Rasim took both gratefully and mumbled thanks around greedy mouthfuls.

Hassin stood beside him when he'd finished eating. Rasim squinted up at the first mate, then sank back against the ship's hull, weak despite the food. "Where are we?" His voice sounded funny, as if it had gone unused for days.

"Half a day from the Morrin river mouth."

"The Morrin." Rasim leaned heavily on the rail, trying to call continental maps to mind. The Morrin River ran through Moran, the city it was named for. "That's an almost four-day sail from Hongrunn. I've been sleeping that long?"

Hassin nodded. "Are the cravings gone?"

"The cravings." Rasim shuddered, then nodded.

Hassin, satisfied, echoed the motion. "Sesin wishes she had some of the drug left to study, or to save for Master Usia. I've seen witches taken with addiction before, Rasim. For some of them, a single taste is all it takes. I wouldn't have put you among them. Not after what you've done."

"What I've done? What have I done?"

Hassin snorted. "Heroics are as addicting as anything else, lad. You keep finding yourself in the midst of them, but you're not seeking them out for the thrill. If you were born to be an addict, I think you would be. So Sesin is curious about that drug, and I admit, so am I. It must have something in it to enhance the need for it."

"Maybe. Everything else—the serpent, the snake, Siliaria, all of it, that was all exciting, but a lot of it was awful, too. More of it was awful. People were dying, or in danger of dying. Breaking up the ice with all that magic was just...it felt wonderful. I wanted to be able to do it forever. It felt like I could. And then when that feeling was gone it was...I just wanted it to come back. Poor Missio."

"You've got a kind heart, Rasim," Hassin said after a moment. "Can I ask you something?"

Rasim waved a hand in agreement, then put it back on the railing, still dizzier than he thought he should be. Hassin nodded, but gathered himself before speaking. "I've never seen anyone use that much witchery. Maybe Guildmaster Isidri, at the harbor. But you've been studying with the Sunmasters. Do you think... now that you know you can use all that magic, do you think you can do as the king hopes? Can you work sun witchery now, do you think?"

Rasim's heart stuttered. He could already work stone witchery along with his native-born seamastery, but no one knew that. No one but Sesin, anyway, and Kisia, who suspected. Neither of them were going to tell. He trusted Hassin as deeply as he trusted anyone, but Hassin was first mate on Nasira's ship, and Nasira had already thrown Rasim overboard once for *suspected* use of sun witchery. A shudder went over him. "No. I don't think so. All the drug did was make me be able to use an awful lot of seamastery."

And if it *had* somehow awakened the ability to use even more magics, Rasim would never say so. Or at least not to anyone but King Taishm, who had set Rasim on this voyage. He should be the first to know, so that no one could ever try to use Rasim against him.

"Probably just as well. The captain wouldn't like it." Hassin grinned at Rasim's nonplussed stare, then waved him off. "Go get some more food into yourself, Journeyman. I think the captain wants to dress you down for being unconscious for three days."

"We didn't hit rough seas, did we?" Rasim clutched his head, trying to remember if any of the pitching had been the ship and not his stomach.

"No, and lucky for you. There's been no sign of a slaver ship, either," Hassin added quietly. "I know they've got a half crew of sea witches aboard, but with our masts and sails, we should have caught them by now."

"We're sailing the main channel? The shortest route to Moran?" Hassin nodded and Rasim shrugged. "The slavers probably aren't. We may get to Moran ahead of them." An angry smile tugged his mouth. "They won't know what hits them. I only wish we wouldn't have to fight our own crew. Because we will. They'll be full of mindkiller, and will fight for the Moranese."

"We'll sail that ship when we find it, Rasim. But first we have to find it. Now go eat," Hassin said again, this time with more severity. "You're pale as a Northerner."

"Aye, Commander." Rasim wobbled belowdecks, where he ate and, to his embarrassment, fell asleep in the galley. Sesin woke him just enough to get him back to his berth, and he slept until hunger awakened him again.

When he made his way onto deck, the shores had closed in: they sailed a river now. A wide and deep river, to be sure, but a river. Nasira stood near the prow, watching the river narrow. Rasim, gnawing on hard bread, went to stand beside her. "I wasn't any use to you after all."

"You will be." The captain didn't look at him, but her tone was certain. "As well that we hit no rough waters sailing in, because they lie ahead of us, sure enough. We are going to war, you understand that, Journeyman?"

Rasim's hunger vanished. "Are we?"

"My old ship's crew may well be in that city, or been sold out of it. This ship's crew is there, or will be soon. We have witchery, Rasim, and I intend to use it."

"But, Captain, we..." Rasim felt like the hard bread had made his tongue too dry and thick to manage. "We're Ilyaran," he said after a moment. "We don't...we don't go to war."

"We've never had reason. No one could threaten us. But now they have, and that needs to be dealt with."

"But what if they've learned magic from our witches? Guildmaster Asindo and I talked about that. We know now that witchery can be learned later in life, and there must be witches who left Ilyara of their own accord. There'd be nothing stopping them from teaching others, or standing against us."

"Do you really think we wouldn't know? If there were other cities with as much witchery to command as we have? Do you think the king wouldn't know?"

Rasim swallowed what was left of the bread sticking to his tongue. "I think they'd try hard to keep us from knowing. I think they'd hide it behind Ilyaran slaves. I'm not saying they *have* magic, Captain, but shouldn't we be careful?"

"You're a strange one to be counseling caution. It's not caution that got you this far."

"It's not recklessness, either! It's just that things keep *happening*!"

"Oh, aye. Leaping from the *Wafiya* to a sea serpent's head wasn't reckless at all. Nor was teaching an Islander magic, or flooding a Northern mine, or—"

"I had to do *something*!" Rasim knew the captain was right, but at the same time, so was he. "I had to make choices, and mostly I had to make them fast. Maybe they weren't good ones, but right now we have the time, Captain. Shouldn't we try to be smart instead of sailing in expecting to meet no resistance?"

Nasira's nostrils flared. "Smart how?"

"Well, we haven't seen the slaver ship yet, right? So maybe they're behind us, which means somebody in Moran expects a ship full of Ilyaran slaves to sail in soon. Maybe we should give them that. Maybe we should pretend to be captive."

"We don't have any Moranese for the roles, Journeyman."

"We've got Prince Lorens." Rasim's stomach dipped. "The Northerners are known to not care very much about slavery, and if the Moranese think we're all full of mindkiller, they'd know Lorens doesn't need a big crew to control us."

Nasira gave him a hard stare, one that said she didn't like what he was thinking, but that she saw the value in it. After a long, grim moment, she said, "I'll talk to the prince about it. We'd need a name within Moran, someone with the power to oversee the purchase of a ship full of Ilyaran slaves. I don't have that information, and if Lorens doesn't, it's a dead end, Rasim. I'm not putting any free man, Ilyaran or no, off this ship to learn those things. These people will make slaves of anyone they lay hands on. I can't risk it. And you're not to sneak off and seek permission later," Nasira added sharply. "Do it and it's the end of your guild career."

Rasim's eyebrows rose slowly. "That's the second time you've used that threat."

"It's the only thing that holds water with you. Asindo admires you, Rasim, but he likes to play a line out to see where it lands. I don't. Cross me, and I'll do everything I can to stopper your dreams."

"I believe you." Rasim left her without making any promises, but neither was he foolish enough to thwart Nasira openly. It was possible that Guildmaster Asindo might forgive what Captain Nasira forbade, but Rasim could almost believe Nasira would leave him in chains on a Moranese shore if he went against orders. Asindo's forgiveness wouldn't matter much then.

He worked the rest of the day with the crew, feeling his strength return even as his mind worried at the problems ahead. Not until the last whistle of his shift blasted did the captain appear and bark, "My quarters," at him.

Rasim winced and the handful of crew in the galley chuckled with sympathy and malice as he ducked his head and followed the captain to her cabin.

Hassin and Prince Lorens were already in the captain's cabin when they arrived. Rasim, stepping in behind her, felt as if he was in enormous trouble. The small, tidy room was crowded with three adults, although Lorens pressed himself into a corner, trying to make the least of his size. A little to Rasim's surprise, Skymaster Arrat followed him into the room, which somehow made the air easier to breathe. Rasim didn't know if it was Arrat's witchery, but he gave the skymaster a brief, thankful smile.

The smile disappeared as Nasira, sounding furious, said, "The prince is willing to listen to your proposal, Journeyman, but I have the final say in whether we try this nonsense."

"Yes, Captain." If he wasn't in trouble now, Rasim was fairly certain he would be when he was finished talking. "You told him about the idea?" At Nasira's sour nod, Rasim took a deep breath and plunged on with what he'd thought about as he worked. "We all know Ilyaran ships aren't going to be casually sailing into Moran, so the way I see it, there are two obvious possibilities. Either somebody's captured the Ilyaran flagship—"

"Hah!" The sound burst from Nasira like she couldn't stop it.

"Well, exactly. So either someone's captured us, in which case the ship would be flying a Moranese banner, or we're coming to get our people back. Those are the obvious possibilities. Or." Rasim took a deep breath. "Or the third possibility is that the captain's turned traitor and intends to sell her crew."

Hassin's mouth fell open. "*What?*"

"I thought Prince Lorens was supposed to be the traitor here!" Nasira remembered to look apologetic after her outburst, but Lorens waved her off, frowning at Rasim.

"Go on, Journeyman. Why the captain and not me? I'm Northern. We're more likely to turn a blind eye to slavery than you Ilyarans are."

"You're the one who put the idea in her head, or who convinced her," Rasim explained. "You're a prince, after all, and the captain's lost a lot. I'm sorry, Captain, but it's true."

Nasira's tight nod told him he was treading dangerous waters, but he'd known that anyway. "So you convinced her to enslave and sell her crew," Rasim went on. "You've promised her a soft life in the North, or something like that, in exchange for the good will it'll buy the North with the Moranese. I think it could work."

Hassin, his voice low, glanced at Nasira as he said, "It has before."

Rasim gaped and Lorens's pale eyebrows drew down curiously as Hassin offered a tight smile in response to Nasira's warning glare. "I was half your age at the time, Rasim. The guild was told that the ship was lost in a storm, but Asindo told me the truth not a year since. Because of all this," he said with a twirl of his fingers. "Because of the fires, the Northern witchery, all of it. He wanted us to be prepared."

Nasira, her nostrils flared with anger, picked up his story. "His name was Matisi. He wanted more than the guilds could give him, and agitated for change. He wanted to earn profits with his witchery, but Guildmaster Isidri wouldn't let him go. So he left, and took his ship with him. They thought he'd been lost at sea until one of his crew escaped Moran the year of the Great Fire. She made her way back to Ilyara and told the Guildmaster what had happened."

"Why didn't we go get them?" Rasim asked, horrified, then closed his eyes. "The year of the fire. Of course." Of all the guilds, the Seamasters had lost the most in the fire: ships and guildhall alike had burned. "Who was it? Is she still with the guild?"

"Masira." Hassin watched in sympathy as blood drained from Rasim's face.

"Masira? The bathkeeper? But she's...how could anyone enslave her? She's so nice."

"Slavers don't care about nice, Rasim. You know that. She's strong, is what she is. She survived, she escaped, and she's happy now. That's what's most important."

"Except to the ones who got left behind!"

"It was the fire, Journeyman," Nasira said in a cold, precise tone. "A lot got left behind."

Rasim clenched his fists and, for a rarity, wished he had something to hit. That was more of something Desimi would want to do. Maybe he and the bigger Journeyman weren't so different after all. "That's part of how it keeps going, though. It has to be. People forget. They have other problems right in front of them and they let the tide wash away the memories, and slavery keeps happening. It's not right. We should be fighting it. All the time, if we have to."

"What do you think we're on our way to do?" The ice hadn't left Nasira's voice.

"Are we?" Rasim thrust his chin at his captain in challenge. "We're going to get our people back right now, sure, but are we going to do anything for everyone else? How many slaves are there in Moran? How many slaves are there across the whole continent? Saving a couple hundred Ilyarans isn't going to do most of them any good at all."

"What would you *have* us do?" Hassin sounded genuinely curious.

"Change things! Stop the slavers! We're powerful, Hassin! We could do it. Maybe not just half a ship of sea witches, but Ilyarans working together. Why haven't we *done* something?"

Hassin tilted his head, considering the question. "Even in Ilyara, once people are used to doing something one way, it's hard to make them come around to another. Look how long the Sunmasters have held sway in the palace. I didn't even know it had been different until Guildmaster Isidri spoke of it. Even there, most people just shrug and say that this is how it's always been. How much harder would it be to get rid of slavery, even if it's to the greater good?"

"Harder," Rasim admitted, but muttered, "but that doesn't mean it's not worth doing."

"You're right," Lorens said, surprising Rasim. "It is worth doing. But Hassin is also right. People resist change because they're comfortable with what they know. Slaves do the housework, women bear children, men do business. It's the way of the world. At least, it's the way of the world outside of Ilyara."

"But changing that would be good for everyone! Can you imagine Inga cleaning house all day?"

Lorens laughed. "No, and neither can our servants. Can you imagine yourself doing it?"

"It doesn't take me all day. Witchery cleans the floors fast, and a Skymaster can take the dust away in a blink. They always do, after sandstorms. If everybody could do that..."

"But they can't," Nasira said flatly. "And neither can we. Not with one ship half-crewed, and maybe not with an entire Ilyaran army, which we neither have nor want. Do you really imagine the crew will go along with this, Journeyman?"

Rasim stared at her, surprised. "If you tell them to they will. You're the captain, and we're trying to get our crewmates back."

"And you're willing to wear chains and use witchery only at my command? Or Lorens's?"

"If it helps keep us safe, of course I am. We all should be. It might even be best if you actually *sell* some of us. It'll help make people believe you've turned coat."

Nasira's thin smile appeared. "Are you volunteering?"

Rasim's mouth twisted. "I'm sure you'd be happy to sell me, Captain. But Sesin would be good, too. She was able to clear the mindkiller from her blood once she knew it was there. And it would look good if you sold Hassin, too."

"If I didn't know better, I'd think you were deliberately weakening my crew with those sales."

"He's right, though," Lorens said reluctantly. "If you've really turned traitor, getting rid of some of your strongest, most potentially rebellious crew members first makes sense. You'd want to hold the rest back, though, until they've proved their worth."

Nasira looked pained. "You two have slave-seller minds."

Lorens looked offended as Rasim's stomach clenched. "It's just like selling camels or bargaining for beads at the market, Captain. Only with people, and that's what makes it wrong."

Nasira shook her head, expression tight, and momentarily turned her attention to Arrat, whose silent presence had all been forgotten. "I think you and your journeymen had better go to shore, Arrat. If nothing else, it'll leave someone to warn Ilyara if this all goes completely wrong."

The tall Skymaster smiled briefly. "We'd be willing to help, Nasira. You know that."

"I do, but it's already madness and I won't bring another guild down with me." She snapped her gaze back to Rasim. "All right, Journeyman. I'll go along with this because I'm afraid it's our best choice, but I hope we don't all regret it."

CHAPTER ELEVEN

Two mornings later, Rasim, at least, regretted it passionately. A heavy collar made of thick anchor rope bruised his collarbones, and his wrists itched beneath the ropes used to bind them. Sesin and Hassin, looking just as uncomfortable and twice as angry, knelt on either side of him. Three others, all volunteers, were also bound and kneeling nearby. A sneering Nasira, backed by Prince Lorens's cool, disdainful figure, stood above them.

The rest of the crew did their jobs, but did them with ropes around their necks and with sullen faces. That, at least, wasn't feigned: everyone understood the wisdom of the charade, but obviously none of them liked it. They had all, grudgingly, even taken a dose of the mindkiller drug, out of fear that the Moranese might have some way to prove they weren't truly inhibited by it. Rasim had rarely felt so helpless, and it was clear that most of his crewmates *never* had.

High above them, the *Wafiya*'s Ilyaran banner had

been disfigured. A circle of thorns, like the pattern tattooed onto many slaves' shoulders, now over-whelmed the Ilyaran colors. Manacles had been drawn on, too, just in case the thorns weren't enough. They'd hoisted that banner a full day out of Moran. Since then, none of them had used witchery without a direct order from Nasira.

The river they sailed on had thick, heavy stone walls built into its banks, giving it structure as it snaked through the city. Docks were built into the sea walls and stretched here and there into the river's width, allowing ships to butt up against docks and walls alike. Above the walls, the city filled a valley and spilled up its sides, creeping over hilltops and fading into the distance. It was built of both stone and wood, and unlike Ilyara, it *smelled.* There were too many unclean people, and more animals. Rasim was used to the warm sea scent and clean streets of Ilyara, or to the frozen stone mountains of Hongrunn. He coughed and tried to cover his face as the stench rolled over them. The ropes at his wrists caught, leaving him unable to wipe his face as tears stung his eyes and slid down his cheeks.

Even from the low vantage of the river winding through the city's center, it was easy to see how the wealth lay in Moran. Large, stately merchant houses, partially hidden behind the sturdy sea walls, lined the river. The houses were walled on all sides, with exten-sive gardens. Rasim imagined private guards kept the premises safe from the crush of cheaper buildings that were built up against those tall garden walls.

Cheaper, but not hovels: those didn't begin to rise up for several blocks away from the river. Rasim couldn't see much more of the city from his vantage, except that the valley hills were also obviously home to the wealthy. The higher the home, the more regal it was. It made sense that the poor were crushed in the middle between two spans of wealth. It was a wonder the poor weren't all slaves themselves. Or maybe they were close enough to not matter.

Back down on the river, a docking berth had been cleared for the massive Ilyaran flagship. Soldiers and slaves lined the river walls there, the soldiers bristling with swords and bows, the slaves—

The slaves were Ilyaran, all of them. Rasim had no doubt they each held witchery ready to use, though he couldn't sense even the water that the *Wafiya* rested in, much less the magic of enslaved Ilyarans. Still, it was clear that whomever it was coming to greet them would take no chances. Rasim was a little surprised the *Wafiya* hadn't come under attack the moment it entered the Moranese valley, despite the circle-of-thorns banner that said slavers sailed Nasira's ship.

Nasira, with lip-curled disdain, swaggered to the captain's deck and stared down at the gathered soldiers and slaves as if they were rotting fish on the banks. Rasim thought she would speak, but she only stared, expression growing increasingly distasteful, until finally the crowd parted and a stout, officious-looking man pressed through. He was beautifully dressed in red and orange, and wore curling hair clipped short across his forehead.

He sounded far more cautious than a man of his bearing should. "An Ilyaran captain and a Northern nobleman. How unusual."

"Pssh. Get me someone who can make decisions." Nasira turned her back on the official, whose eyes bugged in outraged offense. But after a moment he turned, scarlet along the cheekbones, and made his way back through a laughing crowd. Nasira shared a smirk with Prince Lorens, whose handsome features wore the expression comfortably, as if he was accustomed to being superior to everyone around him. With casual arrogance, Nasira sauntered off the captain's deck to root around in a barrel and return to the deck with an apple in hand. Her back still to the crowd, she sat on the deck's curve and took noisy, crunching bites of the fruit.

She was nearly finished when the crowd shifted again. This time a woman of middling years and dark eyebrows approached. Her clothes weren't as colorful as the man's had been, but she carried an air of unshakable authority emphasized by the half-dozen large men who deferentially escorted her. She stood, hands clasped behind her back, and watched expressionlessly as an unimpressed Nasira glanced her way, then finished her apple before bothering to get to her feet. They sized each other up, Moranese and Ilyaran, before the woman's gaze moved to Lorens.

"Prince Lorens. This is certainly an interesting scenario." She spoke Northern flawlessly. Rasim, despite his chains and the whole dreadful situation, felt a pang of envy at her fluency.

Lorens sauntered to the *Wafiya*'s railing and leaned against it, his hands folded lazily over the water. "Lady Amdria. It's been a long time."

A sparkle shone in the woman's eyes. "Surely I'm not old enough for it to have been *that* long, although you've aged nicely, your highness."

"I've grown up," Lorens corrected. "You, however, haven't changed at all. Perhaps it hasn't been so long as all of that."

The amusement in Amdria's gaze grew. "Still charming, I see. Perhaps you'd like to enlighten me as to why you're on an Ilyaran ship, flying a slaver's flag and humoring an ill-tempered water witch as a...companion?"

"It turned out Captain Nasira and I had a few ambitions in common." Lorens sent a languid smile toward Nasira, who somehow managed to look fond of the Northern prince in return.

Or maybe not just 'fond of'. She looked at him in very much the same way Hassin and Princess Inga looked at one another.

Rasim couldn't imagine how she could *pretend* that look, even if he also couldn't imagine how she could mean it. He shot a nervous, confused glance at Sesin, whose scowl, fixed on the deck, was so tight he thought she must be giving herself a headache. Hassin, who might have understood Nasira's acting ability better, was glaring at the captain so hard that Rasim was surprised she didn't catch on fire from the heat of his anger. Rasim thought maybe he didn't understand adults at all.

Amdria murmured, "Fascinating," which drew Rasim's attention back to her. "I would love to hear about these ambitions, your highness."

"Captain?" Lorens purred the word and Nasira's thin smile appeared momentarily.

"Hassin. Offer the lady a bridge. *Politely.*"

Hassin's nostrils flared, but he did as he had to: a gentle water spout spun out of the river and danced to the woman's feet, then rose to her waist. She sent a startled glance toward Nasira, who gestured grandly. "Step in, madam. Feel free to bring two or three of your men. You'll none of you get a drop on you."

Amdria's cautious gaze went to Lorens, who opened his hands as if in invitation. Eyebrows lifted, Amdria stepped forward. The waterspout rushed around her and lifted her. Rasim could see her jaw stiffen, but she didn't tip over and Hassin certainly didn't spill her into the river as he carried her and two of her escort forward. In a moment or two they were gracefully deposited on the *Wafiya*'s deck, directly in front of Hassin.

Lady Amdria traced a fingertip over his jaw. "That was you, my sweet?" Her Ilyaran, like her Northern, was spoken without an accent.

Hassin, through clenched teeth, muttered, "It was."

The woman's smile flared unexpectedly. "And you're angry about it. Tell me why."

"I'm not a dog to perform tricks," Hassin snarled, and the woman laughed.

"Are you not? Then why do as your captain instructs?"

"*She's not my captain.*" The hatred in Hassin's voice made Rasim flinch. "She's a traitor to us all. She's a backstabbing, underhanded, conniving—"

"Hassin, choke yourself," Nasira said coolly, and his power surged, water gagging in his throat. He clawed at it, unable to reach with the thick rope collar he wore. His face flushed an ugly red, foam starting at his mouth. Rasim watched in horror, afraid that Nasira might actually kill the first mate to prove her power, but at what seemed to be the last possible instant she said, "Hassin, stop choking yourself," just as casually as she'd given the order.

His magic cut off as quickly as it had started. He collapsed into a heap, tears staining his cheeks as he heaved for breath. A coil of rage spun in Rasim's chest and his hands shook as he struggled for some way to retaliate against Nasira, even if she, too, was performing a role.

His fury, reflected across the whole deck, made the Moranese woman laugh, though. "How angry your crew are, Captain. Freshly enslaved, I think. We know you didn't raise a slaver's banner until a day ago. Lorens...?" She turned her attention to the tall Northern prince, who stepped forward and offered his hands. Amdria took them, and they bowed slightly toward each other in a formal greeting.

Lorens's voice dropped as he obviously moved closer than formality required...or even allowed. Curious interest flickered across the Moranese woman's face again as Lorens murmured, "You're the heir to your family's fortunes, are you not, Lady

Amdria? Perhaps it's hard to understand the frustrations of being a younger sibling. There is very little for me to *do* in the North, lady. My duties are to charm and delight, not to rule, and I find it...tedious. If I am to be nothing but ornamental, I would like to do it on my own terms, at least, rather than perform for my sister and mother's convenience. And the captain here—" he cast Nasira an appreciative look— "afforded an opportunity to become my own man."

"An opportunity laden with Ilyaran slaves." Amdria still sounded, and looked, curious.

Nasira finally spoke again. "I would like to offer a gift to you, madam."

Amdria twitched an eyebrow upward. "A gift."

Nasira made a dismissive gesture at the bound witches on the main deck. "If any of them pleases you, I would be glad to offer that one as a tribute to you and your fair city."

"Really." The woman's eyebrow arched higher. "It's clear they've had no time to resign themselves to their fate, so you wish to offer me an untamed gift. And one in ropes, not chains. There are those who would not consider that a kindness."

Nasira leaned forward, a nasty smile in place. "There are those who wouldn't, but you're not one of them, are you? Fresh, angry and powerful, all at your disposal. I might beg the generosity of chains from you, rather than ship's rope to bind them with, but take your pick, my lady. Grant us leave to enter your city and to make our sales. If, in a few days, you are satisfied with your new property, perhaps you might be willing to help me establish a residence in Moran. I will not," she said in a suddenly low and flat voice, "be returning to Ilyara, for obvious reasons."

"Ah, yes. That ship has, as you Ilyarans say, sailed, has it not? You've made your choices. What happens, Captain, to Ilyaran guildmembers who flout guild law this way?" Amdria glanced at Lorens, but immediately returned her attention to Nasira.

Nasira's lip curled. "Exile. It's the choice we make."

"Few of you make it."

"Few have nothing left to lose."

"Have you nothing?"

Nasira, with soft intensity, said, "Nothing."

"And the prince?"

The captain's gaze and voice changed again as she glanced toward Lorens. If Rasim hadn't known better, he would have honestly thought she was in love with him, although there was a slightly hard edge to Nasira's expression. "What's between us is nothing to do with what I left in Ilyara."

"But perhaps it's to do with what you've found since," Amdria murmured.

Nasira's gaze sharpened as it returned to the Moranese woman. "Perhaps. I would say, at least, that his highness opened my eyes to possibilities I had never considered."

Amdria looked thoughtful. "My memory of Prince Lorens is of a clever youth who wished to be part of all the political goings-on. This is a dangerous way to do so, your highness. Do you not risk the wrath of the Ilyaran guilds coming down on your people?"

"The Ilyarans are famous for not making war," Lorens replied with confidence. "My sister and mother will declare me a rogue element, acting without their permission—which is of course true—and the Ilyarans will accept their apologies rather than fight."

"And if they should mount a rescue mission, or make war on Moran?"

"They never have before." The flat truth in Lorens's voice made Rasim's stomach clench. It was hard to remember, listening to Lorens's answers, that their goal right now *was* to be a rescue mission. They needed the Moranese woman to believe him, but Rasim wished it wasn't so easy. "I have some degree of personal wealth, Lady Amdria," Lorens continued, his tone very royal and condescending now. "*If* the Ilyarans come for their people, the Moranese would have two choices: fight, using their own enslaved Ilyaran witches, or release those slaves back to the Ilyarans. If it comes to the latter, I will personally guarantee the return of the purchase costs for every slave sold off the *Wafiya*."

"And for those who do not come from this ship? Who will repay the cost of the labor we might have had from those now-freed slaves, if we hadn't risked you and this ship in our port? Who will repay the costs of purchasing them in the first place, and the cost of the mindkiller to keep them pliant?"

"No one," Nasira said flatly, obviously cutting off anything else Lorens might have suggested. Amdria's eyebrows rose as she looked toward the captain, but Nasira's expression was unforgiving. "Those slave owners will have had many years of use from their slaves to justify the cost of purchasing them, and future labor is unknowable. A plague could sweep Moran and kill every slave here tomorrow. You cannot claim losses on what might have been."

Amdria's eyes narrowed. "There are many who would disagree with you."

Nasira spread her hands expansively. "I welcome the discussion."

The Moranese woman barked a laugh, then nodded at the captain and the prince. "Very well. I regard your presence and your propositions interesting enough that I will arrange for you to speak with the Council. If they approve, you will be free to then sell your wares. I will provide proper chains, and will—for your benefit, of course—leave guards on your ship."

"And I will leave slaves ordered to defend themselves at all costs."

Amdria's mouth pursed, then turned to a smile. "Of course. I admire your forethought, Captain."

"Nasira," the captain said. "If we are to be engaged in business together."

"Nasira," Amdria repeated. "Very good. I'm pleased that we shall be friends. Now, as to your delicious offer of a gift..." She trailed her fingertips against Hassin's cheek again, igniting rage in his black eyes. "This one is lovely. I shall be pleased to accept him. And if I might make a suggestion, Nasira...?"

"I'm listening."

"You might choose one or two of your less valuable slaves to enter in the Arena. It's a splendid way to show off your wares, and might fetch you a better price for your more impressive merchandise."

"This Arena. Tell me about it."

Amdria shrugged. "A slave pit, where the inconvenient, old, or bold are brought for the city's entertainment. There are a few professionals, of course. Gladiators. It guarantees almost none of the new slaves survive more than a day or two, but no one puts them in the Arena if they want them to survive. Ilyarans are rare in there, though. You'd earn good will for the entertainment, and get bidders excited over owning a witch."

Nasira's smile was a knife's edge. "You say they don't survive long?"

"A day or two at most."

"Then I have the perfect witch for your pits." Nasira flicked a finger toward Rasim. "That one."

CHAPTER TWELVE

The casual flick of Nasira's finger felt like it plunged a fist into Rasim's belly. This was the plan, this was *his* plan, but his breath left him and the rope he'd held slipped through suddenly numb fingers. They weren't friends, he and the captain, but he'd thought her hatred of him had faded. He had never imagined she might jump at the chance to have him killed. For a sick instant he cast his mind backward, wondering if Nasira had, after all, had something to do with him being thrown off the *Wafiya* as it sailed north.

It didn't matter now, not really. Rasim's shoulders were jostled as two of Amdria's men came on board and cut his ropes, then pulled his arms behind him and chained his wrists together. Sesin cried a protest, but Rasim, still stunned, didn't even try to fight. He had nothing to fight *with*, anyway: he was small for his age and his magic was stunted by the mindkiller. All he could do was stare at Nasira, waiting for some sign that this was a terrible joke.

No such sign came. When he couldn't command his legs to walk well, Amdria's men dragged him past the captain, who watched with her nasty, cutting smile still in place. Only Nasira's cackling whisper followed him as he was hauled off the ship. "Remember, slave. No sea witchery."

A wild hope blossomed in Rasim's chest. He shot one look back over his shoulder, taking in Nasira's smirk and the hopeless gaze of the rest of the crew. Only Sesin had any other expression, a fierce triumphant joy that she quelled almost before Rasim was certain he'd seen it flash over her face. He let his own gaze drop again and allowed himself to be hauled away without protest. Excitement strong enough to be sickness pierced his gut, and he couldn't stop the shiver that wracked his body.

One of his captors snorted and said something clearly mocking, even if Rasim couldn't understand the actual words. He didn't care: they could assume his trembling was fear all they wanted.

Nasira had forbidden him the use of sea witchery. *Specifically* sea witchery.

He had no idea if she knew whether he could command stone witchery, and for a horrible moment thought perhaps he should have told her as they hatched their plot. He still believed King Taishm should be told first, so he could decide if Rasim's talents were a threat, but...well, Nasira had been so careful to make sure he heard her order. Their secret, their *plot*, might not be discovered, if he utilized his other magic. He *might* be able to use stonemastery under the very noses of his captors, because they wouldn't be looking for it.

But it was too soon to try. He needed to be out anyone else's range of command, because he couldn't risk being seen working magic at all. Which meant he needed—terribly, frighteningly—to be in the Arena. He kept his head down, thinking ferociously, and barely protested when he was thrown into a shallow cart. His guards spoke to the driver, a man whose thin face looked as though it had never seen a smile, and Rasim was chained into the cart's belly. One of the guards prodded him until he knelt up, able to see—and be seen—over the cart's low sides. He was bumped and thudded over the Moranese streets to shouts of interest and curiosity, though if any of the callers asked questions, the driver didn't respond. A woman pitched an apple core at Rasim when he met her eyes, and after that he kept his gaze on the cart floor.

There would be some way, inside the Arena, to free himself. There had to be. He would have the use of stone witchery and his own wits, and that would be enough. Rasim told himself that as his knees began to ache from kneeling on the cart's wooden belly, and as his shoulders began to hurt with the weight of chains. It wouldn't be for long, and then he would find the Ilyaran slaves, free them too, and perhaps together find some way to break the back of Moranese slavery. Conviction burned in his chest, filling him with confidence and the fever of wanting to act.

A shadow fell over him. Rasim looked up, and his conviction faded into awe.

An impossibly tall wall rose up above him. It was not stone, as it would have been in Ilyara. Rasim thought it was mostly mud, maybe with sticks woven within it as support, but it was *hard* mud, almost stone, and it was taller than any building in Ilyara. Its thick sides bulged outward as they passed through a door so deep and broad it was more of a tunnel. Wondering how he'd missed the vast wall in his inspection of the city, Rasim glanced backward and saw they'd been traveling down a shallow hill for some time, so the enormous structure stood in a dip in the valley floor.

The cart rattled through into a sand-floored arena more than a hundred feet across and at least twice that deep. Its back wall was a natural amphitheater in the valley hills. The Moranese had simply completed it as a gigantic oval to build their circus pit. There were hollows in both the valley wall—caves, Rasim thought —and in the man-made walls. All of them were fronted with heavy iron gates through which there could be no escape.

He had never even imagined a structure like the arena. Faced with it, his plans to free himself seemed naive. The driver, unimpressed by the view, seized his chains and dragged him from the cart. He hit the sandy dirt hard on his knees before scrambling to his feet and following in the driver's wake. The driver threw Rasim in front of another keeper, whose gaze was disdainful as he looked on the Ilyaran. The two Moranese spoke for a moment, their language swift and unintelligible to Rasim's ears. When they were finished, the other keeper took Rasim's chains. This time he was faster and kept his feet as he was hauled across the sands and finally thrust into one of the iron-barred cages. The door banged shut behind him, and Rasim fell against one of the stick-and-mud walls, gasping at the suddenness of his imprisonment.

"Well, well. Fresh meat for the ring," said a woman in a familiar tongue, from the back of the cage. A Northerner emerged from the darkness, and Rasim took an instinctive step back. She was as tall and nearly as broad across the shoulder as the Northern guard Gontor, the biggest man Rasim had ever seen. Her skin, where it wasn't marked and notched with scars, was as browned by the sun as any Northerner could get, and her hair, which she wore in a braid as tight as any Seamaster's braid, was white from the sun. Looking him up and down, she added, "Ilyaran. You won't have understood a word of that. Just as well."

"I speak your language," Rasim said in a voice gone hoarse. He had met many politically and magically powerful people, but this woman looked like she could break him in half without trying.

The woman's eyebrows, which were so white they stood out against her tanned face, quirked upward. "Where did you learn my language, Ilyaran?"

"Mostly in Hongrunn. Where did you learn mine?"

"My partner in the pits taught me, until the day I had to kill him to stay alive. My advice? Don't get too attached to anyone." The giant woman stalked to the back of the cage.

Rasim sank to the floor by the barred entrance, staring at thick cage walls. They looked like dried mud, not stone, and he didn't know if he could work with it. Even natural-born Stonemasters had trouble working with earth, and found metal, like the bars across the cage's entrance, nearly impossible to shape.

The danger he was in hit him suddenly, sharply, and made a pit of fear in his gut. He should have been much more frightened before this, having been captive twice already, but he'd had such confidence in his dual magics that he'd forgotten to be afraid. He lowered his head against his knees, shivering and trying to imagine how he could survive this mess.

"No spark in you," the Northerner said from the darkness. "Like this one. You'll never last."

Rasim turned to see her gesture at another boy, perhaps a few years older than Rasim, who sat huddled at the back of the cage. He was both small and quiet, and his coloring, even in the faded light, was extraordinarily beautiful. His hair and eyes were black, and his golden-toned skin had a translucent quality that gave it an unearthly depth. His cheeks glowed with red warmth, as if he was lit from within, and he looked, all in all, like he had already given up his grip on this world. Siliaria would welcome him, Rasim thought, and then, as the boy shifted, saw that he was draped with a horse's pelt. Only the Shenryalan clans wore those. Siliaria wouldn't come for this boy, then. His gods would be led by the Horse King, whom the Shenryalans said ran across the sky each night and lit the stars with each fall of his hooves.

"I'm Rasim," he said to the Shenryalan boy, and while the boy didn't answer, the Northerner did. "He doesn't talk. Can't or won't, I don't know, but he doesn't. Won't fight, either. He sits against the wall of the arena, and nobody dares come close to him."

"Why is that?" Rasim looked at the woman, who shrugged.

"One part the way he looks, all gold and ghostly, I reckon, and he's only little when he stands." She was silent a moment. "And maybe one part that there's a Northern giant with a blade between him and them."

"He's your new partner?"

"Aye, he's my partner now."

"So you'll turn on him, when it's your life or his?"

The big woman shrugged again. "Maybe. Or maybe I'll win the hearts of the crowd by defending him, and we'll both go free."

Rasim straightened, his spine scraping away from the rough walls. "What?"

"It's the sweet they dangle for us, to keep us fighting. Once in a while, a crowd favorite is granted their freedom. Almost nobody lives long enough to become a favorite, though, never mind fight their way free."

"Have you? You've been here long enough to betray at least one partner."

The woman gave him a hard look. "They know me."

"But do they love you?"

Her jaw tightened and Rasim turned a faint smirk toward the sands outside. "Not since you betrayed your partner, right? And that's the real reason you're hoping you don't have to kill the Shenryalan. They'll never forgive you for killing a boy and you'll never be free. How'd you end up here?"

"You've got a lot of questions, Ilyaran."

"Rasim. My name is Rasim."

"I don't care."

Rasim, under his breath and in his own language, muttered, "No wonder they don't love you," and aloud in her tongue said, "Maybe if we work together we can all go free."

"Escape, you mean? No one escapes. There are two exits at ground level, Ilyaran, and only one is used by the living. That's the one you came in through." The Northerner came forward again, dangling her fingers through the bars to gesture around the arena. "Everybody who's not noble—merchants, commoners and slaves alike—all enter through those gates. The animals are brought in the same way, but on different days."

"Animals?"

"Big cats. Wild dogs. Birds taller than a man that kick like mules. There are half a dozen or more cages just for the animals, like kept with like to keep down on the killing. Slaves come straight to these pits, eight or ten of them. At Festival, there are thirty or forty in each cage like this one."

Rasim looked around the confines of their cell in shock. "They'd have to be stacked."

"Aye. They allow betting on who or how many will still be alive every morning. You're lucky. The cages are as empty as I've ever seen them, right now."

"Lucky? Doesn't it make us more likely to die out there?"

"Better there, for the crowds, than in here over a scrap of earth to sleep on."

"You have a strange idea of luck."

"My luck has kept me alive this long," the Northerner said. "Don't scoff at it."

"I still think our chances are better if we make a team." Rasim left the cage doors to examine the walls. They weren't mud after all, or if they were, it was the hardest mud he'd ever seen. He knocked on a section, then nursed his knuckles. Water could wear it down eventually, but it was almost stone. He might be able to work it. "What is this stuff?"

"Sticks bound together and slathered with some kind of hardening mixture. You can chip your way through it, but not fast enough to escape, if that's what you're thinking. They're always reapplying it. The cells get new coats about once a year."

Rasim looked over his shoulder at her. "How long *have* you been here?"

The Northerner shifted one big shoulder. "Long enough. Look to the sky, Ilyaran. The sun's coming up high. Rest while it's hot. There will be fights tonight."

CHAPTER THIRTEEN

He slept, and woke a little before sunset. It came early to Moran, though not as early as it had in far-northern Hongrunn. Not as abruptly as it came to Ilyara, either. Rasim was used to a quick end to the day in his desert homeland, but in Moran it lingered a little while. Well-dressed men and women came through the gates as the light faded, and torches were lit to illuminate the arena. Poorer folk in less-handsome clothing came later, once it was dark. Even entry into the arena seemed to be done by rank. They were all loud, though, poor or rich. Rasim looked for Nasira, but didn't see her, and wondered if he was glad or not.

"Ilyaran." Rasim turned away from the door to catch a water skin the Northerner threw his way. "They'll bring us out to show us off and start the fights soon. You may not get another chance to drink."

"Thanks." Rasim took one sip of warm, sour water and curled his lip. An reflexive, unplanned whisper of witchery purified it and he drank deeply, then coughed and pulled the skin away from his mouth to stare at it.

"It's foul," the Northerner said with a shrug, "but it's better than being thirsty. Drink up."

"No, it's..." Rasim handed her the skin, still staring at it. Nasira had forbidden him the use of sea witchery, and mindkiller didn't wear off that fast. In fact, he'd be surprised if the water in the skin hadn't been laced with the drug, to keep him compliant. He watched as the Northerner took a cautious sip, then a deeper draught before gazing at him in astonishment.

"It's sweet." She strode to the Shenryalan boy and offered him the skin, saying something in his language. Suspicious, he shrugged one arm out of his horse hide blanket and took the skin. Rasim finally saw what the Northerner had meant when she said the boy was only little when he stood: his head and torso were about the same size as Rasim's, but his limbs were short, maybe only about half as long as Rasim would have expected. There were a dozen or so people in Ilyara with that shape to their bodies who visited the Seamaster healers when aches settled in their bones. The boy took the skin and tried a tentative sip before his face cleared. He drank more deeply, finally lowering the skin to frown between Rasim and the tall woman. After a moment he wet his lips, then spoke roughly. The Northerner rocked back on her heels, eyebrows lifted. "You *can* talk." To Rasim, she said, "He says you're a sorcerer."

"We call ourselves witches, but it might mean the same thing. I'm a journeyman in the Seamaster's Guild. You speak Shenryalan too? Can you teach me?"

"You're not going to live long enough to learn. What can you *do* with that magic, Ilyaran?"

Rasim shook his head. "I shouldn't be able to do anything with it at all. I..." He trailed off, trying to reach for the Moranese river. He should be able to get a sense of it, at least, even from the distance they were at, or maybe an awareness of water in the mountains that the arena backed up to, but his sensitivity seemed to end at his fingertips. "There's a drug they give us. Mindkiller. It stops us from using our witchery unless we're commanded to, and I was forbidden to use it at all. I shouldn't have been able to cleanse that water."

"But you did." The big Northerner was suddenly in Rasim's space, crouching so she looked a small distance up at him, instead of looming over him. "What does that mean?"

"I really don't know. I...let me..." Rasim moved away from her to place his hands on the mixed-mud wall. He had no sense of stonemastery anyway; even when the witchery flowed through him he couldn't tell until the stone moved, so there was no distress in *not* sensing it as he pressed against the wall.

A change so imperceptible he might have imagined it shifted the wall beneath his hands. Dizziness swept him and he stepped back, gesturing at the wall. "Is it...different there?"

The Northerner, frowning, stood to run her hands over the space he'd touched, then flattened her palms against the wall. "Here. There's a—I can feel the shape of your hands. Small hands," she said with a sniff. "Mine are twice the size of yours. What'd you do?"

"You're twice the size of me." Rasim sat down hard, still woozy. "I—I've learned a little stone witchery. It's...unusual to be able to use more than one magic, but I can. I thought I might be able to use the stonemastery because I'd only been forbidden to use water magic, but I can use it too. Just not very well."

"Are you usually good with it?"

A laugh tore from Rasim's throat. "Sort of."

"How was I to know?" The Northerner sounded offended.

"You weren't. Nothing. It wasn't you, it's..." For a moment Rasim considered trying to explain his former weakness with water witchery, and how he'd come to be strong in it, and almost as swiftly, rejected the idea in favor of simplicity. "Yes. I'm usually good with sea witchery, and I'm sorry I laughed. I'm scared and confused and I don't think I have enough magic right now to protect myself out there, so I think I'm prob-ably going to die tonight, which isn't helping."

"You just used two magics, Ilyaran. How strong do you need to be to survive?"

"I just used two magics and now I can hardly stand up," Rasim snapped. "I need to be able to move, and I need to be able to feel the magic past my fingertips. Usually I would expect to be able to feel the river, or maybe even farther."

"Gods of night and stars." The woman sounded impressed for the first time. "That far? And now it's only what you can touch?"

Rasim nodded grimly and the Northerner fell back a step. The Shenryalan boy spoke again, gaining her attention, and from her expression, she didn't like what he said. She responded and the boy shrugged, looking away. After a few seconds a familiar look crossed the Northerner's face, and Rasim scrambled to think where he'd seen it before.

When it came to him, he almost laughed. Desimi. It was the look Desimi got when he'd reluctantly come around to deciding Rasim was right about something. Whatever the Shenryalan boy had said, the Northerner had agreed without wanting to. "All right," she said sharply. "I'll keep you alive tonight, but, Ilyaran? I expect this to pay off."

"It will." That, Rasim decided, was probably not a promise he should make, but he was determined to keep it. "What *is* your name?"

The woman scowled at him, then sighed explosively. "Agnet. Can you use a blade, boy?"

Rasim turned his palms up, searching for the faint calluses that had been there. "Not well."

"Heh. At least you're honest. They'll give us a range of weapons to run for. Get something with a long handle and get your back to the wall. I'll do the rest." Less audibly, but clearly still meant to be heard, she muttered, "How I've ended up watching over two little boys after all this time..." and shook her head.

Rasim couldn't even protest the phrase. He was, whether he liked it or not, small, and though the Shenryalan boy hadn't risen yet, his short limbs meant he probably wasn't taller than Rasim. Besides, compared to Agnet, even Prince Lorens was little. Rasim shook his head. "How do you know we'll be selected to fight?"

Agnet tilted her head, a motion somehow like a shrug. "You're new meat. They probably wouldn't let you die tonight, but if you acquit yourself well, tomorrow we'll have a huge audience."

"Aquit..." Slow realization sank through Rasim and raised chills despite the warm evening air. "Do you mean, if I kill somebody?" At Agnet's nod, sick resolve formed a knot under Rasim's breastbone. He was not going to kill anyone. Even if it cost him his own life, he was not going to kill anyone. It was no use telling Agnet that. At best she would think he was a fool, and she'd certainly spend a lot of time trying to convince him he was wrong. Neither of them needed the distraction. Rasim nodded and turned his face away, gazing at the arena through the iron bars.

Shadows leaped and danced on the sand, making monsters of a half-dozen men who walked out, in formation, to deposit the promised weaponry in the middle of the arena. Their mere presence woke a roar from the crowd, though none of them so much as smiled as they broke apart to walk purposefully across the sands to half a dozen cages, including Rasim's. He scrambled to his feet, backing a few steps away, and ran into the Shenryalan, who had risen to stand behind him, silent and wraith-like. Rasim was nearly a foot taller than he was, although the other boy's shoulders were as broad as Rasim's. He smiled faintly at Rasim's apology, and brushed past him as the cage door opened. Rasim, heart pounding, followed him into the arena.

HE'D THOUGHT the crowd was noisy when they passed through the gates. He'd thought they were loud when they cheered for the guards who had placed the weapons and released the slaves. But the cage walls had muffled the sounds then, protecting him from their intensity. Outside in the open arena, their cries were a physical blow, an impact that struck Rasim and rattled his breath away. He faltered, but Agnet pushed him forward relentlessly. Struggling for air, he glanced back at the giant Northerner and saw, to his shock, that she was grinning. Not a grin to hide fear, but a broad, anticipatory grin that only grew wider when a portion of the shouts turned to jeers and hissing.

She lifted her arms, fingers flickering inward, toward herself, like she was inviting all their attention. Like she wanted it, whether it was good or bad. Rasim faltered again and Agnet stalked past him, taking the lead. Her skin glowed reddish under the torch light, the fire's colors bringing out the sunburned undertones that Northerners couldn't seem to avoid even when they tanned. The boys fell into her shadow, into her *shadows;* there were many, born from the ever-changing torch light. Rasim relaxed just a little, as if he'd stepped into a safe place, although he knew the Northerner's shadow could no more protect him than a stray bolt of sunlight might.

The audience was impossible to see as anything more than a seething black mass. What light there was focused on the arena, making them the bright spot at the heart of a vast dark circle. Rasim wondered if any of his crew were out there, or any other Ilyarans, free or slave. Wondered if Nasira was there, shouting for his death like thousands of others. His hands worked themselves into fists so tight that his fingernails, short as they were, cut into his palms. He felt small and even more powerless than he'd been when he fought the sea serpent. He wanted to run, but there was nowhere *to* run, and his pride wouldn't let him cower before the shouting throngs.

A voice thundered across the stadium, so loud it had to be carried by sky witchery, though Rasim had no sense of the flitting, incessant power that he associated with Skymasters. Nor could he understand a word of the announcement, but its meaning was clear enough: *Here are slaves, prepared to die for your entertainment.* The speaker shouted something: a name, Rasim realized, as a slave across the arena stepped forward to renewed shouts and cheering. Six names were called, in all. Agnet's was the last. She swept Rasim and the Shenryalan boy along with her as she stepped forward into the light. Rasim kept his feet through force of will alone. He had never heard anything like the pounding roar of so many voices. Not even the worst storms the *Wafiya* had weathered beat at him the way their voices did.

Four of the names were repeated, and those four—as well as the slaves with them—retreated to their cages again. Agnet was left with her cellmates, and across the arena, another, larger group gathered in anticipation. "Dennel," Agnet reported. "He and his are ruthless.

They'll go for the range weapons, the maces and the spears. Get to the spears first and get your back to a wall." She caught the Shenryalan's eye and he nodded, but before Rasim could ask if he'd understood, the skywitch-assisted voice boomed out again and suddenly everything was in motion.

Agnet surged forward in flat-out run, astounding Rasim with her speed. No one that big should be that *fast.* He had thought she would move like a lumbering buffalo, all heavy slow mass, but she had the speed and elegance of a lioness at the hunt.

He sprinted along in her wake, the Shenryalan at his side, but Agnet's long legs and determination let her outpace them handily. By the time they reached the stockpile of weaponry, Agnet had already seized two sheathed swords and slung their belts over her shoulder. She snatched up two more unsheathed blades and spun them in a glittering, deadly circle as Rasim grabbed a stave of his own and, shoulder to shoulder with the other boy, began to back toward the distant arena wall.

The man Dennel reached the weaponry at about the same time they did. He was thicker than Agnet and not as tall. He took up a flail that looked like it weighed as much as Rasim did and swung it a few times, his grin showing several missing teeth. The ones he had left were healthy and strong: violence, not sickness, had taken the ones he lacked. Then he selected a mace for his off-hand weapon, and nodded with satisfaction.

He had three others with him, two men and a woman. The men looked confident as they took up their own weaponry—swords, like Agnet had chosen— and the woman looked terrified as she selected a spear like Rasim's own.

Agnet and Dennel moved away from the weapons, sizing one another up. Agnet's hands loosened and tightened around her sword hilts, her head lowered as she watched her opponent. His mouth pulled an open sneer, like he was tasting the air. He could probably taste Rasim's fear, despite the fact that the boys had backed up against the arena wall and were as far away as they could get from the thick slave.

The two other swordsmen circled toward them, knowing easy targets when they saw them. The woman, gripping her spear as if she could squeeze life out of it, edged around Dennel and Agnet, her frightened gaze locked on the Northern woman. Rasim wanted to cry out a warning, but knew if he drew Agnet's attention, Dennel would press the advantage and attack with his terrible flail. He had to trust Agnet knew the other woman was there.

Metal clashed, so fast Rasim barely saw the attack. Dennel's mace smashed one of Agnet's whirling swords, and as the blade broke, she lunged forward to drive the other sword at his fighting arm. She scored blood and the audience screamed again. Arrogant and smiling, Agnet fell back to encourage their cries, then shook the sheath off her third blade as Dennel came in again, his flail swinging blindingly fast.

The other woman was behind Agnet now, her breath coming hard as she lifted a shaking arm to aim her spear. "Throw it," Rasim whispered encouragingly.

Untrained, she had less chance of hitting her target if she threw the spear than if she kept it in hand and charged Agnet with it. Then the two swordsmen were in front of Rasim and the Shenryalan, their blades glittering in the firelight. New cheers rose up and Rasim felt the hot breath of dozens of observers wash over him as they leaned over the arena's edge to watch the fight just below them.

Rasim battered a sword away as the bladefighters pressed their attack, and swung the blunt end of the spear toward a fighter's head. His heart beat so fast he could hardly breathe, and he was afraid that his sweating hands would let the spear's haft slip. The swordsman ducked and Rasim flung himself sideways as the man drove his sword down. Rasim caught a handful of sand and threw it into the man's face, then surged to his feet again, gripping his spear. He had sworn he wouldn't kill anyone, but suddenly he wasn't sure he could keep that vow. If it was his life or the other slave's, he might fight to survive even if he thought he couldn't.

Only a few feet away, the Shenryalan fought with a serene expression. He only defended himself, never trying to strike his opponent down. Admiration surged through Rasim, but was washed away as his own opponent came at him again. Rasim caught the man's blade on the spear haft and squeaked in terror as the sword cut halfway through the haft. The man, smirking, withdrew to strike again. Rasim, as quickly as he could, snapped the haft and shoved both broken ends toward the man's stomach.

He caught him in the diaphragm, knocking the wind from him. The man's eyes bulged in surprise and dismay. He tried to gather himself to strike at Rasim again, but his own body was working against him now: all it wanted to do was breathe, and his fingers, clearly numb from a sudden lack of air, fumbled his blade. Rasim slammed one half of the haft into the soft spot in the man's wrist and the blade fell to the sand. Rasim kicked it away and bashed the man in the temple, sick with relief as the man collapsed.

That sickness turned itself into a twisted grin. He glanced up to share that grin with the other boy, and went cold as he saw the Shenryalan had lost his spear. His opponent stood over him, blade lifted over his head to drive it downward into the boy's chest.

Very suddenly, a spear sprouted in the swordsman's spine. He dropped to his knees, then fell forward, all slowly enough that the Shenryalan boy was able to scramble out of the way. The crowd's screams were incessant now, the sound of a people surprised and delighted by the turn of events. Rasim, gaping, offered the other boy a hand, then looked toward the center of the arena.

The frightened woman, no longer looking in the least bit frightened, nodded once as she met Rasim's eyes. Admiration flashed through Rasim again. She had put on a show. Her fear had been a performance, and she had played it well. She could be an ally, if he could only talk to her.

A smile of relief rushed his face and, as quickly, turned to dismay. He let go a hollow shout of warning too late. Dennel's mace whistled past Agnet and caught the woman in the back. She fell without so much as a change of expression, while behind her Agnet redoubled her attack against Dennel.

They had been playing with each other before, Rasim saw now. They'd been performing for the raucous audience, whetting their appetite for blood and death. Now with the distractions removed, they could focus on the serious business of trying to kill one another.

The audience sensed the shift as well, and for the first time, became quieter. Not quiet, but quieter, more intense and more divided: both Agnet and Dennel clearly had supporters within the viewers, and their names rang out as their weapons connected and came apart time and again.

Agnet had the speed and the reach; Dennel, the brute strength. Rasim could see it wearing on the huge Northerner each time the blunt man slammed his mace into her swords. Only her swords: she was too fast for him to connect a bone-breaking blow to her arm or leg. But the reverberations through the blades were enough; soon she would slow, and then she would die.

And so would Rasim and the Shenryalan. Agnet had agreed to protect them. The least he could do, Rasim thought grimly, was *try* to help her. He picked up his broken spear again and glanced at the other boy, who took up his own spear with a nod. Rasim moved to the right, Shenryalan to the left, both of them skirting Agnet widely. Dennel saw them and smirked, but didn't disengage from Agnet. He clearly didn't consider them a danger.

Rasim could throw a rope; any sailor could. His broken spear wouldn't fly like a rope at all, but if it went near where he aimed it, he might distract Dennel a moment. He caught the other boy's eye again and they moved as one, flanking Dennel and raising their spears in threat. The thick warrior watched them from the corner of his eye, not fearfully, but appraising. A sneer flickered over his mouth as he saw Rasim's clumsy hold on the broken spear. Irrationally insulted, Rasim flung the weapon at him.

It went so far off-target that Dennel didn't even bother to knock it away. But at the same time, the Shenryalan loosed his own spear, and if Rasim couldn't throw one, the other boy could. It flew swift and true, true enough that Dennel *did* stop advancing on Agnet to knock the oncoming weapon away.

Agnet needed no other chance. She stepped inside the other slave's guard and slammed her blade through his chest, then stood, panting, above his body as it fell from her sword. Her face was empty, Rasim thought: no triumph, no sorrow. A job that needed doing was now done. This time the audience's roars *did* drive him to his knees, and there he sat, gazing blankly at the fallen, until the guards came to take him, at arrow-point, back to the cage.

CHAPTER FOURTEEN

The fights went on long into the night. Rasim turned his back on the arena and slept, although he didn't think he would. He was bothered by nightmares, with danger always just too far away for him to face.

The silence after the arena emptied awakened him briefly, and he found that Agnet had draped a blanket over him. The other boy had one, too. Agnet herself, standing watchfully by the cage door, wore one wrapped loosely around her shoulders as well. Rasim thought she could be Coluth, the Stonemaster god, although usually Coluth was depicted as male. Still, she had that kind of aura, strong and broad and certain.

Knowing she was there helped somehow. Rasim rolled back over and went back to sleep, his nightmares vanquished. He woke at dawn to the sounds of food and water being thrust through the cage doors. Even from where he lay at the back of the cage, Rasim felt the slosh of water in the skins, and hope lightened his heart.

Agnet had cast away her blanket and wrapped her hands high around the bars, letting her weight pull her down and back a little as she spoke quietly to the slave bringing their food. She nodded once, then tore one of the haunches of bread in half and returned it to the man, who tucked it inside his tunic and ducked his head in thanks before he went on to the next cage. Rasim, sitting up with his blanket around his shoulders, said, "What was that?"

Agnet tossed him a water skin. "He says we won't fight again for three days. I paid him for the information in bread, although I'm not surprised. After a big kill like Dennel, they like to whet the appetite for the next round. Is three days enough?"

Rasim turned the skin in his hands, feeling the water inside. It had to be laced with mindkiller. There was no way they would stop drugging him. But any sea witch could purify sea water and it couldn't be harder to take a drug from water than salt. A touch of witchery sweetened the water and he sipped, then drank deeply. Then he turned and, without much thought, sank his hand into the wall.

Agnet inhaled sharply. Rasim took his hand out of the wall, pulling the stone back into the shape it had been, and stared at his fingers. "It'll be enough. The mindkiller—either they're not drugging me or it isn't working. I don't know why they wouldn't drug me, so I have to think it's not working."

"Then let's get out of here."

"In broad daylight?" Rasim smiled faintly. "Even if they're not checking on us every half hour, someone's going to see a tunnel opening up on the outside wall and be standing there ready to kill us. We don't have any weapons, and..." He turned his attention toward the arena sands, which were warm and dark in the shadows cast by the rising sun. "We have to wait until the next fights. That way you can get weapons and if my witchery is at full strength I can...create a distraction. Free all the arena slaves at once. We'll escape in the chaos."

"Free *everyone*?"

Rasim's expression hardened. "I didn't come to Moran to rescue a handful of Ilyarans and leave everyone else in chains."

Agnet laughed. "Did you not? What profit is our freedom to you?"

Rasim stared at her. "It's the right thing to do, Agnet. People shouldn't be enslaved. It's wrong."

Tolerant humor swept her face again. "And you, a child from blessed Ilyara, are going to change it?"

"Blessed?"

"Blessed Ilyara of the Golden Sands, where no one breaks their backs in menial labor. Don't you know how people talk about your homeland, boy? They won't appreciate you saving them. They'll think you're just putting yourself above the rest of us, deciding what's best for us because we lack the magic to make those decisions ourselves."

"Well, maybe you *need* it, then! The witchery, I mean, not Ilyarans making decisions for you. We have enough to do in Ilyara without telling everyone else what to do. But I don't believe that they wouldn't appreciate it. Wouldn't you rather be out of here? Free? Isn't that why you haven't already killed me?"

"Aye, but I'm making the decision myself."

Rasim clenched his fists in exasperation. "Fine. If I manage to break everybody free, anybody who wants to keep their chains can. I don't know how I'd stop them anyway. But I still think you're wrong. I think most people want to be free, if they're given a chance. I think maybe they don't think about it with every change of the tide, because they'd go crazy at being enslaved, but given a chance? I think they'd take it. And I'm going to do everything I can to give them that chance. Not just for my people, but for everyone."

"All by yourself, eh?"

"With other Ilyarans, and with anyone else who will help me. You're right. Ilyarans do have a lot of power, and we should use it. We should *do* something. I don't know why we haven't!"

"You must drive your elders mad," Agnet murmured. "Look, boy. Even in your blessed country, I'm sure that once people are used to doing something one way, it's hard to make them come around to another."

Rasim startled, thinking of the Sunmasters, and how long they'd held sway in the Ilyaran palace. He hadn't even known until recently that it had once been different. Agnet was right. Even in Ilyara, most people just shrugged and accepted that the world worked one way, and always had. "It is," he admitted grudgingly.

"And I guess even if slaves want to be free, the people who own them won't want it, so that's going to make it harder still. But that doesn't mean we shouldn't try."

"You're an optimist, and you're going to start a war, Ilyaran. You're going to start a war and get everyone around you killed."

A protest formed and fell away from Rasim's lips. Agnet was right. Again. Maybe not about getting everyone around him killed, but if he kept doing what he was doing now, it seemed likely that he would start a war. King Taishm wouldn't appreciate that at all. Even as he thought it, though, Rasim shook his head. "My crew, my best friends—they're out there. They've been taken slaves. Even if I *just* get them back, it's going to make a lot of people angry, maybe even angry enough to come after us and, yes, start a war. But what choice do I have? Just let them stay in chains? I can't do that either."

"There's a funny thing about people," Agnet said after a moment. "They think having a choice means choosing between a good thing and a bad thing. Often it means choosing between a bad thing and another bad thing. You have no good choices here, Ilyaran. Stay in the arena and die. Free yourself. Free all of the arena slaves, sowing chaos for cover as you find your friends. Free everyone you can and start a war, sowing chaos over the whole continent."

Rasim, under his breath, muttered, "The brightest dawns are after the storm." That was true. Dust and grit in the air were knocked away by storms, making the following day unusually clear and bright. But true as it might be, even if the analogy followed, war was worse than any storm. It might be worth it, but Agnet was right, too. It was the kind of decision that should be left up to the people, or at least their leaders.

Then again, the leaders in Moran put people in chains, and the leaders of every other country weren't here. Rasim slumped against the stone wall, looking glumly onto the sands. "Maybe I'll think of something clever before we fight again."

"Maybe," Agnet agreed. "Or maybe you'll get us all killed, like I said." She stretched to her full height and returned to hanging on the iron barred doors. "On the other hand, I never thought I'd make it this long, or see a spark of hope at the end of the day. You're going to get us killed, Ilyaran, but at least it'll be an interesting way to die."

THREE DAYS of hard thinking offered Rasim no better ideas than the one he already had. They did offer more skill with a sword than he'd had, and even a smattering of the Shenryalan language. Having spoken once, the other boy—whose name was Bayar—had decided to continue doing so. Having Agnet's language in common made it easier for him to teach Rasim his own. He would say nothing of his own history, but Rasim couldn't blame him for that. He didn't much want to talk about his own circumstances.

They drove him, though. The fear of the crew being sold, or things going as wrong for his friends as they'd gone for him, kept Rasim from sleep. When he couldn't sleep, he practiced with the mock swords, loosening muscles stiffened by Agnet's lessons and improving his sword work until he thought he might be able to fight and survive a round or two in the arena.

Bayar improved too, but he retained the sense of emotional calm that Rasim had noticed before. *He* might falter, and kill to save his own life. He didn't think Bayar would. He wished he could ask the Shenryalan boy about it, but when he tried, Bayar only shrugged as if he magically didn't understand the Northern tongue anymore. If they survived the next few days, maybe Bayar would talk about it then. Rasim couldn't blame the other boy for not wanting to become friends, when they might be forced to turn on each other at any moment.

When Agnet insisted he rest, Rasim hunched at the back of the cage, testing his returning witchery. His stonemastery couldn't get him more than forearm-deep into the walls. They were riddled with too much other material, sticks and straw and debris that, while hardened, blunted his witchery. He would not be escaping through the walls after all.

His sea witchery was still weaker than it should be. He had gained some faint sense of the river, but he could no more dredge it up than he could fly. There was water deep beneath the arena, too, but it was no more accessible than the river. After Siliaria's kiss, Rasim had been able to command more witchery than he'd ever imagined. *Then*, he would have been able to draw the water from the hills, or from the river, without effort.

Well. Not without effort, because he had slept for the better part of two days after flooding the Northern mines, but it would have been possible. But now the faint sense of distant water mocked him with what he could no longer do.

One thought kept climbing up from the deepest parts of his mind where he tried to keep it buried: he wished he had more of Missio's drug. With it, he would be able to shatter the arena, free the slaves, and send Moran itself into the far-off sea, regardless of how weak his power was right now. It was so easy to believe that the post-drug collapse would be worth it.

Every time the thought arose, he tried to remember Missio's ravaged, dying eyes, but even those memories couldn't quite convince him that the risk was too great. He guessed it was lucky that it didn't matter. The drug was gone.

The sun wasn't long up on the third morning when the gates flew open. Rasim got to his feet, astonished, to watch hundreds of people pour in. "I thought we fought at night."

"We will, or late afternoon, at best. There'll be smaller matches all day, though, to keep the appetite whetted. Slaves against animals, first, and then the survivors pitted against each other."

Sickness swam through Rasim. "You mean we have to sit here and watch people die all day before we have a chance to—to do anything?"

"Better if you don't watch," Agnet said wisely. "Nothing you can do, and it'll make you lose your nerve."

"But I could do something."

She gave him a hard look. "Could you? Use your magic now, Ilyaran, and you'll get us all killed. Not in a fair fight, either. They'll shoot us down with arrows and feed our bodies to the beasts. Once we're out of the cage you can bring the walls down for all I care, but until then you hold your water, boy. You're our one chance."

"So you don't really think you can work your way into the hearts of the people and earn your freedom that way," Rasim murmured.

"I think we'd all get killed before they loved me enough for keeping you alive to free us, or even me, aye. I think this is a bad wager and that it's the best I've got. So go to the back of the cage, Rasim. Plug your ears and try not to listen, and when they call for us, unleash witchery."

THE SAND HAD BEEN RAKED over time and again already, but it was stained red anyway, with the scent of blood and offal rising under the increasing afternoon heat. It still wasn't nearly as warm as Rasim expected it to be, but the amphitheater captured the sunlight and warmed itself. The crowd, which had grown quieter during the last few fights, suddenly rose up again, screaming their ecstasy.

For a sickening moment, Rasim thought they were the only three in the arena and that they were intended to turn on one another immediately. He gathered what witchery he could, feeling for the water in the hills. It was there, waiting for him. Springs and small streams trickled downhill, but no deep well existed for him to draw on. None, at least, that he could reach. Not yet, at least. He guessed the mindkiller had done its job too well, for all that it had been days since he'd last been dosed with it. He breathed, "I don't know if I can do this today."

Agnet shot him a daggered look over her shoulder. "If you can't, then you're going to have to do whatever else it takes to stay alive until you can, boy. You're still the only chance we've got." Then she lifted her arms, once more inviting the cheers of the crowd to rain down on her, and for a few moments they were at the center of that maelstrom, pounded by it. Rasim still hated it, but Agnet clearly thrived on it. She seemed to grow larger with each step she took toward the middle of the arena, her red-tinged brown skin and white hair glowing under the sun.

There was no mish-mash of weapons awaiting them this time. There were four swords, all of far better quality than the ones Agnet had used three nights ago. She buckled two of the blades onto a belt at her hips, then lifted the other two, as if asking the crowd what to do. Incoherent answers responded, then redoubled in cheers of approval as she turned and offered Rasim a long-bladed sword and Bayar a shorter one that he could wield more easily. "There will be other weapons provided for us if these break," she said under the roar. "Take them, lift them, and look brave. It's what they want."

Rasim, hesitantly, took his. It weighed more than

the sticks they'd practiced with, if not quite as heavy as the blades Lorens had taught them with aboard the *Wafiya*. Those lessons now seemed like they'd taken place a lifetime ago. The blade felt well-balanced, though. With an uncertain glance toward Bayar, he turned away from Agnet, thrusting the sword toward the sky. He glimpsed Bayar turning the other way and echoing the gesture. The Shenryalan boy looked like a painting, all gold and black beneath the burning sun, with the blade lifted high. The crowd roared, and both boys stabbed the air again, lifting the audience's voices higher and higher into a frenzy.

For the time between heartbeats—a time that seemed to draw on unnaturally long, as if the cries of the masses had stopped his heart—for that space of time, Rasim understood Agnet's love of the arena. Their voices all but lifted him. If he'd dared to look down, he wouldn't have been surprised to see that his feet barely touched the ground anymore. It felt...not like food or drink, but like a different kind of sustenance, something that could sustain him past the edge of reason and endurance. It felt like unbridled power, raw and energizing.

It felt, he realized with a shock, like Missio's drug.

That brought him back down to the earth, a physical thump that had more to do with his heartbeat than his feet, but the effect was the same. The sun was warm enough, this late in the afternoon, but chills ran over Rasim's arms and left him trembling.

It was bad enough to want another taste of that drug. It was worse by far to find something like it in the arena. Shuddering, Rasim lowered his sword and looked away, like there might be somewhere safe to rest his gaze. Somewhere away from the crowd, even if they were surrounded.

Off to one side, roughly across from the enormous tunnel-like gates that allowed egress and exit from the arena, a single man stood alone in the sands, waiting to be noticed.

His hair was long and worn in myriad strands that swayed like black ropes around his shoulders. From the distance his features were indistinguishable, but his skin tones were a familiar Ilyaran brown, and a gold slave's collar glinted against his collarbones. Cool, calming dread washed through Rasim as he looked for the man's backup.

He had none. Rasim hadn't really expected him to, but he'd almost hoped for bladefighters. If they had only sent one man against them, they thought one was enough. And if they'd sent an Ilyaran, they didn't intend for Agnet to lead the fight at all.

Maybe they *hadn't* drugged Rasim with mindkiller. They had wanted him able to use his witchery.

Of course they did. The Moranese woman Amdria had said as much. The anticipated profits from selling Ilyaran slaves would be higher if Rasim acquitted himself well in the arena. He just hadn't thought they would set him against another Ilyaran. He hadn't thought at *all*, not about this, not about *their* plans and motivations. He'd been too focused on his own. His voice cracked, even in a whisper. "Agnet."

She shouldn't have been able to hear him beneath

the screaming crowd, but she did, glancing casually at him and then more sharply in the direction he was looking. Her incredulous snort was loud enough to be heard, too. "One man? They don't think much of me, do they?"

"He's Ilyaran," Rasim whispered. "He's a witch. This isn't your fight at all."

The huge Northerner didn't even blink. "Have you got enough magic to defeat him?"

"I don't think so." He *should*, though. It had been days since he'd last had mindkiller in his system, and he knew experience that it didn't last that long. His witchery should have returned full force by now.

Unless it wasn't the mindkiller at fault. Rasim's knees buckled. Agnet lashed her hand outward, catching him so he didn't fall, and hissed, "What is it?"

"I used a drug," Rasim whispered thickly. "A week or so ago, I used a drug that made my witchery stronger, and I did something impossible. Something the whole crew together couldn't have done. I fainted afterward, and when I woke up I couldn't reach my witchery at all. I thought it was the mindkiller stopping me since then, but...what if it's the other drug? What if I used up all my magic?"

Agnet's expression went flat. "You've been lying to me all along."

"No! No. But I might..." Rasim faltered. "I might have been wrong."

The death of hope and the lack of forgiveness in Agnet's eyes was worse than the idea of being left with what little witchery he'd once commanded. "If you get out of this alive, boy, I'm going to kill you myself." She turned away from both the boys, facing the sole opponent far across the ring, and lifted her swords as she shouted defiance at him.

In response, a howl ripped through the arena, drowning out even the crowd. A familiar howl, the shriek of a killing wind. The arena wasn't large enough to let a wind like that kick up, not really. Agnet nearly fell back a step. Rasim saw her stance change, and then how she stiffened, refusing to let anything like fear show. Bayar came to stand beside Rasim, and said, carefully, "Wind sorcerer."

"Skymaster," Rasim agreed in a whisper. "I don't even know *how* to fight a sky witch."

"He's only a man," Agnet snapped. "He'll die like any other." She surged forward with the same astonishing blur of speed and grace she'd shown three nights ago, leaving Rasim's cry of protest far behind.

The invisible force of wind snatched her up and threw her halfway across the arena. It cushioned her fall, too, catching her just before she hit the sand so that the impact would jar, not kill, her. Admirably, she came to her feet again almost instantly, a combination of rage and fear contorting her features.

To Rasim's surprise, the audience, so passionate in its opinions, roared disapproval. Agnet's anger turned to instant agreement. She spun to face the nearest tiered seats and, through body language alone, expressed her disbelief and outrage. The gestures couldn't have been more clear. She, like the audience, was offended by the use of magic, against which she had no defense. They were in this *together*, she and the audience: they were *all* being cheated by a witch in the arena. Hisses and jeers turned to agreement, and then, slowly, a word became distinguishable in the noise: "*Il-yar-an! Il-yar-an! Il-yar-an!*"

As they chanted, two more slaves joined the Skymaster. Both of them carried blades: one a spear, the other, two swords. Agnet spoke over her shoulder, somehow knowing the slaves were there without ever seeming to look away from the crowd. "They're calling your name, Rasim. Bayar, stay behind me. I'll take the spear first. Don't engage the swords. Go!"

She and Bayar both broke into a run, with Agnet pacing herself so the boy's shorter legs could keep up. Rasim gasped, expecting another onslaught from the commanded winds, but the Skymaster ignored them, clearly watching for—waiting for—Rasim's response.

He had to try. Even if he didn't know how to fight a sky witch, even if his witchery was weak, he had to at least try. Rasim braced and reached deep into the Moranese hills, calling the streams to his need, searching for the stone itself beneath the soil, and commanding it to move.

Nothing happened.

CHAPTER FIFTEEN

A quiet cry of despair slipped through Rasim's lips. The bladefighters were mere seconds from engaging. Agnet bore down on the spear-carrier, who spun her weapon with ease and confidence. Rasim barely saw the flash of metal before their clash jarred the whole stadium. The other woman was clearly as strong a fighter as Agnet, who also watched the swordsman. Bayar had not put down his own sword, but neither did he look prepared to use it.

The Shenryalan boy was going to die, if Rasim couldn't waken some kind of witchery. Agnet would, too. They were counting on him, and he'd effectively led them into a trap.

The other Ilyaran came closer, not with any obvious intent. His head cocked to one side in apparent curiosity, and when he was certain Rasim was looking at him, he raised one hand and beckoned, as if inviting Rasim to strike back. Rasim shrugged, then, on impulse, called out in Ilyaran. "What's your name?"

His opponent's mouth twisted. "Mikkel."

It was not a Skymaster's name. Pain tugged at Rasim's heart, but he didn't press it. Perhaps the man didn't remember his Ilyaran name. More likely, though, that it was dangerous to even acknowledge he'd ever had another. "I'm not your enemy. I don't want to fight you. If we work together maybe we can escape. Will you try?"

Harsh, soundless laughter broke from Mikkel's mouth, and a shocking blast of wind forced Rasim back several steps. The Skymaster kept coming, though, and Rasim unconsciously tightened his fingers around his sword's hilt. "Fool," Mikkel said, his lips barely moving. They didn't need to, though. His witchery carried the words to Rasim's ears easily enough. "You think any of us will survive if we try to fight our way out? I don't want to fight you either, Journeyman, but there are men out there with killing knives."

"You're a sky witch," Rasim said in disbelief. "None of them can even get through your winds, if you want to protect yourself."

"They're not at *my* throat," Mikkel replied flatly. "I've been permitted a family. Now fight with whatever witchery you have before they decide we're conspiring, or I have to kill you in cold blood."

"I have no power left," Rasim whispered, and with sudden ferocity, rushed the other Ilyaran with his blade.

Genuine surprise flickered over Mikkel's face. He swept his hand across his chest, sending wind to knock Rasim's feet out from under him. Rasim collapsed in a heap at Mikkel's feet, panting and angry. If he'd waited another second or two, he might have been close enough to strike before Mikkel could react.

And then what? he wondered. Would he have killed Mikkel and broken his promise to himself? There were no good answers here. The crowd was screaming, either at him or the bladefighters, he couldn't tell. Mikkel, standing over him, looked uncertain. "You're supposed to be a sea witch."

"I was never much of one anyway." Rasim swept his feet around, knocking into Mikkel's knees and—well, anyone but a sky witch would have fallen. Wind leaped up, steadying Mikkel before he collapsed, but Rasim launched himself from the sand to attack the other Ilyaran again.

His hands were empty: he'd dropped the sword. That was all right. It was harder to kill someone with your fists anyway, and he didn't *want* to kill the other Ilyaran. Rasim swung hard, and struck with no more power than any boy of thirteen might.

It was still enough to stun Mikkel, although Rasim was certain the other man's wobble came more from surprise than pain. Rasim had a chance to land a second punch before irritation—not even anger, much less rage; just irritation—flickered over Mikkel's face and he twitched his fingers.

Wind snatched Rasim and threw him halfway across the arena. He landed in a skid of sand not far from Agnet and Bayar. Agnet's swords blurred against the spear-bearer's attacks, but the other woman stayed just far enough out of Agnet's reach that the giant

Northerner couldn't end the fight. Bayar gripped his blade with an expression caught between resolution and despair, as if he was no longer certain that he should abide by his own code. The swordsman approaching them flinched at Rasim's sudden arrival, and Rasim, with a shout, scooped a handful of sand and flung it at the swordsman's eyes.

It flew with unerring accuracy, as if guided by more than chance, and Rasim froze in momentary surprise. The swordsman snarled and wiped his forearm across his eyes, never letting go of his blades. Rasim cast another handful of sand at him, thoughts churning. He had no sense of stone. He never had. And he had been reaching for it from so far away: from the hills, beneath the topsoil, through the knobbled roots of trees, because that was where the nearest stone seemed to be.

But sand was nothing more than ground-down stone, and the arena was full of sand. Heart hammering, Rasim looked at his palmful of golden grains.

He had sculpted a stone monument in Hongrunn from the side of a mountain. There had been no doubt that it was all one single piece. A grain of sand was an individual stone, tiny but unique, not belonging to a whole. Shaping that into a wall or a shield—even the thought fell apart into grains, slipping away before he could do anything with it.

It didn't matter. Rasim flung another handful of sand, watching it strike the swordsman's face with pinprick accuracy. Even that shouldn't be happening, not really; he didn't think he could guide it through the air so precisely, not unless—

Bayar cried, "Rasim!" and so many terrible things happened at once.

A fresh sky witchery attack slammed Rasim into the sand. As he fell, the swordsman surged at him and Agnet, with flawless accuracy, spun and threw one of her swords. It caught the swordsman in the chest, but as he collapsed, the spear-fighter closed the distance and thrust her weapon at Agnet's back. Bayar dropped his sword and jumped on the woman's back, an arm around her throat.

And then Rasim saw nothing else as the wind pressure drove him face-first into the sand.

He didn't have enough air. In a few seconds he was going to try to breathe, and then he would start the swift business of dying. He struggled to hold on to his clarity of thought, and an unexpected memory came to him.

He had lain in the awful heat of the sea-witch prison in Ilyara, surrounded by licking flames. Those flames had died momentarily, just long enough for him, Desimi, and Guildmaster Isidri to escape. Rasim had thought that Desimi and Isidri, working together, had somehow reached a little water, and quenched the fires, but he remembered now that they'd looked confused when he'd said as much. He hadn't thought anything of it then, though. They were all exhausted and dehydrated then, and almost nothing seemed to make sense in the moment.

But if their confusion had been real, if *they* hadn't freed them all, then either a Sunmaster had freed them...

...or Rasim had.

If he, untrained, unaware it *could* be done—because by common Ilyaran wisdom, it couldn't—had used a second magic that day...or if he had, indeed set fire to the *Wafiya*'s ropes as Nasira believed he had...then he had now used *three* magics.

And if he had used three, he could use a fourth.

Rasim dug his hands into the sand, struggling not to take a desperately needed breath. Sand was stone, and stone was all but immutable. It couldn't be forced where it didn't want to go, not easily, not even by pummeling winds. He willed that strength into his own muscles, into his own *bones*, as if he could turn himself to stone, and then, stubborn as the stone itself, he pushed himself up to his hands and knees.

For a shockingly quiet instant, the wind stopped, and Rasim imagined he could feel Mikkel's surprise flowing across the arena. He had that instant, the space of a gasping breath, to see the lay of the land, and tears rose in his eyes.

Agnet's sword had flown true, and the swordsman was dead, but she had taken the spear thrust to her left arm and had dropped her other blade. She held the spear that had pierced her in her right hand now, and knelt in front of Bayar, whom the spear-bearer had thrown off. Agnet leaned heavily on the spear she'd taken, so heavily that Rasim couldn't tell if it was theatrics or real pain, but Bayar was behind her, and she looked prepared to defend him to her final breath.

They would love her, Rasim thought in heartbroken horror. The crowd would finally love her, for dying to save a boy. But it would be too late for her, and that was no good at all. He turned away from them, one hand still deep in the sand, as a new screaming attack of sky witchery rushed across the arena.

Head lowered, Rasim lifted his other hand and sought the leading edge of the shrieking wind with witchery.

It felt nothing like the other magics. Sunmastery lived, in its bright and fatal way. Sea witchery endured, the most abiding element in the world. Stonemastery held fast, a huge vast silence that didn't speak to him at all, even in the throes of its power.

Sky witchery *danced.*

It darted and spun like eddies in the water, but with an exhilarating lightness, impossible to even see unless it carried particles in it. It laughed and teased, ruffling over surfaces; it shoved, taking unwilling partners in its dance. It gusted and jumped, as if taking pride in its capriciousness. No wonder Skymasters flew only in legend, Rasim thought. Air was mercurial, unreliable. It would take tremendous witchery and the steadiest soul in the world to coax it into calm flight.

Lucky for Rasim, he didn't want calm.

It felt as though a wedge extended from his fingertips, a somehow-sharp edge of *air* that cut apart the screaming, rushing wind that hurtled toward them. It was barely wide enough to allow Rasim's narrow shoulders through, but it broadened swiftly, leaving Agnet and Bayar in a safe and silent space behind him. For long moments, he didn't even dare look up, just stayed where he was, one hand in the sand, the other stretched out in front of him, slicing the attacking wind into two.

Agnet and Bayar were still in danger. The spear-fighter was still back there. Rasim clenched his eyes shut, trying desperately to feel the filled space in the air. It was possible with sea witchery. A talented Seamaster could tell where there were obstacles in the water. Sandbars interrupted the flow of sea water, threatening ships. Even the vast ponderous whales that sometimes breached the surface could be felt as filled-in spaces within the water by a sea witch who knew how to look for them.

If it could be done with water, it could be done with air. If a whale was an interruption in the shape of water, then the people should feel like interruptions in the air. Rasim clung to that idea, *feeling* for the other people in the arena.

Agnet and Bayar were low interruptions, close to the ground. It was easier for the air to flow over them, like they were part of the sand. The spear fighter, near them, was higher, vertical. The air had to split around that, rather than flow over it.

Rasim, breathing through his teeth, pushed at Mikkel's attacking wind until it ran into the tall, upright person space, and heard the woman's scream of surprise as the air itself seized her and flung her away from her prey.

He finally got to his feet, leaning forward even though the wind itself was no longer pressing on him. Over his shoulder, he said, "Stay alive," before turning his full attention to Mikkel.

The Skymaster's stance had changed entirely. His feet were wide, his arms spread, and he, like Rasim, leaned forward a little, as if bracing himself against attack. A terrible, mad smile contorted his face. With a shock, Rasim recognized it as the same smile Nasira had had when she said she had nothing left to lose. "You don't have to die today, Mikkel."

He hardly spoke the words, but the air carried them at his whim. Mikkel's smile grew even more awful. "I have to win, or I have to die. They promised they would set my family free, if I died."

"And you believe them?"

Mikkel screamed, a sound as loud as his windstorm, and sent the smashing power at Rasim again. It hit like a blow, but Rasim's toes were deep in the sand, borrowing its strength so he could stand fast against the attack. Stonemasters were notorious for their strength. Rasim had always supposed it was just from working heavy stone. Now he thought he knew better.

Mikkel's family was out there somewhere. Here, at the arena, probably, because his masters would want him to have seen them. Here, where his masters could see if he failed in his part of the bargain, and slay Mikkel's family instantly. That family was probably also enslaved, so they would either be in the arena itself, in the cages, or...

...or watching from the best vantage in the arena, where they too could know whether they would die through Mikkel's actions, or if he would.

A profound hatred filled Rasim. It was unforgivable to own other people. It was unforgivable to force *him* to think like slavers, to try and imagine how he would be most cleverly cruel to those he owned. He glanced toward the seats, searching for the colors that indicated wealth, and the most luxurious of the sitting spaces. There were a handful of them scattered around: covered boxes to keep the viewers cool, banners flying to proclaim nobility or money.

Skymasters on the *Wafiya* used a trick they called bending light to make distant things seem closer than they were. Rasim had seen the same kind of effect with water droplets. He pressed the two ideas together in his mind and caught his breath as the audience suddenly magnified, sky witchery shrinking the apparent distance until he could easily see the features of each person in the box.

None of them were slaves with knives to their throats. He looked into another box, and then another, and another. In the fourth he found two children with light, sun-golden brown skin, much like Rasim's own, kneeling in front of a spear-bearing guard. Behind them stood a Moranese woman. A guard held a blade at her throat, although her features were so calm and composed that Rasim wouldn't have guessed she was terrified, if it weren't for the way her gaze was locked on the arena below.

He didn't want to risk slamming anyone around, not with knives and spears in the guards' hands. Not without more certainty of his ability to control sky witchery. But he'd created bubbles of air within water many times, by pushing water away from himself. Maybe he could do something similar with sky magic.

It took longer than he hoped. Finally, though, as Rasim himself struggled with the unfamiliar power, the nobles within the box became woozy. Rasim's head began to pound, and a sudden surge of witchery sent the nobles to sleep, but made Rasim himself stagger. For a moment there, it had felt like he was using Missio's drug again: like he was unstoppable. But that sensation left him as quickly as it had come, leaving him wanting more and also suddenly afraid. If using more than one magic could make him feel that rush of addiction, then doing so wasn't safe for anybody but the royal family, after all.

Even as he fought the memory of that heady use of magic, the guards in the nobles' box collapsed. The woman flinched as the knife dropped away from her throat. Rasim sent words to her on the air, hoping she would understand. "Dress yourself in noble clothes, *quickly,* and go to the docks. Find an Ilyaran ship called the *Wafiya* and get on board, if you can, or hide nearby. I'll send Mikkel to you as soon as I can."

To his astonishment, the woman didn't even hesitate, much less question orders arriving out of thin air. Either she understood him, or knew how to seize an opportunity when it presented itself. Whichever it was, within seconds she had arranged someone else's dramatic headpiece to fall over her own head and shoulders, obscuring her slave's collar, and was dressing the children similarly. Rasim turned away, aware that both very little and also too much time had passed since Mikkel's attack. The audience was losing patience.

The witchery he held at bay yearned to fly free. It wanted to dance. Air was not accustomed to restraints, and neither, it seemed, was the magic that commanded it. Air moved like it was alive, all on its own. That was different from the other two magics he'd knowingly used. Water pooled in things, collecting itself together, and stone, left on its own, didn't do much of anything, at least not within a human lifetime. Air flowed constantly, though, and all Mikkel was doing with it was throwing slabs. Rasim twisted his fingers and sky witchery caught in them, spilling upward.

A funnel of air appeared. The audience shrieked with delight, and Rasim sent the funnel whipping around the arena, keeping it high enough to pick up very little sand. It *did* snatch light bits of cloth from the audience, who roared with protesting laughter as their scarves and cloaks made brightly colored streaks in the funnel. Those colors lashed around each other, beautiful, deadly shapes, like wings in the spinning wind. Like something alive inside it was shaping it. Concentrating so hard his head began to hurt, Rasim whispered across the distance to Mikkel. "Your family is safe. Look to their box."

The Skymaster glanced sharply at him, then turned on his heel to stare incredulously at the empty box above. "They'll be waiting for you at the docks," Rasim promised. "*Now* will you help me?"

"My name is Karluk," the Skymaster whispered back, "and I will do anything you ask."

Rasim grinned so widely his face hurt. "Let's bring the arena down."

CHAPTER SIXTEEN

Karluk's shock was clearly visible even without witchery to enhance it. Rasim couldn't stop grinning. "A sandstorm, first, to drive everybody out. I don't want to kill people, Karluk, Skymaster of Ilyara. We have to be better than that. A sandstorm and then we shatter the locks." Rasim brought his funnel down to the arena's surface. Sand whipped into it, creating a sifting, roaring sound that the audience echoed. There were moments where Rasim could almost see through the sand, as if speed turned it to glass in the same way heat might. Those were just the bits of cloth, though, creating flashes of brilliance even in the dusty yellow of the rising dust. But it seemed like there was something _in_ it. Something living, something invisible, something powerful....

"And I thought you didn't have magic," Karluk said across the distance. "Keep it out of my way, and I'll make as much of a mess as I can. Then—"

"Then go after your family," Rasim said suddenly.

"Get out of here before the panic starts. Tilarea keep you in her arms, Karluk. Good luck." He broke his funnel into two as he spoke, and that was as much as he could do. They were eager to leap around and create chaos, and he got dizzy if he watched them too long.

The audience, though, was on its feet with outrageous delight. People were throwing things into the funnels now: food, clothes, even weapons, and Rasim realized they had never seen a sandstorm. They had no idea how much damage wind funnels could cause with bits of straw, never mind daggers or arrows. He brought one of the funnels as near to Karluk as he dared without breaking the Skymaster's concentration, and the audience roared even more loudly. They were so excited to see impending death, Rasim thought sickly. They wanted so much to see him swept up and destroyed. That was awful, to take so much joy in someone else's pain.

A sudden staggering sweep of power answered his whirling funnels. Karluk ripped the one nearer to him apart with such ease that Rasim staggered. Then Karluk wrested control of the other one away, sending it spinning across the arena. Rasim protested so loudly his chest hurt, but the audience stomped their feet, shaking the air itself with their cries. Chastened, Rasim flung himself into the fight, more concerned with creating a mess than hurting anyone.

Karluk seemed to be performing with the same gusto, and the onlookers, unaccustomed to the treat of witches doing battle, didn't seem to care. That was good. Just maintaining the sandstorm overwhelmed

Rasim, and he had a brief, longing thought of working with water again. Their whirlwinds slammed together, almost collapsing with their own power, then suddenly surging into a massive tornado that finally got a few shrieks of terror, rather than delight, from the viewers.

Color flashed in the cyclone, bright clear hues that made it absurdly beautiful, despite its deadly potential. He had the sense again that there was something alive in it. Something that was now awakening, having slept before. Across the distance, as the twister grew, Rasim caught a glimpse of fear in Karluk's face before the Skymaster's voice sounded in his ear. "We have a mess. Now, how do you mean to bring down the arena?"

"Let me worry about that. Get out of here. Make sure my friends get out too. Take them to the *Wafiya*."

"The Ilyaran flagship is *here?*" Astonishment sharpened the Skymaster's tone.

"Aye, but the captain is playing a long con, so be careful." As Karluk and the others ran for the exit under the protection of the lashing sand, Rasim bent all his concentration on the storm. He wanted to spill it into the seating, but at its current power and speed, he didn't dare, not if he expected to keep everyone alive. And as Karluk retreated, he released his control over the enormous working, leaving Rasim to hold together a magic he'd barely even touched before that day.

Barely. Barely, but he *had*, or at least he thought he might have, now that he was thinking about it at all. He'd shouted through the storm when the Seamasters had found Captain Nasira's old, wrecked ship, the *Sinaz*. He had believed then that one of the Skymaster journeymen on the voyage had helped him, making his voice carry, but he'd never gotten the opportunity to ask about that, and then he'd forgotten. And his voice had carried strangely far only a week or two ago, when he'd commanded the *Wafiya*'s crew to fight against the slavers, too.

Now, standing rooted in the earth through stone witchery, struggling to contain an immense act of sky witchery, he wondered how many times in the past few months he'd used a magic he didn't think he could even touch, much less master.

Not that he dared think he'd mastered sky witchery. The funnel of air fought him with every spin, as if a living thing inside it clawed to get out. Rags and cloaks and daggers glittered within its depths, lashing toward the tornado's outer edges. If even one of those weapons came free, someone would almost certainly die. Rasim shot a desperate glance toward the exits, but Karluk had fled, the other gladiators in his wake. No one would help Rasim break the massive show of power into pieces and send it hissing through the stands to chase the audience away. No one but he could drive the wind into narrow cracks in the arena's thick walls, finding weak spaces to break apart so he could tear the whole monstrosity down.

A shrill bit of humor sliced through Rasim at the idea that he could even do any of that. Getting himself and everyone else out of there without anybody dying would be a wonder all by itself.

The tornado, or something within its tight-wound center, was *fighting* him. He'd felt it awakening while he and Karluk tangled with each other. Now it seemed like the roaring, sand-filled winds were trying to expose something that had always been hidden in the air. Eyes clenched shut, teeth set together, Rasim put the backs of his hands together and pushed them forward, like he could reach into the cyclone's heart. Sweat spilled into his closed eyes, tickling his nose as he struggled to unwind the twisting winds.

The windstorm shattered with a thunderous silence, and in that silence, people began to scream.

SAND SPRAYED in Rasim's face, blinding him for long seconds. He wiped it away, tears dripping from the sting. He only slowly realized that he'd fallen to his knees, that his hands were buried in inches-deep sand. He shook it free and wiped his face again to the sound of screams, and lifted his gaze in baffled exhaustion.

A creature of glass shimmered in the air above the arena, threads of color spinning through four rapid-beating, translucent wings. It was cousin to a dragon-fly, but a hundred times larger, and with a body more serpentine. Its legs, though, were slender and segmented, bunched together at the beast's chest. Wings rode high on its shoulders, leaving it mostly lashing tail that broke sunlight into a thousand prisms as it flickered through the air. Given the size of the thing, its neck was comparatively short. Its head was small and dominated by huge faceted eyes.

Eyes and *teeth*, Rasim saw in horror. Innumerable pin-like teeth, so clear they could hardly be seen, at least until the creature spun in the sky and plunged toward the sand to land, all six legs driving downward into one of the fallen blade-users. The fighter's body convulsed under the impact and the glasswing serpent lifted a bloody, spear-like foot to stab the dead person again. People screamed, Rasim among them, but unlike those who sensibly ran from the arena, Rasim searched the sand near himself for a weapon. A spearhead, half buried in the sand, glinted in the sun, and he seized it, then, trembling, ran at the glasswing.

It sprang into the air as if it saw him coming. As it whipped around, its many-faceted eyes glittering, Rasim realized it probably *had* seen him. It hissed, a terrible gas-filled breath that made the air waver with its foulness. Then its tail slashed toward him, and thin, glass-like shards flew from its tip. Rasim dove to the side as daggers of clear, shimmering *air* hit the sand and blackened it. Heat rose from the delicate weapons, which cooled almost instantly, even as more of them sprayed toward him. Rasim flung up a wall of air, desperate to protect himself, and the air itself turned solid when the glass daggers struck it.

Of course it did. That was what the glasswing was. A creature of solid air, like the sea serpent had been a thing of the water, like the stone snake had been made of the mountain itself. Rasim thought the glasswing had been called by the battle of magics within the cyclone, as if so much sky witchery concentrated so fiercely had drawn its attention. It screamed, a thin sound like glass scraping, or like wind through narrow canyons, and dove at Rasim. At least it was going after him, not the audience running from the arena, but he was one boy with an inadequate weapon and a magic he barely understood.

He threw his spear at it anyway, aiming for one of the swiftly-fluttering wings. The glasswing spun around and snatched his spear from the sky, breaking it between its needle-like teeth. Its tail slammed toward him, trying to catch him with a deadly blow, but he threw himself to the side again, landing in a spray of sand. The glasswing pounced, its feet driving toward him with unnatural points. Those feet were weapons, meant only to kill. Rasim slid away from them feet, scrambling down the length of the creature's belly to hide beneath its long thrashing tail. He could see the sky through it, distorted and shot with the glasswing's brilliant prisms, but still blue, as if he looked through thick glass or heavy air.

The glasswing bent double, looking under itself with its astonishing eyes. Then its tail twitched inward, the stinger spraying shards of solid air again. One of them caught the glasswing in its own belly and it squealed, another high horrible sound of howling wind. Rasim gave a panicked laugh, glad to know it was vulnerable to *something*, while also all too aware that he, too, was vulnerable to witchery.

He threw another wall of air, trying to protect himself, and the glasswing danced above him, stabbing with its vicious feet, slamming its vast tail, snarling with glittering teeth, but not, Rasim noticed, shooting its spikes at him again. A few lay near him and he scrambled toward them, seizing their hafts to turn them into weapons of his own. They turned to air in his hands, leaving him grabbing handsful of sand. The glasswing drove a spear-like foot toward him and caught the leg of his trousers, scoring blood but not really hurting him. He yelled anyway, and the great creature screamed in delight, its feet smashing blows toward him faster and faster.

Rasim rolled toward its tail again, but the glasswing danced back with him, the wind crying through its voice sounding ever-more triumphant. He flung a handful of sand up, trying to command it to turn to stone, to protect him. Although the wall it made was as thin as paper, the glasswing's driving foot caught in it, and would not come out.

Its triumph turned to rage as it swiveled, trying to free itself. The fragile leg snapped and the glasswing flung itself into the air, its broken limb dripping color that dissolved into wind. Rasim stared for the space of a heartbeat, then, with a clarity of mind that went beyond thought, he ran across the sand toward the fallen blade-wielders.

The glasswing followed, its vast form casting clear shadows on the golden sand. Rainbows glimmered around him and he threw darts of air backward, in the direction the shadow came from, not daring to stop, look, and aim. He knew to duck when the thin shadow, cast by sunlight through the glass wings, gathered as it prepared to pounce. The huge beast landed hard in the sand and bounced up again, shaking itself as if confused. A few steps later, Rasim skidded to the earth beside one of the blade-user's bodies, seizing her sword and rolling to his feet again. This time, he waited until the glasswing gathered itself, waited for it to drop from the sky like a weight, and drew on stone witchery to throw a tremendous splash of sand into the air as the glasswing fell.

It flung itself backward, seeing danger too late, but sand turned to stone, catching its many feet just above the first joints. The glasswing opened its mouth, hissing poison air at Rasim, who batted it away with a weak gust of wind. Then he slipped behind the glasswing's head so it couldn't try to poison him again, and sent more sand upward to catch its bashing tail. Its wings beat harder, trying to buffet him, but he was inside their range now, and knelt at the glasswing's shoulder, putting a weary hand on its head.

The touch almost hurt. The beast was completely mad, all war and fury within. It felt like magic fighting itself, just as Rasim and Karluk had fought with magic. Rasim could imagine a different kind of glasswing, a creature called by magic that merged instead of fought itself. That kind of glasswing might not have been driven mad by the witchery that had drawn its attention. He thought that perhaps a real Skymaster, or maybe even a master healer, could have helped this raging beast out of its insanity back toward wholeness. Maybe even he could have himself, if he had the time.

But he didn't have time, and as it was, the creature was a danger to everything around it. Gods forbid the Moranese should capture it, somehow. At best, it would be forced to fight in the arena. At worst, it would be used as a weapon against their enemies.

Regret lanced through him, but, as with the sea serpent, he didn't see that he had a choice. With the serpent, he'd been fighting for his own life, which made its death a little easier, but if he left the poor glasswing alive, its future would be even worse than its brief existence had been. He didn't want to kill anything, but at least this creature wasn't human.

"I'm sorry," Rasim said helplessly. "You should have been beautiful, and we broke you. I can't fix you, and I can't let them use you. I'm so sorry."

He rose, and, teeth bared with effort, smashed his sword through the glasswing's fragile neck.

The blade slammed to the earth in a rush of air, and the glasswing was gone as if it had never been.

CHAPTER SEVENTEEN

Rasim, numb to the bone, stood for what felt like a long time, staring sightlessly at where the glasswing had been. Sounds beyond his own battle finally began to filter through, and he raised his gaze, aware of what was happening around him for the first time in minutes. People fled the arena, no longer caring that the danger was past. There would probably be ringmasters coming for him soon, a thought which jostled him into motion. He had meant to free everyone in the arena, and had succeeded in bringing a monster into their midst instead. Only a few people had been freed, and others had died, because of that. But if he didn't go now, he wouldn't be able to do anyone any good at all. He was already exhausted, and if he didn't lose himself in the crowd, he would be easy to recapture.

His feet made the decision for him. Rasim found himself running, joining the last throngs of people fleeing the arena. He had no magic left to hide his presence with, no way to reawaken the sandstorm, and he wore a slave's collar and no shirt. No one was going to help him and everyone would try to turn him in.

There were merchants just outside the gates, selling beer and wine and food. Some sold linen parasols to help keep the day's heat off, and others offered loose-woven tunics that would fend off both sun and rain. There were dozens of other things for sale, but most of them were being hastily dragged back into carts and shut away as thousands of people poured from the arena. Rasim, with an apologetic mutter, snatched one of the tunics as he ran by, and stole a floppy straw hat from another cart as he was jostled past it. He fell twice, deliberately, making a mess of both tunic and hat so they didn't look new, and caked his hands with as much pale dust as he could to change his skin color a little. His bare feet were already lighter than usual from the coating of arena sand. It was as much disguise as he could manage quickly.

The crowd swept along swiftly for a considerable distance beyond the arena gates. Rasim kept his head down, judging their direction by his sense of where the river was. It grew stronger at times and faded at others. Both filled him with hope, because at least he could tell where it was. But he didn't want to go straight there, because the Moranese might expect him to try to return to the *Wafiya*. Too late, he realized he shouldn't have instructed anyone else to go there, either. Agnet and Bayar's height and coloring made them both incredibly distinctive, if in completely different ways.

A ripple of discontent moved through the crowd as

shouts arose. The general forward motion slowed a moment and Rasim peered under someone's arm to see a scuffle being subdued. He was moving again before he fully understood what he'd seen, and when he did, hope jolted through him.

A free man was bearing a slave to the ground, squashing the fight out of him, but the slave's expression had been anything but defeated. He'd looked willing to try again, like he was going to fight for his own freedom. And there were more scuffles like that breaking out. It had only been minutes since people had started running from the arena, and already slaves were in rebellion. They'd been given hope.

They needed more.

There had to be a way for Rasim to offer it. There had to be, but running across the city was no time to think of a plan. He caught scent of a marketplace and ducked to the side, following another part of the crowd through the narrow streets. Apologizing under his breath with each theft, he stole lemons from one stall, waxed bags of honey and oil from two others, and then, actually succumbing to hunger, a stick jammed full of roasted lamb and onions from a fourth. It was almost full dark now, making it easier to slip into the shadow under a set of rickety wooden steps so he could shove the lamb into his mouth undisturbed. It was tender and rich, and he licked his fingers gratefully before scooping a generous glob of honey into his mouth as a sweet treat before tending to the other things he'd stolen.

With a scoop gone from the honey, there was a bit

of room to spare in its waxed bag. Rasim mixed as much oil into it as he could. His hair, already unwashed and dirty from living in the slave pens, had stayed in its loose curls, but lay flatter than usual, more like Desimi's or Kisia's. Their hair remained resolutely black no matter what, but his, before it had been cut journeyman-short, the ends had been dark gold from exposure to the sun and salt. People had commented on it as a mark of his Northern blood and right now, it offered a chance to disguise himself better.

Making a face at the mess, he dabbed oiled honey through his hair, rubbing it into every curl and strand. When his whole head was slick and sticky with the mess, he made as much of a bun of it as he could, and put his hat on top of it. He would have to get to the river or a trough before morning to rinse it out, but a night's worth of honey bleaching would lighten it a little more. Then he'd use the lemon juice and hope for a brilliantly sunny day to brighten it. He'd need days to get it truly yellow-gold, or even to achieve the reddish coppery tones that Ilyaran hair often turned when bleached, but it was at least a step toward making himself look like someone else.

None of which would matter if he couldn't get the slave collar off before dawn. Stomach full and hair attended to, Rasim slipped back into the crowd, now looking and listening for the sounds of a forge.

Instead he found soldiers, city guard in imposing black uniforms that let them come out of the increasing dark like wraiths. They shoved their way through the crowd, cuffing anybody who looked twice at them and grabbing slaves by their collars to examine them. Rasim's palms ached with sudden fear. He tried to remember to breathe as he fell into step with a man whose belly was large enough to provide cover for someone twice Rasim's size. As the guards swung around to have another pass at the market square, he stepped nimbly in front of a woman with ample skirts and several children. Heart in his mouth, he glanced back and couldn't see the guards from where he was. That meant they couldn't see him, either, which somehow did nothing to settle his stomach. Hungry as he'd been, he wished he hadn't eaten the lamb, which now felt heavy and greasy in his belly. Trembling with the fear of a mis-step, Rasim left the square by slipping from one group to another, trying not to stay with anyone long enough to draw attention.

He didn't even dare slump against a wall while he decided what to do next. He'd be investigated for loitering, and his slave collar would be discovered. Cursing under his breath, he chose the darkest alley he could find, and followed it away from the market.

In Ilyara, a forge would be near a stream or water mill of some sort, in case of fire. Here in Moran, where the buildings were made of wood and there weren't witches everywhere to keep things from burning, that seemed like an even more important idea. Rasim clung to the shadows, following his sense of the river and its tributaries more than any particular path. That prob-ably kept him safer anyway. It meant he wasn't taking a predictable route. It was difficult enough to keep moving at a reasonable clip, neither too slow nor too fast. Exhaustion was settling into his limbs, turning them to stone, although he thought he'd worked harder on the *Wafiya* many times without feeling so weary.

Of course, on the *Wafiya* he hadn't made heavy use of a new kind of magic. The realization made him stumble, fatigue suddenly overwhelming him. Using massive witchery was tiring in the best of circumstances. Using huge amounts when he'd never tried that kind of magic before was probably a good way to accidentally kill himself. He'd been lucky.

More than lucky. He had accomplished what King Taishm had hoped for with the King's Guild: he could probably use every kind of Ilyaran magic. It *was* possible, even for those who weren't of royal blood. They had put so many rules in place that no one had ever tried, perhaps to Ilyara's detriment.

Rasim rejected that thought immediately. If it had been widely known that anyone could learn multiple magics, the Ilyaran royal family would have been challenged time and again, and Ilyara's peace destabilized. It was better for the country to leave multiple magics in the hands of the royal family.

Too bad half of Moran had just watched him use sky witchery, then. Rasim wasn't exactly going to be able to keep that a secret. Not that most people here knew he was supposed to be a sea witch, but Nasira and Lorens certainly did, and they were out there, maybe telling people right now what a prize he'd turned out to be.

Or maybe not such a prize after all. He'd instigated at least some level of rebellion in Moran. Maybe they would hold that against Nasira. Maybe they wouldn't want her slaves at all, and the rest of his crew would be safer than he'd ended up being.

Or maybe they would just kill them all in retaliation for what Rasim had done. He stumbled again, then lurched into an ivy-lined alley to huddle, shivering, amongst the concealing leaves.

He hadn't thought any of it through at all well. He'd imagined he could somehow single-handedly bring down the arena, and when he couldn't, he'd fled. He'd started something like a rebellion, but he hadn't considered what might happen to his crewmates as a result. Most of his previous adventures had only endangered himself, and he'd mostly been endangered anyway. This time, other people were affected.

Agnet had tried to warn him, in her way. She hadn't done a very good job, but Rasim was supposed to be clever. He was supposed to think of things before other people did. He'd seen how he could perhaps change the whole world, but he hadn't thought of how trying to make those changes could potentially hurt his friends. Desimi was right. Rasim thought too big sometimes.

He had to get the slave collar off. Fear for the *Wafiya*'s crew burned Rasim's tiredness away. He got to his feet again, no longer willing to skulk in the dark. He needed to really look for a forge, or even more alarmingly, ask someone for directions. Another slave would be his best bet, assuming he could find one who spoke Ilyaran or Northern.

Despite his worries, a crooked smile crept across his features. He was more likely to find a forge on his own than find an Ilyaran-speaking slave who would be willing to help him. At least he was a fair distance from the arena. Hopefully no one would be looking for him in a wealthy quarter. Moving purposefully, he left the alley and strode down the road, once more searching for streams. Even if he only found a stables, he might find something there to cut through the collar, and that would be enough.

Voices behind him made his chest tighten, but he didn't look back. A scent of horses caught his attention and he turned up a twisting road that started with paving stones, turned to cobble, and then finally to dirt marked with hoof prints. The voices were still behind him: following, maybe, or maybe just on the same path. Rasim quickened his pace every time a curve gave him a moment or two unseen, and in the darkness nearly ran into the opening door of a stables.

He crushed himself against its wall as the door banged back and smacked him in the nose. Tears flooding his eyes, he snatched the door's leather handle, trying to keep it from bouncing shut again and revealing him. Horses were led out and a rough voice called out. The men who'd been behind Rasim shouted in response. The one at the door grunted and shouted again. Rasim wondered if they were talking about him, and wished desperately that he spoke the Moranese language. If he got out of Moran alive he would ask the Sunmasters to teach it to him. Seamasters should speak a lot of languages, he thought furiously. They traveled everywhere. They should know the tongues of the places they visited, instead of relying on Sunmasters for translation, or using the cobbled-together common language that had bits of everything, and not enough of anything. If he got out of here alive, he'd tell Guild-master Asindo that, too, and make sure language classes were included at the guild from then on.

The man at the door swung onto his horse and rode down the street, leaving the door gaping open. Rasim, wedged behind the door, stared after him, amazed at his terrible manners. Even Rasim, who had grown up with ships, not horses, knew better than to leave a stable door open. As he wondered if he dared leave, someone else came out of the stables. Rasim didn't need to speak Moranese to know the other person was cursing the rider. Without ever looking beyond it, the other person pulled the door shut and latched it, leaving Rasim pressed against the wall and fighting back a giggle of relief.

Just beyond the stables was another alley. Rasim scurried into it and was rewarded with a mist in the air and the sound of running water. He choked down another nervous giggle and crept forward, embar-rassed that his fear had overwhelmed his sense of where the water was.

A small open yard lay behind the stables. A stream welled up in one corner next to a small forge. Horse-shoes and short bars of metal were tidily stacked beside the forge, and innumerable tools hung against the back wall. Rasim vaulted the short fence and ran to the tools, searching for anything like clippers. Different-sized tongs were everywhere, along with hammers and small nails, but none of them could be used to get his collar off. He fell back against the forge wall in despair, searching one final time, and saw a huge pair of clippers on the ground in the anvil's shadow.

Someone, he bet, would get in trouble for leaving those there instead of putting them away. Shaking with gratitude, he scooped them up and found out just how difficult it was to clip a collar off your own throat without taking half your skin along with it. After several tries he sat down, bracing one handle of the clipper between two stones, and carefully maneuvered the pinchers onto his collar. The clippers were *sharp*: the skin he'd already scraped off could easily be joined by a tremendous amount of blood if he wasn't very careful indeed. He wrapped both hands around the wedged clipper handle to make sure it stayed in place, and, feeling awkward, used his feet to pull the other handle closed.

The snip of metal sounded loud enough to bring every guard in Moran running. Rasim froze, wide-eyed, hardly breathing as he waited to be caught. When, after long moments, no one came to investigate, he cautiously unwound his hands from the clippers and put them back under the forge where he'd found them. If he knew which hook they belonged on, he'd put them away and save someone a scolding—or worse—in the morning. As it was, he muttered an apology as he put them back, then hesitated as he started to leave.

The forge would be a safe enough place for several hours, and sneaking around at night in an unfamiliar city—especially one being searched for misbehaving slaves—would likely get him in trouble. His friends and crew were out there somewhere, probably in trouble themselves, but Rasim didn't know what he could do for them in the dark with no resources or plans. Sleep might do him—and them—more good than anything else he could do right now.

There were burlap sacks under the forge's half-roof. Rasim tucked them around himself and went to sleep instantly.

HE WOKE BEFORE DAWN, partly out of self-preservation and partly because his scalp itched so badly he gasped with the effort of not scratching it. He crawled to the little spring and scrubbed sticky, oily honey from his hair until it felt less disgusting. The cold water helped wake him up, and he was almost cheerful as he found a small knife to cut one of his lemons in half. He rubbed the juice into his hair and threw the lemon peels into a moldering heap of straw near the stables. If the sun was strong today, it would help brighten his hair, and he'd keep reapplying lemon as often as he could. It would take a while to really be effective, but between the honey and the lemon, it was a start.

As an afterthought, he went back to the straw pile and buried his collar at its base. Then, before the sun had broken the horizon, he leaped the low fence again and hurried toward the river. If he was lucky—very lucky, he admitted aloud, but under his breath—the crew would still mostly be on the *Wafiya*. Failing that, at least he could find Agnet and the others.

An air of unease remained in Moran as the city

awakened. Rasim passed by sullen slaves and edgy masters, and wished again that he spoke the language so he could understand the gossip that passed around him. City guards were everywhere, and anyone who wasn't dressed in the fine clothes of the rich avoided meeting the guardsmens' eyes, or getting in their way. Rasim followed their example, looking meekly at the ground as he walked through the streets. Keeping his head down helped hide the scrapes he'd gotten while taking the collar off, and he let his tunic slide backward a little so his bare nape was exposed.

More merchants and fewer guards were visible as he approached the docks, but Rasim circled the long way around to find the *Wafiya*. Smart guards wouldn't be obvious, and he was better off assuming they were smart. His stomach rumbled as he passed a cart selling warm, sweetly scented bread that reminded him of home. Kisia's family owned a bakery, and he'd often helped her work the bread dough very early in the morning, before she joined the Guild.

The man walking the cart caught his hungry glance and spoke. Rasim shrugged and the man spoke again, this time in Ilyaran. "A clipped copper for a bun, lad, if you're hungry."

An answer nearly spilled from Rasim's lips before he realized a *smart* guard would do something like this to tease out a missing slave boy. He shrugged again and spoke in Northern. "I don't speak your language."

"No?" The baker switched to Northern as easily. "You look Ilyaran."

"My ma was. She died birthing me and me da

brought me back to the North where he's from. I've never been there, but he's told me about it a little. He says it's hot and that almost everybody is brown like me."

"Browner, even. Where's your da now?"

There were at least three Northern ships docked farther down the river. Rasim pointed that way. "I'm the cabin boy on his ship."

"His ship? He's a captain, is he?"

Nonplussed, Rasim shook his head. "Nah, I didn't mean it that way. He's only third mate. Captain says he's got too much temper to be in charge." He'd led himself down a dangerous path, answering the baker's questions. Putting on his best beguiling face, he asked, "How come you talk so many languages?" and hoped the baker would go with the change of subject.

"Useful for selling wares, lad. Who's your captain? What's your ship?"

Dread sluiced through Rasim. Chances were the baker was only curious, but if he knew the ships and their captains, Rasim had just talked himself back into a slave's collar. He forced a broad grin and thrust a finger toward the *Wafiya*'s distinctive masts. "That one, eh? I'm gonna take it like an Ilyaran pirate and be captain of the whole wide ocean! Arr!" He brandished an imaginary sword and pretended to skewer a bread roll, then ran off laughing at himself. The baker's tolerant chuckle followed until the crowd had separated them, at which point Rasim fell against a cargo box and tried not to wheeze too audibly.

He had been stupid *again*. No one here was his

friend, and everyone was likely to know more than he did. Any conversations would lead to trouble. All he needed to do was find his friends and then huddle down to make a plan. He squished between two cargo boxes, trying to get a look around without being seen.

The baker passed by again, just within earshot as he spoke with a Northern man whose hard face was at odds with the baker's more genial nature. "Around eleven," the baker was saying. "Likely looking. Said he was from one of the Northern ships, but wouldn't say which one. Might be a stowaway, yeh? The sort nobody will notice if he goes missing." He passed out of hearing range again, leaving Rasim a mixture of offended and relieved. The baker wasn't looking for escaped slaves; he was looking to make new ones. But Rasim was thirteen, not eleven!

Faintly insulted, he glared after the baker, then turned his attention back to the *Wafiya*. He had friends there, if they were still on board. If they were, he could save *them*, at least, and together they would have more chance at anything than Rasim did by himself.

Nervous and feeling very alone, he concluded he wasn't quite foolish enough to walk up the gangplank, although the boldness of the move made it almost tempting. Instead he went far enough up river that he could slip into the water unnoticed and swim back to the *Wafiya*.

To his relief, his witchery responded as he dropped down the walled-up bank of the river and sank. It wasn't as strong as it had been after Siliaria's kiss, but it was enough to keep air with him, and to propel himself through the water with its currents. The water wasn't especially clean—it never was anywhere except in Ilyara—but its murkiness helped hide him, so he didn't have to swim too deep.

The *Wafiya*'s keel was unique, making the Ilyaran ship easy to distinguish amongst the others. There were also markings to identify it, since because young apprentices and journeymen—and sometimes not-so-young ones!—often needed to identify their ship from below, after swimming in the oceans. Rasim swam up beneath its hold, glad that the *Wafiya* protruded well into the river. Only a handful of boats nearby would even be able to see its stern, where he intended to climb up.

As he swam toward the surface, it struck him that the entire population of the city on the river's far side would *also* be able to see the stern. There wasn't, he realized now, a very *good* way to sneak on board, not in broad daylight. Despite having needed the sleep he'd gotten, it now seemed like a bad idea. He might have snuck onto the ship under cover of dark, if he'd risked it last night.

He also might have been caught by patrolling guards, which even now seemed more likely. In the ship's shadow, hoping he looked like a seal—hoping Moran *had* seals!—Rasim poked his head above the surface for a quick look around. He sank down a moment later, convinced that either witchery or the anchor chain were his best bet. Neither of them seemed like a very *good* bet, but his alternative was paddling around the ship until sunset, which was even less appealing. Besides, that would mean he'd lost an entire day since escaping the arena. He didn't want to waste that kind of time, not after causing so much trouble. Odds were that he'd landed his crewmates in hot water already. Dawdling would only make it worse.

The anchor chain was half as big around as he was. If he could cling to its underside as he climbed up, that might be the most subtle way to get on board. But witchery would be faster, which might be smarter.

On the other hand, he could stay in the water all day, frowning at the water-wobbly lines of the ship, and never make a decision. Determined to act even if it was the wrong act, Rasim swam to to the anchor chain and hooked his arms around it, hauling his weight upward. Every body length he moved, he expected to hear a shout that betrayed him, but he clambered up without notice and swung himself over the ship's rail to land with a quiet thump in the stern's shadow.

A hand snaked out of the shadow and clapped itself over his mouth.

CHAPTER EIGHTEEN

Rasim choked off a yelp as he was hauled around by a strong grip on his face. Within a heartbeat, he'd been dragged inside a cabinet at the ship's stern, where spare sails and other necessary shipboard repair materials were kept. Early morning sunlight slipped through the narrow slats, illuminating the small hold space just enough for him to see the wide-eyed, determined face of Karluk's wife. Behind her, in shadow, were their children, whose interested expressions suggested they thought they were having an adventure.

The woman gradually released her grip on Rasim's face as she became confident he wasn't going to shout. Nor did he, though when she finally let him go, he did let out a slow breath, murmuring, "You're very strong," in Ilyaran.

Because she'd come to the *Wafiya* like he'd told her to, Rasim wasn't really surprised when she responded in Ilyaran. "I work every day cleaning house. Lifting water bucket, heavy curtain, beds to—" She made a gesture like sweeping, and Rasim offered, "Dust?"

She nodded once, firmly. "Beds to dust below. I have strength. You save us, but where is Mikkel?"

Rasim nearly bared his teeth in dismay, but, remembering the children, stopped himself just in time. "He should be nearby. We got separated. How did you get on the ship?"

The woman shrugged. "I took off good clothes and told ship's guards that captain had—" She snapped her fingers, searching for a word. Her Ilyaran was strongly accented, but, Rasim thought, very good. Much better than his non-existent Moranese, obviously, and probably better than his limited Northern. "Buyed. Captain had buyed us. Captain was not here to say no, so when guard changed I took children and hid here. There is trouble in city. What have you did?"

"Karluk and I drove everybody out of the arena with a sandstorm to give us a chance to escape. My name is Rasim."

"Karluk. He has taked back his name?" Pride flashed in the woman's eyes as Rasim nodded. She gazed at him a moment, as if assessing his honesty, then said, "I am Zyterna. Are we safe here?"

"I don't know," Rasim admitted. "For the moment, probably, but there's probably going to be backlash for what I did, and it might affect the ship. I'll find something on board to cut your collars off you—"

Zyterna's hands flew to her collar, strong fingers wrapping around it as if she would pull it off herself.

Then, more composedly, she loosened her hands again and nodded. "That would be best."

"I can find you clothes, too, and some money, probably. Tonight I can slip you off the ship and we'll find you somewhere to stay until I find Karluk and can figure out a way to get all of us out of here."

Zyterna murmured, "Karluk," again, and then, as if her husband's name helped her come to a decision, lifted her chin and said, "We accept your help," proudly.

Rasim smiled. "I'm glad. Stay here while I search the ship, all right? Is anyone else aboard?"

"No. The witches, they was taked away before I arrive. I am sorry," Zyterna said as Rasim felt a wince of disappointment cross his face.

"It's all right. At least I know, so I can stay hidden instead of walking out in the open. I'll be back soon." He slipped out of the cabinet and crawled swiftly across the deck. A pang of homesickness struck him as his hands passed over the *Wafiya*'s familiar planks. Nothing had gone the way he'd imagined, when he'd laid out his plan to the captain. After the mess he'd made in the arena, he wasn't even sure if Nasira was still free. There was a real chance the flagship, the one place Rasim had always wanted to belong, would never return to Ilyara.

He put the thought out of his mind and got his feet under him as he entered the hold. There were clothes and coins aplenty, though both were Ilyaran. Well, so were the children, so perhaps it wouldn't seem strange to anyone if a Moranese woman adopted those styles and had that coin. Rasim collected outfits that he thought might fit the children, his own among them, as he was easily the smallest member of the *Wafiya*'s crew.

Mostly they had knives aboard, not clippers, because they used rope far more than metal. Chewing his lower lip, Rasim went through his crewmates' belongings, searching for something that could be used to cut metal. If he'd known he'd be cutting collars off people, he'd have stolen the clippers from the forge.

On a second thought, the idea seemed both impossible and improbably funny. Rasim began to imagine himself lurching around the city trying to disguise a pair of clippers almost half his own height. Maybe he could have pretended they were trousers, or perhaps that he had a hurt leg and lash them to his leg. Giggles began to fight their way up. Rasim clasped a hand over his mouth, muffling his laughter, then seized a blanket from one of the berths and giggled hysterically into it. Tears wet the blanket and the air he sucked in through it was too warm, but every time he thought the laughter was under control, he re-envisioned himself hobbling around with clippers tied to his leg, and collapsed into hysteria again. Twice he whispered, "It's not that funny!" to himself, fiercely, but that only served to heighten his amusement.

It took a long time for the giggles to pass, and when they did, Rasim lay on top of the blanket like a wet rag himself, numb with exhaustion. Shivers wracked him then, until he had to sit up and find something to wrap himself in. None of it was funny, not really. He knew the strange reaction was from being scared and alone, and probably from having used far too much witchery lately. He'd escaped the arena, but nothing else at all had gone to plan, and in the end he was only a rather young and small Ilyaran journeyman. Slave rebellions and toppling empires were all beyond him, even if he kept ending up neck deep in them.

That reminded him, viscerally, of having shoved his knife through the sea serpent's eye, pushing his arm in all the way to his own jaw, until he reached the monster's brain. Its eye had been gelatinous and cold, sucking at his skin like it would draw him in. That was *exactly* what being neck-deep in this mess felt like.

Wrapped in two cloaks to fend off a chill that came from within, Rasim went to the galley to find food—hard tack and oranges and, to his relief, a bit of dried fish—and set out to return to Zyterna and her children. On the way he passed Nasira's cabin and stopped abruptly, then ducked inside. She had the keys for the crew's slave collars somewhere. Maybe she'd left them in the cabin.

The last time he'd been inside the captain's cabin, it had been to convince Nasira of his plan to get them into Moran safely. He hadn't really looked around then, but now Rasim pulled cabinet doors and drawers open, searching for anything—even metal cutters—that would let him free Zyterna and her children.

One of the drawers held a copy of a familiar book, and a great upswelling of loss rushed through Rasim. Its cover was a carefully etched image of the guildhall, with color added by a steady hand. The guild had a dozen copies of that book, which told the story of how the Ilyaran guilds were created. Children and the youngest apprentices heard its story every night, as it was read to them again and again, helping to build a sense of community and continuity and place for orphans who had no other. Homesickness brought stinging tears to Rasim's eyes. He pushed his hand over them, trying to ease the ache that coursed through his whole body.

Instead, he caught a glimpse of himself in the captain's brass mirror. It showed him a boy who could easily be mistaken for ten or eleven; the slave-seeking baker had been right after all. His hair looked strangely *big*, worn loose instead of in the short, tight ponytail that would someday become his braided braid. The honey and lemon had already done a little of its work: the loose curls were more golden than he was accustomed to, although the mirror's tint made them look greenish. His eyes were bright green instead of hazel in its tint, too, and he wished he could carry that through as part of his disguise. There were hollows under his eyes, like he hadn't slept enough for a long time, and his cheeks and shoulders were thin. "Some hero," he said aloud to his reflection, and stepped backward, frowning around the room. If he was the captain, if he wanted to hide a spare set of keys….

His gaze lit on the mechanisms tacked safely in their cases on one of the shelves. Maps, compasses, sextants...and another case shaped like it would hold a sextant, but the captain only had one. Rasim opened that one, and let out a gasp of disbelief and relief to find a ring of keys nestled in a bed of coins and small jewels. He scooped up the keys and a handful of money, and with food, jewels, clothes and keys bundled in his arms, he scampered back to the cargo hold.

Zyterna's expression was stern when he returned. "You were gone long time."

"Sorry. Are you all right? I have food and water." He offered them to the woman, whose children scrambled forward eagerly. Zyterna parceled the oranges out first, peeling them as Rasim lifted the keys and asked if he could try them on their collars. She nodded with the dignity of a queen.

He discarded five keys before one fit her collar well enough to pop it open. Her spine stiffened and she put both hands on the collar, pulling at it softly, as if she couldn't believe what she'd heard. Rasim loosened it further, watching it shift against her collarbones, but didn't remove it; it seemed like she might want to do that herself.

After a moment she did, and seemed to gain two inches of height with its removal. She held it a few seconds, staring at it, then dropped it to one side as if it wasn't worthy of looking at again. Then she returned to breaking off pieces of oranges and hard tack for the children, who gaped between Rasim and their mother in fascination. Rasim, grinning, scooted around behind them and tried the same key that had worked on Zyterna's collar. Within a few seconds, all of their collars lay to one side, and Zyterna captured the children in her arms, her expression so hard Rasim suspected she was holding back tears.

"I think we should get you out of here sooner rather than later," Rasim confessed. "I'd rather wait until we have the cover of night, but I don't like leaving you here. I think we should just go over the side of the ship and find a quiet place on the river bank to surface."

"We cannot—" Zyterna frowned. "We cannot water. We cannot..."

"Swim?" Rasim made a swim stroke gesture or two, and Zyterna nodded. "That doesn't matter, as long as you can trust me. *Really* trust me. You know that Karluk commands the air? I can do that, but with water. As long as we all hold on to one another and don't panic, I can get us to shore." He could, he told himself sternly. He'd done it in the North, in much colder water, before Siliaria had graced him with her kiss. He could do it again here in Moran.

"There is no quiet." Zyterna gestured, taking in the length of the river. "Up and down, all busy. How to sneak out without being see? No. We wait for dark. Maybe, though—we leave here? Go below?"

Rasim nodded slowly. "That's probably safe, and it's more comfortable. And there's a necessary down there, which I'm sure you need. We'll have to crawl, all of us, to stay low and unseen. All right? And stay quiet," he admonished the children, who eyed him with disgust. They were raised slaves, Rasim reminded himself. They probably knew more about staying quiet than he ever would. They hadn't, in fact, said a word in the time he'd spoken with their mother. "Sorry, you already knew that. It was a silly thing to say."

Their disgust vanished, turning to skeptical interest. Possibly no one had ever apologized to them before. Rasim smiled to hide his dismay at the idea, and then led the trio across the deck and into the hold below. "The necessary is at the back. Th—" Before he got any farther, all three of them ran for the back of the ship.

By the time they emerged again several minutes later, all looking less tense than before, Rasim had put berths together for each of them. "Mostly just stay away from the portholes—the windows—and stay quiet. There's more to eat in the galley, and—" He poured coins and jewels into Zyterna's hand. "In case I don't come back tonight to get you. You're resourceful. I think you'll find your way to safety. But I'll try to be back just after sundown, to take you to an inn."

"Where will you go?"

Rasim spread his hands. "To find Karluk and tell him you're safe. To find my friends and make sure *they're* safe. To find my crewmates and rescue them."

The corner of Zyterna's mouth twitched, as close to a smile—as close to an expression—as Rasim had seen from her. "All before sunset?"

Rasim smiled back crookedly. "I guess it'll be a busy day."

CHAPTER NINETEEN

I t was easier to get off the *Wafiya* than it was to get on it. Rasim peered through the ship's railing until he was reasonably confident no one was looking, then swiftly dove over the edge. Sea witchery kept him from splashing, and the water enveloped him smoothly.

Zyterna was right. There was nowhere particularly good to exit the river, but it would be simpler for him alone than with three others. His chance came as a small ship docked. Everyone was busy throwing ropes and shouting at one another, giving him the opportunity to scamper up a ladder and join the work. Moments later he slipped away into the bustle of the city, thinking hard as he walked along. The sun, warm on his head, made his hair smell of lemons, which was considerably more pleasant than Moran's general odor. He tested a strand or two and found it stiff and dry, so he ducked into an alley to rub more lemon juice into it.

By the time he emerged he had a plan, although after the past few days even he didn't put much stock in his own plans. Still, it was a course of action, and that was better than nothing.

He had to assume the worst had happened with the *Wafiya*'s crew. That his escape from the arena had endangered all of them, even Captain Nasira. The whole crew might be enslaved by now.

But no one would dare enslave Lorens. A Northern royal might have some explaining to do, or even some damages to pay for, but Rasim was fairly confident Lorens wouldn't be chained up and sold, or worse.

And it couldn't be *too* hard to find the Northern prince in Moran. Probably. Rasim knew Lorens had presumed on his youthful friendship with the lady Amdria to establish his and Nasira's credentials. Finding Amdria might lead to the prince.

It was a place to start. Rasim worked his way back toward the docks, because he'd watched Amdria's approach from the *Wafiya*'s deck, several days before. He couldn't follow her path back very far, but he could go a block or so, and then start asking for directions.

The instructions he was given were far too complex for his limited understanding of Moranese, but he got enough from hand signals to travel another few streets, where he asked a shabby woman sitting on a corner for directions again. The woman held her hand out expectantly and Rasim gazed at her, uncomprehending, until her face twisted in disgust and she spat at Rasim's feet. Rasim jumped back, surprised, and went on for some distance before he realized the woman had wanted payment. She'd been a beggar, a sight so rare in Ilyara Rasim hadn't even recognized her need. Embarrassed, he returned to her, put a coin in the woman's palm, and asked again.

Neither of them could understand the other well enough to be useful. Finally, the beggar woman, clearly exasperated, drew a picture in the dirt. Rasim memorized it, wiped it out, and gave the woman one of Nasira's jewels. She was gawping and holding it to the light when Rasim left her.

Amdria was wealthy, living in one of the enormous houses with even larger gardens that lined parts of the river. There were ivy-lined walls everywhere, and climbing roses that fell over the ivy like sweetly-scented waterfalls. Rasim skulked around the alleys, hoping for a quiet one that would allow him to climb one of the walls, but there was almost as much traffic in the narrower roads as on the main one as tradespeople and merchants made deliveries. He slipped along behind a brewster delivering barrels of beer, and wedged a tiny stone into the garden door of the house before Amdria's, preventing it from closing all the way. Then he waited for traffic to die down enough to allow him to slip inside.

Instead a heavy hand fell on his shoulder, and a viciously smiling Moranese guard said, "Got you."

AMDRIA HERSELF, smiling coolly, came out of her house at the guard's shout. She carried a flagon of water, and told him without hesitation that it was laced with the heartbreak drug that Nasira had once mentioned.

Prince Lorens came in her wake, his gaze dark with anger that Rasim hoped hid worry.

"Drink it," the prince told Rasim flatly. "Don't try to purify it. Don't try anything at all. Your crew's lives depend on it, and so do my profits."

Relief swilled through Rasim's stomach, making him want to throw up. "They're alive?" His voice broke on the word.

"So far," Lorens said in the same flat tone. Rasim couldn't hear any hint of regret or apology in the prince's voice. "If you didn't have a particular reputation for being trouble, they'd all be dead already. Be grateful Nasira spent her first evening here complaining about all the difficulty you'd caused her. Your troublemaking hasn't killed your crew."

The unspoken *yet* was very loud. Rasim drank the drugged water. Neither Lorens nor Amdria could tell if he purified it, but Amdria might have a sea witch hidden nearby. Rasim couldn't risk using his magic and run the chance of jeopardizing his crew.

Amdria gestured, and someone handed her a cup. Even its scent was brackish as she waved it in front of Rasim's face. "Purify this, witch."

Rasim stared at her. "How can I? You just gave me heartbreak. I can't use any magic."

Satisfaction pulled at her lips and she handed the cup away again. "I gave you mindkiller as well, witch. If you were faking the heartbreak's effect, you would have been forced to use your magic by my command. I'm convinced," she said to the guard. "Take him."

"Take me? Take me where? Lorens? Prince Lorens?"

Rasim let the words tumble out, afraid that otherwise he might accidentally confess that the mindkiller hadn't been working on him since the arena. Besides, pleading to one of the people who had apparently betrayed him seemed just the right amount of terrified and pathetic.

Amdria seemed to agree, her smile growing nastier, and Lorens only looked at him coldly, as if Rasim was a thing, not a person. It was hard to remember the Northern prince had an act to keep up just like Rasim did. Very hard, given that Lorens's act kept him warm and comfortable and surrounded by wealth, and Rasim's involved chains and fighting for his life.

A second guard joined the first, and they dragged Rasim out of Amdria's garden and through the streets of Moran to an imposing building he'd never seen before. It looked important, although he didn't expect chambers in important buildings to have places to chain people up. This one did, though; Rasim was thrown to the floor and put in chains, then left to wait what seemed like a very long time indeed. His forehead pressed against the floor as his mind raced.

When he'd been on mindkiller, he had felt like his will had been sapped, but as if his power was still there. Being on Missio's drug had felt as if someone had released all the potential power he might use in his whole life all up at once. And Nasira had said the heart-break drug felt like something, too. Like something was missing inside her, like something important had been cut away.

Rasim, who had just been given water laced with

both mindkiller *and* heartbreak, didn't feel any different.

It could be that Missio's drug had left his witchery so weak that there was nothing for him to feel. That would make sense, except his sea witchery was slowly coming back, and the other magics he'd used hadn't been affected by the grey dust at all. But either way, Amdria had specifically *ordered* him to use his feeble sea witchery, and he hadn't felt a compulsion to do so.

So either the heartbreak was working, or the mindkiller wasn't.

But unlike mindkiller, heartbreak was supposed to cut off access to all witchery. Mindkiller just kept him from using it except when commanded.

He was afraid to try using sea witchery. Someone might be waiting, *feeling* for him to do that, and they might even be watching to see if he could use skymastery. But stone witchery should be safe. Not even Nasira fully expected him to be able to use that, even if she had her suspicions.

Or maybe it was more than just a suspicion. He supposed Sesin could have mentioned his stone witchery while he'd been sleeping off Missio's drug, on the *Wafiya*. But he was going to have to assume she hadn't, or that Nasira had been wise enough to not bring it up to Amdria.

Cautiously, Rasim tried to send stone witchery into the floor beneath him. Stone witchery, the magic he couldn't feel even under the best of circumstances.

On the other hand, it wasn't as if he had anything

else to do. Not until someone came to tell him what his fate was, at least.

All he wanted of the stone was for the stretch of it beneath his cheek to rise a little, a bump to tell him he commanded its power. And after a long time of nothingness, it did. If he slid his cheek across the floor, he could feel the irregularity he'd built. He smoothed it back out and lay still again, eyes closed, heart racing.

Heartbreak didn't work on him.

He didn't know why. He didn't *care* why. Maybe it was the different kinds of witchery he'd learned to use. Maybe Missio's drug had done something to all of his magic. But it meant he had a weapon, and he didn't dare let anybody know.

Doors banged open around him and people came in, bearing torches that they set into sconces on the walls. Rasim lifted his head, squinting as the light changed. He was in a chamber of some sort, one filled with comfortable-looking seating. As the torches were lit, more people came in, all of them well-dressed. Amdria was among them, as was Lorens, whose pale, handsome features were petulant and frustrated.

To Rasim's surprise, Nasira, looking furious, joined them. Not in the seating, though. She wasn't exactly chained in the middle of the floor like Rasim, but she was obviously on the defensive. The look she threw toward Rasim was rage-filled, and she snarled a wordless curse that twisted his stomach. Even if she was acting, it scared him.

But he could use stone witchery, and maybe not

even she knew it. He held on to that, hoping it would give him a way to break himself out of this situation.

When the nobles had gathered, a deep-voiced man said, "Lady Amdria, you may speak for the Council."

Amdria's sweet smile appeared. "Of course. Captain Nasira, you cannot expect the Council to demand no recompense for yesterday's activities. Slaves *escaped* yesterday, Nasira. Slaves do not escape the arena. It has caused trouble all over Moran. Our members have had to kill dozens of other rebellious slaves in the hours since that little performance."

Rasim shuddered violently. He hadn't wanted anyone to die, no one at all, much less those with the least power. Trying to help and making it worse was awful.

Nasira's voice was dismissive. "You have all the recompense you need, Amdria. You've taken my crew, and I have assured you time and again, that Skymaster who fought Rasim in the arena is the source of that storm, and all of the troubles it brought. That boy is a sea witch and spent his life barely able to fill a bucket with piss, never mind working a magic he's never studied."

"And as I have asked you, how can you possibly expect me to believe that a man enslaved for fifteen years and with a family to protect seized a fool's opportunity in the arena?"

"It's more likely than a journeyman with little magic did the same, isn't it? And your Skymaster's family escaped, didn't they?" Nasira shrugged. "You people are the fools who chose to set witches to fighting without mindkiller limiting them. That man was born free, Amdria, and the freeborn don't give up on hope easily. Maybe slaveborn don't either, I don't know, but I would never stop looking for a chance to fight back."

"And yet you're selling your crew."

A thin smile stretched Nasira's lips. "Isn't hypocrisy wonderful?"

"It would be even more wonderful if I trusted your hypocrisy. How, Captain, am I to ever trust you again? Ilyarans don't often turn against their city, and none of those who have in the past have ever brought with them the kind of trouble you have. Perhaps you have a plan to sow dissent."

"Yes," Nasira said sourly, "because that would be to my profit and longevity. Lady Amdria, Council members, I understand your concerns, but I didn't even know you had slave fights to begin with. How could I expect him to overthrow the fights with magic he doesn't have, against odds no one could reasonably prevail against, as some sort of clever plot? I just wanted to be rid of him, without putting anyone who might buy him through the trouble of dealing with him."

"If your purpose is to be rid of him, Captain, and the Lady Amdria's is to be able to trust you, then I have an idea," Lorens said, his voice soft but clear.

Rasim's stomach turned again, his heartbeat suddenly too fast and sweat breaking out all over him. Nasira and Amdria both looked to Lorens, whose expression held a kind of serene calculation. "Captain Nasira, why don't *you* just kill the boy?"

CHAPTER TWENTY

To Rasim's relief, his captain recoiled with genuine horror. "Are you mad? I'm no murderer."

Amdria, though, began to smile. "What a splendid solution. So tidy. Yes, I think the prince's thought is worthy, Captain. I see no reason you should not execute the boy immediately."

Terror slammed through Rasim, each beat of his heart smashing against his ribs until he thought he would throw up. He struggled to his knees, staring fearfully at Nasira as tears began to roll down his cheeks. He didn't *really* think she would kill him. Not really. Not exactly. Except—except if it was his life over the lives of everyone else on the *Wafiya*, if it was the only way to save the enslaved *Sinaz* crew, then...then it might be a bargain worth making. A bargain he could understand, at least, even if he was scared to death of it.

Lorens cleared his throat very softly and everyone's gaze, even Rasim's, snapped to him. "Forgive me," he murmured, "but surely this isn't the place for it? I'm sure the Council watching him die would be very satis-fying and all, but if he dies in anything less than the public eye, I fear it might make a legend out of him. There are those who would fight back in his name, never believing he had died for his audacity."

Amdria's mouth pinched as she considered that. "You suggest the arena, then?"

"If you think it wise, Lady," Lorens murmured.

Disbelieving amusement touched Amdria's face before she considered Nasira a moment. "Well, then, Captain. I believe you have a choice. You'll either be executioner or among the executed, in the arena."

Nasira's fists clenched and she lowered her head, teeth bared and eyes crushed shut, as she stood rigidly before the council. Rasim felt a whisper of her witch-ery, and could almost hear her weighing the odds before she lifted her gaze, grimly. "So be it. I've come this far and I can hardly afford to go back. I'll do it."

Rasim whispered, "Captain," in helpless fear, and she gave him one cold, hard look.

And she had to. He knew that. To keep up their charade—assuming they still had any chance of pulling off their plans—she had to. But knowing that didn't make it any easier. Knowing that this wasn't the time to show that he still had access to his witchery didn't make it any easier, either. There would be a moment when he could dare. There *had* to be. But right now the best either of them could do was play along, and hope that Lorens had some plan in mind.

His plan might just be to get both Nasira and Rasim out of the council chambers alive. They were far more likely to survive an escape attempt outside of the heavily-guarded chambers than inside, at least, even if it was hard to believe Lorens's cool tones and calculating suggestions were on their side at all.

It was hard to believe *anybody* was on Rasim's side right now, though. He wished Kisia and Desimi were with him. Well, not *with* him. It wouldn't do anybody any good for them to all be chained up in the council chambers. But he wished he knew where they were.

He wished he knew if they were safe.

A guard came in and went to Amdria's side as Rasim and Nasira stared at one another. Amdria's smile sharpened as she listened to the guard, and she sent him away before returning her attention to Nasira. "Well, Captain, you'll be able to prove yourself today. The other three missing arena slaves have been found. There will be a public execution before sundown."

Rasim went boneless, unable to hold himself upright anymore. Agnet. Bayar. Karluk. They were going to die because of him. Sickness twisted upward from his belly, choking in his throat.

"You propose I execute them all," Nasira said softly.

The words shot through Rasim like needles, awakening prickles of pain across his skin. His chest hurt terribly, and a sudden heartbeat felt like it was the first one in minutes. He struggled for a gasp of air, keeping it quiet, and the pain in his chest lessened.

"I do indeed," Amdria replied with a smile like knives.

"If I must." Nasira's voice remained quiet, but filled with resolve. "I have no real choice, do I."

"None at all. Really, Nasira, what a lot of sentiment you have for the enslaved. I'll be surprised if you can live with yourself when it's all said and done."

The captain met Amdria's gaze and pulled a nasty smile from somewhere. "I'm sure a fine house and servants will lessen the guilt."

"Servants." Amdria snorted. "You have to *pay* servants, Nasira. That's not how the Moranese work."

"I am not Moranese."

"That," Amdria said dryly, "is manifestly obvious. The executions will be held in the arena. I'm sure you'll understand if you remain under quite significant guard as we journey there."

The arena. Rasim put his forehead down to hide a grim smile. They had gone to so much trouble to get out of the arena, and they would die in there anyway. There had to be a way to get them out. There had to be *something* Rasim could do, because he wasn't about to leave them to die.

"I've made my choices," Nasira said in a dark voice. "Guard me if you must, but these are the seas I've chosen to sail."

"It appears our escapees hoped to sail different seas themselves. They were found near the *Wafiya*," Amdria replied with arch amusement. "Perhaps there's something you'd like to tell us, Captain? Ought I inspect that ship again."

Rasim's heart lurched again and he bit his arm to keep from crying out in alarm. Nasira, apparently oblivious to him, now only sounded irritated. "If you must, I can't stop you, but it's a *ship*, Amdria. There are no secret rooms on a ship. Your own people inspected it when we removed the crew, and they wormed their way into every space a living creature could possibly fit." Nasira paused, studying the Moranese counselor for a moment. Then her tone became more natural, even casual, as if she'd actually come to terms with what she'd agreed to do. "I owe you some coin for that, in fact. They killed a handful of rats that had slipped on board. I loathe rats on my ship."

Amdria gazed neutrally at Nasira for a moment, then suddenly laughed. "I'll accept your coin and thank you for it, and I confess that having walked the *Wafiya* myself, I saw no wall or door out of place. Even a Seamaster needs all the room a ship provides, I suppose, and Ilyarans aren't known for smuggling...anything." She sounded a bit sour, as if Ilyarans were in general too law-abiding to be trusted.

Rasim, relieved beyond measure that the *Wafiya* would not be inspected, buried his face against the floor. His stomach and heart were flip-flopping and their violence made a cold sweat stand out on his whole body. Of all the trouble he'd gotten himself in over the past year, this spying was the most terrifying.

"Our lawfulness is why my crew didn't imagine I would sell them until it was too late," Nasira said flatly. "I imagine they now wish they'd been more suspicious. That Skymaster slave of yours ought to have been, too. He's a fool to have been drawn to the one Ilyaran ship at the docks."

Rasim silently cried, *I'm sorry!* and wished he could undo the advice that had sent Karluk to the docks. At least Nasira had dissuaded Amdria from boarding the *Wafiya* again. Zyterna and her children were still safe, even if Nasira hadn't known she was protecting them.

"He is," Amdria agreed. "Well, we had best go to the arena early, before the inquisitors have done their job too thoroughly. We'll want to know exactly how they escaped, and the inquisitors often remove their tongues before the end."

"Inquisitors?"

Amdria's eyebrows rose. "We can hardly send escapees to a clean and simple death, Nasira. An example must be made. They'll be alive enough for you to drown with your magics, or however you choose to do the deed, but not much more than that."

Rasim shuddered and Nasira stared at Amdria a long moment before speaking slowly and clearly. "You people are barbarians. I may have thrown my lot in with you, but I will never accept that torture and murder are the actions of a civilized people."

Unkind mirth danced in Amdria's eyes. "Then we had better get there *very* early, so your poor delicate sensibilities aren't offended by the state of the slaves we must speak to. They're being brought up through the city now. We'll meet them at the gates, and this one," she said with a lip curl directed at Rasim, "can be thrown in with them." She tilted her head and guards came to surround Nasira, making it clear that she was, at best, only cautiously trusted. Two more guards came to drag Rasim out into a well-appointed but empty square in front of the council buildings. Even the street beyond the square was comparatively empty, as if someone was keeping it that way, so for a few minutes, he and Nasira were outside alone, save for their guards, underneath the bright, chilly Moran sun.

Rasim, unable to help himself, said, "Captain?" in a small voice. She and Amdria had been speaking Ilyaran in the council room, and he supposed the rest of the Moranese council knew his language, but it seemed less likely that their guards did.

Nasira gave him a cutting glance that silenced any hope he had of talking with her. Of strategizing.

He couldn't believe he was simply on his own, not when he was right there beside his captain, but...she wasn't wrong, either. They shouldn't talk. Certainly not to plot, at least. He let his fear fill him, turned it to anger, and spat a curse at her.

Whether the guards understood the words or not, they certainly understood his tone. A mean chuckle went through them as Nasira gave him a look of such disgust it bordered on pity. Then she turned her attention away again, visibly hardening herself. Rasim guessed that was necessary, if she was supposed to kill him in a little while.

He had no idea how she was going to get out of that. And he was the clever one. The one who was supposed to come up with plans *to* get out of things like that.

The awful idea that maybe Nasira was counting on him to come up with a plan dawned on him. Not just a plan, either. One that would get *her* to safety as well as himself and the other three arena slaves. He said, "Captain," again, and this time Nasira snarled, "Shut up, slave," to the obvious amusement of their guards.

So they probably did understand, or at least, Rasim had better act as if they did. A voice barked from somewhere nearby and Rasim was hauled up again, dragged toward a low, open carriage that someone led into the street beyond the council hall square.

"Come," Amdria said from behind them, in a voice like water running over smooth stones. "Join me, Nasira. Show the people of Moran that you have nothing to do with this little revolution."

Nasira murmured, "Of course," and went with the Moranese woman as Rasim was dragged to the back of the carriage. A guard lashed his wrists to a hook on the carriage's back, baffling Rasim for a moment. Then he thought he understood: Amdria wanted to be seen as his captor, but wouldn't lower herself to riding in a cart where he might be chained to its floor. This way she got to be seen, and he still got dragged along behind in the most humiliating way possible.

But it meant his bare feet were on the stone cobbles of the street, and that gave him a chance at using his stone witchery, if he had to.

The cart turned on to the main road leading to the arena. Agnet and the others were probably going to be taken this way, too. The greatest number of people would see them that way, and making sure they were seen was obviously an important aspect of their punishment.

But they weren't just going to be punished. They were going to *die*.

All of Moran seemed to already know the slaves had been recaptured. People thronged in the streets again just as they had the evening before, but with a different urgency now. Then, they had been afraid and angry. Now that fear was being given an outlet, and they were eager for blood. Rasim could tell it from the sounds of voices, even speaking a language he didn't know, and from the hard edge to their laughter. Everything was going back to how it had been. The escape had been sheer chance. No one really broke free of slavery, not in Moran, and those who tried were being punished. The air felt taut, stretching toward breaking.

Agnet had been right. No one really wanted to be rescued by outsiders. Not even if it was a clean victory, and Rasim couldn't deliver that. The people lining the streets were fraught with tension, ready to be pushed one way or another: back into the familiar patterns that they knew, or into explosive change.

And by Siliaria's fins, Rasim wasn't going to allow his friends to be delivered into the hands of torturers, no matter what the cost.

A roar was building down the road. Rasim twisted, trying to see, and caught a glimpse of traffic on the road behind him. The crowds crushed around it, and things were being thrown, probably at his friends.

Rasim, hopeful but not confident, reached for the river with his power and was relieved to feel the under-street tributaries that carried the city's waste into the main river. That was more than he'd been able to feel earlier in the day. Maybe his sea witchery was returning, although not fast enough. He wouldn't be able to rely on it to stage a rescue. And skymastery might be easier for him than stone witchery, but short of scooping everyone up and flying away with them—a skill that was far beyond him—Rasim didn't see how it could get them out of there.

Which left him with stonemastery. Rasim sighed, wishing that particular magic came more naturally to him, and then, despite everything going on around him, muffled a laugh. He could almost hear Kisia saying, drolly, "Yes, your life is very hard, Rasim. You can probably work all four Ilyaran magics, but you have no sense of *one* of them. You poor thing. However will you manage?"

Fighting off a grim smile, Rasim began to build an image of what he wanted in his mind. He poured the stillness of stone witchery into it, wondering, as always, if he was doing anything at all. Usually he was trying to do something immediately, so at least he found out fast whether he'd succeeded. This time he had to wait to release it. Without a sense of the building magic, he could only hope something was actually happening.

A headache built behind his eyes. If he'd been at sea, Rasim might have thought the air pressure was changing. That was how it felt, like pressure looking for an outlet. It made holding the image of the magic he was working more difficult, but the thought of Bayar and Agnet kept Rasim focused.

He was still trembling with the intensity of holding a single thought in his mind by the time the caravan of captured slaves caught up to him. He looked over his shoulder, trying to see what he had to deal with.

There were three wagons, drawn by plodding oxen, and, unlike the carriage that pulled him along, they were all heavily made and surrounded by even heavier armament. There were no fewer than six guards for each wagon, bristling with spears and grim faces. The guards walked along more than an arm's length from the wagons, like they wanted to be sure the slaves could be easily seen. Slaves with downcast eyes led the oxen, so there were more than twenty people surrounding the captured trio. It seemed a little excessive for three slaves, although Rasim knew he would put his money on Agnet if she had only her own half-dozen to face.

But not chained as she was. All three of them, Agnet, Bayar and Karluk, were chained, standing, in the middle of their wagons. Agnet had a fresh wound on her forehead, blood drying crimson in her white eyebrows, and a tightly wrapped length of cloth around her upper left arm where she'd taken the spear blow. Her sneer of defiance was so potent that people looked away to avoid meeting her eyes. Bayar had lost his resolute calm. Tears rolled down his face, although he wasn't sobbing. Karluk looked defeated, worse than either of the others, and Rasim realized he didn't even know if his family was safe. The jeering crowd threw fruit and heels of bread at them. Nothing more, though. City guards cuffed a couple of youths who flung rocks. The city councilors didn't want the slaves accidentally killed before they could be executed.

And they certainly didn't want them to escape. Rasim stopped looking over his shoulder, and released the first wave of witchery he'd been building.

He *expected* it: all the stonemastery he'd tried so far had worked even if he hadn't felt it building. But even expecting it, the way stone exploded upward in the road was shocking. A jagged circle shot up well above Rasim's head, all the cobbles and paving stones jamming together to make walls around them. It smashed through the carriage, pulling him along. Nasira and Amdria's screams were audible above everything else, for a moment. They were on the other side of his barrier, though. Nasira would have to rescue herself. Rasim had too much else to do. His chains had come free from the back of the carriage as it flew apart, but his wrists were still bound to each other. He'd try to get them off later.

He'd placed the magic just right. It was a narrow box surrounding the wagons, and only two guards were caught inside the ring. The rest, having been walking more than an arm's length away, were stuck outside, though their sword hilts and spears were already banging against the wall Rasim had constructed. The two inside the wall were so astonished it took them a moment to react.

In that time, Rasim caught Agnet's eye and held it as if the intensity of his gaze could promise her he had a plan. "Tell the drivers to unhitch the oxen!"

Her eyes were bright, fiery blue as she met his. She nodded, a smile pulling at her mouth as she bellowed Rasim's command at the drivers. Then she crouched, wrapped her chains around her forearms, and with a roar, put forth an effort beyond comprehension.

The chains ripped free of the wagon's floor. Hands clasped together, chain gripped between them, Agnet spun, and, still roaring, slammed the freed end of the chain into the nearest guard. The strength of the blow knocked him into the other guard and they both fell. Agnet leaped out of the wagon and onto them, out of Rasim's sight.

At the same time, the terrified slave boys handling the oxen quailed and refused to free them. Probably smart, Rasim thought, but he didn't want the innocent animals to get hurt. He scrambled to release the first one himself, slapping its haunch to send it as far away from the wagon as possible. The walls meant they couldn't run very far, but it would have to do. He went after the second beast, racing over Bayar, who had fallen to the floor of his wagon, hiding. Karluk had the look of a man desperate to waken his witchery through mindkiller's fog. Hoping he hadn't been primed to take orders from only one person, Rasim called out, "Use your witchery to save yourself, Karluk!" and then, as he freed the second ox and leaped to the third and final wagon, he whispered, "Your family is safe," to the other Ilyaran. "Use your magic, Karluk."

Karluk's mouth twisted. "They gave me heartbreak, not mindkiller. I'm defenseless."

Dismay slammed through Rasim as a spear clattered across the wall he'd shaped. Karluk snatched it up and began working his chains free. "Keep my family safe, Rasim. Nothing else matters to me."

Rasim nodded. "We still have a chance. Hold on. This is going to get bumpy. Agnet! Get Bayar!" He slapped the third ox away and finally, gasping, released the last stone witchery he'd prepared.

For a glorious moment it seemed it would work. The ground beneath them sagged as the stone under the street softened. There were river tributaries down there: all Rasim needed was enough space to drop them through, and he could get them to safety. He thought he could drop the whole section of street down, if he had to, but Agnet was already free and Karluk was halfway there. If Agnet could grab Bayar in time, they would only need a space wide enough to fit the big Northerner's broad shoulders, and they would be free.

Agnet bounced up, bloody from her fight with the guards, and, roaring once again, ripped Bayar's chains free of the wagon. Rasim saw it more clearly this time, how the old wood, uncured and softened by time, gave up its grip on the heavy nails that held the chain base into place. She scooped Bayar up and all but threw him at Rasim, a triumphant grin bright and beautiful across her face. That was how Rasim would remember her forever: sun-white hair loose and wild around her tanned face, her eyes brilliantly blue under the streaks of red drizzling from her forehead, her muscles shining with sweat and blood.

And that was how she died, free and defiant under the Moranese sun, as a guard finally lurched over Rasim's barrier and shoved a spear through the back of her neck.

CHAPTER TWENTY-ONE

Rasim screamed. Bayar, stumbling toward him, spun to see what was wrong, and screamed as well, even more heart-wrenchingly than Rasim. Even Karluk cried out in horror. For a heartbeat, that was all any of them could do. Then Bayar flung himself back toward Agnet's body and Rasim went after him. He was —they were both—still screaming, though Rasim's screams turned to pleas: "No, no, Bayar, we can't help her, we have to go, we have to *run—!*"

But the road beneath them was no longer caving in. Rasim struggled to regain his concentration so he could rebuild the magic. Instead he could do little more than keep Bayar from crawling to Agnet's body. Karluk broke his chains free too late, and drove his spear toward the guard who had slain Agnet. The guard fell back, but there were too many of them. Rasim knew it and so did Karluk. Another, and then many more, would come over the wall in a moment. If Rasim couldn't break through the road, they would all die, just like Agnet had died. Holding Bayar so hard it hurt, Rasim tried to force witchery into the street below, searching for the softness that had been there before.

Nothing happened. More than nothing: resistance met him, as if his lack of skill with stone witchery had suddenly made the bedrock below resentful. He was still struggling to waken it when one of his carefully constructed walls melted away. A thin Ilyaran with a collar of thorns tattooed over his shoulders stood in the street, his face turned away from the trio he'd just exposed. Rasim let out another cry of dismay, and the slave flinched, but refused to look their way.

Sea witchery wouldn't work. Not here, not this far from the river. Desperate, unsure if he could even manage it, Rasim snatched at the wind currents, trying to bring sky witchery into play. Maybe he could drive people away with vicious enough winds; maybe he could force a passageway for the three of them and make a run for the docks.

But the air wouldn't respond either, as mute as the stone. That was wrong, Rasim thought in a panic. He might not have much practice with it, but sky witchery had felt much more natural than stonemastery did. He should be able to command the air currents the way he'd done in the arena, the way he could have once commanded the river currents. But they remained resolutely muffled, and only slowly did Rasim realize that another witch already had the wind—and perhaps the stone—in their grasp. It wasn't that he couldn't command the magics. It was that they were being deliberately kept from him.

Still slowly, much too slowly, it came to him that the street was unexpectedly empty. There had been thousands of people lining the roadsides. He'd known some of them had run, but there was no one visible from where he stood with tears streaming down his face. No one except the Ilyaran slave, and then, gradually, shadows that joined the slave.

Two of them: one woman, one man, and a third person pushed to her knees between them. The one on her knees was Nasira, now in chains herself and full of rage as she tried to throw off the hands of those who held her down.

To throw off Amdria's hands, of course, and Prince Lorens's.

Amdria's expression was one of furious pleasure. "You were right," she half growled at Lorens. "He does command more than one magic, and the drugs don't work on him."

An agony of betrayal slashed through Rasim's chest, taking his breath away. His voice broke on a wordless cry, and Lorens glanced at him with no regret, no concern. Not even a flicker of remorse touched his eyes as he said, "I hardly believed it myself, but I couldn't allow my own future to be jeopardized. I was afraid Nasira would prove too soft for this game, and I was right."

Nasira lunged at Lorens, snarling, and the Northern prince barely stopped himself from skipping back, even though the chained Seamaster captain obviously couldn't get to him. "Tsk," Lorens said to her, soft and mocking. "It was stupid enough of you to try to help them and end up in chains yourself. Try again to harm me and your crew will die slowly and painfully in the arena." He turned his gaze to Amdria. "The boy is useful, Lady. You should consider a stay of execution."

Amdria shrugged easily. "His usefulness ends with the knowledge that it's possible for Ilyarans—and perhaps others—to command more than one kind of witchery."

"We already knew that," Lorens pointed out. "Their royal family has always been able to do."

The Moranese woman turned a flat look on the Northern prince. "Are you suggesting I've happened on the lost Ilyaran heir, Lorens? That out of the hundreds who died in their great fire, the heir somehow survived the flames, was raised in their Seamasters' Guild, and ended up in chains in *my* arena?"

Nasira's eyes bulged and she stared at Rasim, who nearly swallowed his own tongue in horror. He didn't want to be a lost prince. He wanted to sail the *Wafiya* and never think about politics again. Lorens's expression reluctantly turned to acceptance. He still said, "It's possible," a bit defensively.

Amdria rolled her eyes. "It's possible," she conceded. "It's more likely that no one has ever tried *teaching* someone outside of the royal family more than one magic. But now we know it's possible, and the slaves we have can be tested and trained without allowing *this* one to escape the consequences of his actions."

A flash of frustration crossed Lorens's face and for an instant his gaze met Rasim's. Rasim couldn't tell if there was worry or apology in the expression, although it was certain that this was *not* how the Northern prince wanted things to go. Lorens tried once more, his voice low and intense. "Knowing how *this* boy did it would help in testing and training others, Amdria—"

"No." The Moranese woman's tone brooked no argument. "These executions will emphasize that we fear no one, not even the Ilyaran guilds, and that will go a long way in quelling any resistance these four might have stirred up. A pity about the woman," she said with a dismissive glance at Agnet's body. "But at least we have Nasira to take her place on the field."

THEY DRAGGED Agnet's body first, making the price of defiance clear to everyone. Rasim, Karluk, and Bayar were no longer even worthy of a wagon, and Nasira had been chained with them. They were driven along with whips, stumbling with misery and defeat. Rasim's tears had disappeared, but he could think of no plan of action, not with witchery being denied to him. They'd forced him to drink more water laced with heartbreak, which, alone, was more bitter than mindkiller. Nasira, at his side, was forced to take the drugs, too, and either they worked on him this time, or the enslaved witches were still keeping the elements locked down. Whichever it was, Rasim could no more work witchery than he could turn into a fish.

Bayar, beside him, wept silently. Strangely, that seemed to soften the tone of the re-gathering crowd. They had seen Agnet fight for him in the arena, and now he walked behind her body and mourned. Perhaps she was beloved by the people in the end, after all. They were surprisingly quiet and respectful as her body was dragged by.

Amdria, riding a long-legged horse just within Rasim's line of sight, didn't seem to like that. She wanted the snarls and sneers of earlier. The silence was a kind of rebellion of its own. Lorens trailed behind her on another horse and looked neither left nor right, his expression unreadable as he helped escort the captured slaves to the arena.

Rasim no longer knew whether he could trust the Northern prince. Nothing had gone according to plan, but the plans he'd helped Nasira and Lorens and Hassin come up with had fallen apart at the very moment Nasira had sent him to the arena. He had no way of knowing if *other* plans had been made in his absence. Lorens might have betrayed them all, or he might be the one person on their side who was still able to move freely through Moran. Rasim had to believe that, even if the weight of fear said it seemed unlikely.

A cold place fixed itself in his heart. If Lorens really had betrayed them, Rasim would get even with him somehow, someday.

That was an ambitious idea for a boy who expected to die in the next hour. Rasim actually laughed at himself, a harsh little sound that caught the attention of the quiet crowd. Someone spoke in a soft but surprised tone, and someone else caught their words and carried them on. "Laughing in the face of death," Karluk said abruptly, his translation surprising Rasim. "They admire you. They think you're mad," he added after a moment, "but they admire you."

The whispers ran through the crowd, which swayed like a living thing, like something ready to be persuaded. Then one voice, louder than the others, broke out with a word Rasim knew. "Agnet!"

It caught like straw kindling, a sudden roar of the Northern warrior's name: "*Ag-net! Ag-net! AG-NET! AG-NET! AG-NET!*" The shout swept down the streets, echoing from the arena to the docks. For a moment, the city shook with it.

Then, as quickly, the silence returned. Before anyone had time to be singled out, Rasim thought. Before anyone could be slain for their boldness. In the cry's wake, though, the quietness seemed far more ominous. If shouting Agnet's name had been the straw catching fire, the silence now said that the whole of the city was tinder, waiting to come alight.

The thought caught fire in *him,* clear and sudden: it was possible that putting them to death was the worst mistake the Moranese Council could make right now. The gathered crowd didn't have the air of a people eager for execution. They wanted action. Action of *some* kind. An execution would do, but maybe Rasim had done as he'd hoped after all. Maybe their dramatic escape from the arena *had* opened Moranese eyes to the idea that the world could be different.

Or maybe there had been discontent simmering under the surface for a long time, and he was only here to see its eruption. But a show of power on the part of the Council had the wrong feeling to it, to him. If they wanted to retain their hold, they needed to be clever. They needed to show mercy, not strength.

Another laugh barked loose from his throat. He was in chains, his back itching with whip stings, his tongue thick and dry from need of water, and he was being herded into an imposing arena to be murdered. But he was Rasim al Ilialio, who had an opinion on everything, and he thought his executioners were going about it all wrong. All he needed was a quick word to explain their folly, and everything would be all right.

Well, he'd only be in Siliaria's arms a few minutes earlier if he spoke and it was badly received. Coughing laughter again, Rasim wet his lips and lifted his voice: "Lady Amdria! Lorens! I have an idea!"

The Northern prince's spine stiffened and he turned toward Rasim so slowly that he wasn't sure Lorens was even going to look at him. Indeed, he met Amdria's gaze first, and the Moranese woman took her time in looking at Rasim. When she finally met his eyes, her expression was disbelieving to the point of laughter. "You do."

"You're making a mistake. You shouldn't kill us."

Amdria's eyebrows climbed upward. "Oh? You must understand, I'm not surprised to hear you say that."

Her disbelieving amusement was infectious. Rasim felt a terrible urge to laugh again, a real laugh this time. Prisoners didn't bargain for their lives this way. "Look at the people, Amdria. They're burning for an excuse to riot, and they've already decided Agnet was a hero."

Agnet's name caught fire again as he voiced it. Another rush carried it down the streets and into silence. Rasim charged on, heedless: "If they kill us too, we'll just be more fallen heroes. Symbols of resistance. If the Council is smart, they'll show mercy."

A momentary pause hung in the air before Lorens murmured, "The boy may have a point, lady."

Amdria looked at Rasim like he was something unpleasant found on her shoe, and at Lorens like he was a simpleton. "I trust the Moranese Council knows what it's doing more than a boy desperate to save his own life does. I wonder, that Ilyara has stood unmolested all these centuries, if they take their guidance from panicked children. And as for you," she said to Lorens, "I suggest you maintain your loyalties as they are, rather than imagine slaves have the right to thoughts of their own."

"Of course, lady," Lorens replied softly. He bowed in his saddle, and Rasim, watching his shoulders set, muttered, "But I'm right."

When he looked away from the prince, Karluk was watching him with an amused twist to his lips. "You don't give up, do you, Journeyman? Keep your mouth shut now, though. Plenty of people here speak Ilyaran, and if you put ideas into their heads, it won't be just us who die today. The Council will stop rebellion however they can, including selecting random people out of a crowd to kill."

"That," Rasim said through his teeth, "is stupid. If the people really are ready to rebel, the Council will only prove themselves worth rebelling against if they do that. Don't worry," he added more bitterly. "I tried. I won't try again. I don't want her to start killing people."

Despite the apparent lack of blood lust, the arena was more than half filled when Rasim and the others were escorted in. There were no cheers at their arrival, but neither was there an outcry to save them.

Hooded men with deadly instruments approached them, and, a little to Rasim's surprise, stopped several feet away, loosely encircling the three captives and Agnet's body. A little dully, he said, "I thought they were going to torture us," and to his left, Karluk chuckled dryly.

"They may yet. Or they may have heeded your words after all, Journeyman. They're not going to spare us, but they might fear anything but a quick, clean death will set off those who cried your Northerner's name. You've been in Moran less than a week, Rasim. Do you always sow this much chaos where you go?"

Nasira, who had remained sullenly silent, abruptly snorted so loudly that Karluk laughed again. "I'll take that as a yes," the Skymaster slave said.

"I don't mean to."

"And yet," Nasira said through her teeth.

"Nasira—Captain—is Lorens...?"

"Playing a part?" Nasira's teeth showed again. "I hope so. This is what he was meant to do if things went wrong, but nothing was supposed to go *this* wrong. I don't know how you make these messes, Rasim."

"I don't *mean* to!"

"I wouldn't have thought Moran was ready for rebellion," Karluk interrupted quietly. "I would have thought we were all too afraid. I was."

"You were also drugged so you couldn't use your

own witchery unless somebody told you to. It's harder to fight when they've taken away all your familiar weapons."

"You found a way."

"I..." Rasim pressed his lips together. The air had gotten heavy and wet since they'd entered, and now it pressed down on him exhaustingly. "I never had much to lose, I think. I wasn't a good sea witch. All I really had was being clever, and if there hadn't been another fire in Ilyara, that wouldn't have been enough to get me what I wanted."

"What did you want?" Karluk sounded genuinely interested, as if they were having a conversation over a cup of wine in a courtyard, not standing in chains beneath the arena's sweltering gaze.

Rasim gave a quick laugh and shot an almost-angry glance at Nasira. Confessing his wish within her earshot seemed like an invitation to mockery, but it wasn't like any of them were going to live much longer anyway. "I wanted to be the captain of the *Wafiya*, of course. Which was never going to happen. I've never even said it out loud before, but I might as well now."

To his surprise, Nasira's mouth twisted in a smile that seemed sympathetic. "It's hard to want what you know you can never have," she said, almost gently. "I know that better than most."

Rasim was silent a moment, staring at her, then nodded before, voice cracking, he spoke to Karluk again. "I had almost no magic then, and nobody gives a ship, never mind the flagship, to a magicless captain. So maybe I've just always taken chances that other people wouldn't. And look where it got me. Look where it got *us.*"

"You saved me," Bayar said in unexpected, flawlessly formal Ilyaran. "Taking another's life is the second-worst crime my tribe acknowledges, even when done in self-defense. If we are forced to kill to defend ourselves, we know that our spirit has been corrupted by the madness that led the other to attack. To be cleansed of that corruption takes many weeks of spiritual guidance by our shamans. When war comes to us, we spend the weeks before it in close contemplation with our shamans, and are cleansed again if we survive. If you had not come, Rasim al Ilialio, I believe I would have killed a man to save my own life. I would have died with that stain on my spirit, and I would not have been allowed passage into the King Horse's realm."

As Bayar's speech went on, Rasim forgot the humidity and the gathering crowds in favor of gaping at the small Shenryalan boy. Bayar's mouth curved in a slight, almost apologetic smile that widened when, instead of asking about his ability to speak Ilyaran, Rasim blurted, "What's your *worst* crime, then?"

Bayar's smile flickered a little wider. "Other tribes have differing traditions on lesser crimes, but all of Shenryal is united on the worst. To slaughter a horse unnecessarily is to lose all honor. A Shenryalan who does so is driven from their tribe forever, or until they can in some way redeem themselves in the King Horse's heart. I am sorry for my deception, in letting you believe I did not speak your language," Bayar added. "My people prefer the isolation of the steppes and believe that to speak long with strangers can...contaminate us. But I wished for you to know, before we died, that I believe you have saved my spirit from wandering the forever-after alone, with no hope but to return to the cycle of life as a lesser creature and begin my journey toward the King Horse's country again. I wished to thank you."

"You're welcome. I wish we could have talked more. I wish I hadn't gotten us killed." The arena was full now, thousands of people looking down at them. They were quiet, though. Quiet, at least, by comparison to the screams before and during the arena fights. Their guards tightened the circle around them, weapons held more purposefully.

Rasim swayed, feeling faint. He couldn't tell if his dizziness was from the heat, which was much worse than it had been after the chill of the past few days, or from pure astonishment, or—most likely—from the encroaching awareness that he was going to die very soon. One of the guards stepped forward and put his hand on the back of Rasim's neck, forcing him to his knees. A sudden spurt of defiance made Rasim lift his eyes to the arena's highest wall. They could kill him, but they couldn't make him die cowering and with his eyes closed. He wanted to see the world until the last possible moment.

Karluk snarled and shook off the hands of the guard who tried pushing him downward. Instead he knelt gracefully, his own gaze lifted in a glare at the arena audience. A cheer rose at his boldness, and Rasim wished he'd done the same. Another guard kicked the backs of Bayar's knees, sending him crashing to the ground, although the Shenryalan boy's attention was also cast upward. He was murmuring. Praying, Rasim thought. He hoped the King Horse would welcome Bayar to their afterlife with pride. Nasira also knelt on her own, her gaze lifted in visible anger. Rasim thought Amdria must have given her heartbreak or she would have freed them all with her witchery by now.

A drum beat banged through the arena, so deep and loud it made Rasim's teeth rattle. It silenced the audience more completely than they'd ever been, and in its wake someone started giving a speech. A woman. Probably Amdria, Rasim thought, although her voice was distorted by the use of sky witchery. It carried everywhere, though, and when Karluk caught his breath to translate, Rasim shook his head. "Don't bother. I can guess. We're criminals, throwing ourselves against the natural order, and we must be punished for our stupidity and so that everyone knows the price of defying their masters."

Karluk smiled thinly. "Close enough." Before he could say anything else, the drums sounded again, this time rolling on long enough that Rasim swayed beneath the onslaught of sound. He would not faint. He wouldn't. The guards were baring blades now, preparing to kill them, but Rasim was not going to do them the favor of falling face first into the sand before they tried. They were going to have to look into his eyes before they murdered him.

"This is duty," one of the guards said in Ilyaran. "I

take no pleasure in it. Will you grant me forgiveness for what I must do?"

Astonished, Rasim looked into the man's hooded face. "Not a chance, and I hope Siliaria drowns you in your sleep!"

The guard recoiled in shock, and Karluk choked back edged laughter. "It's considered good manners to forgive your executioner. It's how they do it in Moran."

"I don't give rotten fish guts for how they do it here! He's going to kill me, and he can carry the guilt of that for the rest of his stinking life!" Enraged, and glad for it, because at least he wasn't afraid anymore, Rasim locked his gaze on the arena's tall upper lip.

Water began to pour over it.

CHAPTER TWENTY-TWO

It sounded like the tide rushing in, and drew the attention of everyone, including—most importantly—the guards about to kill them. More than one of the guards pulled the black hood from their heads to see more clearly as they gaped upward at the ever-widening stream that broke over supports and rushed onto the roofs of the wealthy's boxes. From there it fell again, spilling down onto those who couldn't afford rooftops and filling step after step of the arena's seats before splashing to the next one. Screams of surprise began echoing through the arena: screams and laughter from children, and shouts of fearful anger from adults.

When it reached the lowest tier that held boxed seating, the water stopped falling downward and began to pool along the steps. It looked as if someone had pressed glass along the back of one of the steps and stopped it from falling any farther, but Rasim knew better. The bulges and shimmers of the flattened edge were the natural tension of water's surface. Witchery held it in place, not glass.

Rasim glanced at his own hands, half wondering if they were somehow directing the witchery, although clearly it wasn't his own working. Even seeing it, he couldn't *feel* it. The heartbreak at work, he supposed, although a shock coursed through him. The heavy humidity that was making him sick was *almost* what sea witchery felt like when others worked it. Maybe it was what it felt like to non-Ilyarans, or to those who weren't sea witches. Gasping at the thickness of the air and the incredible magic being worked, he glanced at Nasira.

A vicious smile smeared across her face as she looked to the high walls. He began to speak, but instead followed her gaze upward.

The water had gotten deep in the moments he'd looked away. It was running around the stadium now, relentlessly filling the upper ranks. It was a *huge* amount of water, at least as much as he'd flooded the Northern mine with. It had to be from the river. There had been no earth-shaking to suggest fissures had broken open and let water spring upward from below. He wondered if the riverbed was empty, and if the *Wafiya*'s keel was strong enough to hold the ship's weight if it lay foundered in mud.

All at once the water leaped into action, as if simply filling the stadium steps wasn't enough. It snatched at people, seizing them into a current that hadn't been there a moment earlier. Rasim cast a hard glance at his guards, then climbed to his feet defiantly, wanting to see what was happening clearly far more than he feared them. The guards either didn't notice or didn't care, and after a moment Karluk and Bayar stood too. Nasira was already standing, her grin sharp enough to cut.

Above them, in the seating, people of rank were being swept away, all of them screaming and thrashing. The water searched for them, nimbly seeking those who were best-dressed or who had slaves attending them. Those with slave collars, either tattooed or iron, were getting wet, but they weren't being carried away. More than once, key chains fell to the steps in wet splashes, and after incredulous moments, slaves began snatching them up and freeing themselves.

As they did, the more distant elite, those who hadn't yet been caught up by the oncoming waves, began to shriek in a whole different kind of protest. Those cries turned to alarm as their own attendant slaves began to understand that their freedom was at hand, and started to turn on their masters. Water crashed toward them all, and more than once Rasim suspected the flow saved a slave owner from a harsh fate. Because instead of drowning, those who were being taken by the water were carried swiftly and without injury toward the exits. Some panicked, flailing in the coursing witchery, and once or twice the water violently ejected those panic-stricken riders. Then it leaped up and snatched them back down again, holding them firmly in its grasp as it carried them out of the arena.

It was an imperfect attack. Some of the beautifully dressed masters escaped, and a few slaves and poorer folk were taken away. But given how many people were in the arena, it was surprisingly precise. The stadium was maybe half-cleared when rivulets began climbing down the steps again, this time to snake across the sand. The guards finally remembered they were meant to be killing slaves, and turned to face their captives with uncertain expressions.

"I'd throw down those blades and run, if I were you," Rasim suggested. "So far, the water's not hurting anybody, but I think if you kill us, you're going to be exceptions to its rule."

"Is this your doing?" whispered the one who had asked his forgiveness.

Rasim extended his hand and smiled as coldly as he could. "Do you want to see what else I can do?"

As one, their captors threw away their swords and ran. The water approaching them hesitated, then suddenly lost cohesion and sank into the sand, no longer animated by witchery. Karluk made an incredulous sound. "*Is* it you?"

"No. No one person could do it." Not even someone using Missio's drug, Rasim thought. Lifting the water into the mines, breaking up the ice—those had been acts of brute force. The witchery being enacted now was full of finesse, and not even Seamaster Isidri could have done it alone. "I think the Seamasters' Guild must be here, somehow. Captain, do you know what's going on?"

Nasira drew breath to answer, but Karluk interrupted with, "The entire *guild*? How?!"

"I don't know. It's been ten or so days since the raid

on Hongrunn," Rasim said absently. The cleansing water rushing through the arena's seats was mesmerizing, its every flow beautifully directed. It reminded Rasim of the water sculptures some sea witches could create: dolphins and flying fish made from the water itself, skimming along beside the ships. Only those were for play, and this had purpose. He'd thought his acts of strength had meant he was finally really skilled with seamastery, but now he saw that the delicacy of this act was equally difficult and impressive. Still enthralled at its beauty, he continued, "If Skymaster Arrat could use the wind to carry a message to the absolute limit of his reach, and find another Skymaster to pass it on to, and again, you could get a message from Hongrunn to Ilyara pretty quickly, I think. And I don't think there's much of anywhere the fleet couldn't get to in ten days, if they were of a mind to."

Karluk made another incredulous sound. Rasim frowned faintly at him, not wanting to take his eyes from the waterworks for long. "What?"

"If a sky witch—carried a message—is that something that's *done* now? Relay stations manned by Skymasters? Is it even possible?"

Rasim's face fell. "Oh. Well, I thought it might be. Don't you do that?"

"I'm sure it's possible!" Karluk howled in exasperation. "But no, we don't do that! No one ever thought of it, as far as I know!"

"Well, that's not my fault!"

"I see now," Bayar said unexpectedly, and with a smile, "how it is you get into trouble, Rasim al Ilialio."

"All I have are ideas!"

"Ideas cause more trouble than anything else." Bayar lifted his chained wrists. "Do you have an idea on how to unlock us?"

"Plenty," Rasim muttered, "but they all require either witchery or a key. Captain—"

"All kinds of things can be a key." Karluk stretched for one of the fallen swords and began to work its point into the lock around Rasim's ankles.

Rasim winced at his feet, afraid of what would happen if the sword slipped. "Maybe we should just wait. If that breaks in the lock it'll be a lot harder to get these off me."

"Wait for what?"

Rasim eyed Karluk, then looked pointedly at the water witchery storming the arena. "For whomever is doing that to come rescue us? I don't think they're going to this much trouble to leave us here. Captain, what's *happening*? Did you and Lorens plan this? Or *is* it the guild? Where is Lorens?" Rasim's heart fluttered hopefully. He'd been gone from Ilyara for months, with no word on Seamaster Isidri's recovery or whether there had been a sea change within the palace or if Sunmasters still held sway there. If the Guild had come to Moran, they would have all of that news and more. Better yet, they would be able to bring Karluk home, and perhaps hundreds of other Ilyarans as well.

"I don't know where he is," Nasira replied. She hadn't moved, other than to stand. Her fists were clenched, and her gaze remained on the skyline. "It's not the guild. We—"

An eruption of sound made Rasim whip around. Sand and water were clashing together near the amphitheater wall, neither able to gain an upper hand in a sudden battle of elements. Bayar's voice shot high. "What's happening?"

"Someone remembered they had Ilyaran slaves on mindkiller to command," Rasim replied softly. "It'll get ugly now." He flexed his hands, wishing again he could use his own witchery, then yelped as Karluk attacked the chains again with more vigor. "Wait!"

"Tilarea's teeth, Rasim, for a clever boy you've got no sense at all. How long do you think it's going to take for them to send one of those witches after us? A sky witch doesn't even have to leave the stands to kill us. We need to get free and out of sight!"

"Oh." Rasim felt heat curdle his cheeks. "Right. Maybe you'd better hurry."

His last words were lost in the sounds of more explosions, this time as steam billowed in huge waves around the arena. Rasim flung his arms up, instinctively trying to protect himself, and the chain between his wrists clobbered him in the face. He howled and fell, clutching his mouth, then looked up over his fingers to see fire slam into the watershed and create new bursts of steam. The sea witchery was under attack everywhere: what had once been seating now curved upward under the power of stonemastery, capturing the flowing water in balls and enclosed tubes. The stands were probably the mud and straw mix, Rasim thought bitterly. Moran's enslaved Stone-masters were better with their witchery by far than he had been. All of this could have been avoided if he'd been able to work the arena's walls well enough to escape through them.

In other places, the sea witchery was being held to a stand-still by hugely powerful winds. Spray splashed from the front, and the water split, and split again, going around the outer edge of the winds, but time and again the sky witches wielding it caught the water's leading edge again and held it in place. One spot was held by someone who looked no older or bigger than Rasim. If they were in Ilyara, he thought, they would become a leader within the Skymasters' Guild.

Here and there, Ilyaran slaves resisted their masters' orders. Rasim saw at least two of them die for it, too, but it seemed that they died with expressions of terrible triumph. A few simply *triumphed*, either too strong or too valuable for their masters to slay. A few more—those whose owners had been carried away— fought on behalf of the Seamasters who had begun the fight. They were the ones who turned the tide, Rasim thought. They were the ones who threw up resistance to the slaves who could not deny their masters. The former slaves didn't harm their brethren. They only broke the stone tubes and balls that held water captive and set up cross-winds to take the power from the sky witches, or quenched the sun witches' flames. There weren't many of them, but there didn't have to be. All they needed to do was disrupt, not hold the line.

Karluk gave a sudden satisfied shout as the lock around Rasim's ankles came free. Rasim danced out of the chains and offered Karluk a distracted thanks. It was nearly impossible to see the stands anymore. Sand and steam and smoke were everywhere, fogging the view. This was what he'd imagined, with his initial plans to free them all. He'd been arrogant to think he could do it all himself, but this was what he had imagined. This was a chance at freedom and at changing Moranese culture. Rasim whispered a promise, wishing the big Northern warrior could hear him. "It's working. I'll try not to let anybody else get killed, Agnet. I'm sorry I wasn't able to save you."

Clouds of steam and sand rolled across the arena floor itself, totally obscuring the stands. Karluk let go another shout as he freed Bayar, then handed Rasim the sword. "It's not too hard, but I can't get the angle if I hold the blade myself. Tilt it toward you, then twist— no, not like that, you'll snap the blade—!"

"Someone is coming," Bayar reported calmly. "Please hurry."

"I'm trying to!" Rasim glanced up as Bayar took up a sword and stepped in front of them. "No, Bayar—here, you try the lock, I'll hold them off." He took Bayar's sword and peered through the swirling gloom. There were at least five shadows in the dust and steam, far more than he could hope to defeat himself. Two of them were big, too, though the leader was slight. Rasim wet his lips and fell into the stance he'd been taught over the past week, ready to fight. It wouldn't be easy with his wrists still chained, but at least he could move his feet. It would give him a chance, however slim.

"Ah!" Bayar's cry came with the sound of metal snapping open, and Rasim's heart soared as Karluk came forward with a sword of his own. Bayar took up his place, too, and they stood united as a gust of wind parted the dust to reveal the people approaching them.

"Hi," Kisia said with a breathless smile. "Did you miss us?"

CHAPTER TWENTY-THREE

Rasim's sword fell from numb fingers as steam and stand billowed away to reveal not just Kisia, but Desimi, too. Desimi, and Hassin and Sesin and, to Rasim's baffled relief, Lorens. The prince's quick grin was the last thing Rasim saw before the mists closed again, leaving only Kisia close enough to be discernible. She held a key uplifted in her fingertips, and wore a smile wider than any he'd ever seen. He put his hands forward silently, still unable to do more than stare, and she unlocked first the chains that bound him, and then Nasira's.

As soon as her chains were released, Nasira slammed an approving punch into Kisia's shoulder. The journeyman rolled with it, then turned to Bayar and Karluk, unlocking their chains too, before asking, "Can you run? Because I think we should run."

Karluk looked hard at Rasim, who croaked, "They're friends. They're friends," before nodding at Kisia. That was all he could do: he couldn't even think clearly enough to really wonder *how*. Kisia nodded back, grabbed his hand, and shouted, "Let's go!" to the rest of *her* team, and all of them bolted for the exit.

"Wait!" Rasim's voice broke and he stumbled to a halt. "Wait. There are slaves in the arena cages. We have to set them free. And the animals—the animals." A sob caught his throat as emotion began to return. Kisia and Desimi were alive. Sesin wasn't enslaved. Lorens was with them, an ally after all. It was more than he could take in, and it left him with tears streaming down his cheeks as he said, "The animals," again, his voice choked. "They don't deserve to be made to fight any more than people do. We have to let them go, Kisia. We have to let them go."

Through the fog of tears and sand-filled mist he saw Kisia exchange glances with the others of her group. There was a strange authority in how she did it. Even though Nasira was the one who nodded, in the end, it seemed as if the decision had been Kisia's, and that somehow Nasira lacked the authority to countermand it.

"I'll do it," the captain said unexpectedly. "Slaves and animals alike, Rasim. I'll get them into the hills. You get to the *Wafiya*."

Rasim made a sound that was barely even a broken word. Nasira's eyebrows rose in question and he forced his thoughts into words. "They drugged you, didn't they? Mindkiller? Heartbreak? I saw them, when they gave me the second—the third—" He couldn't remember how much he'd been given, now. A lot. His mind didn't seem to be working very well. "When they gave me more. They gave you some too. And I didn't feel you purify it, someone would have stopped you—"

Nasira cut him off with a fierce grin. "You were full to your eyeballs with the stuff, lad. You wouldn't have felt it if I'd run a current up your nose, and there were no other sea witches at hand to be sure I didn't purify it. I'm fine. Who do you think was directing *where* all that water went through the stands?"

Rasim stared at the water-filled arena seats briefly, then back at his captain. "But I can't feel…"

"Rasim, for Siliaria's sake, *go*. I can handle myself. Now run." She spun on her heel and disappeared into the mist, leaving Rasim to gape after her, shaken and shaking. Kisia took three running steps herself, then realized Rasim wasn't with her and came back to grab his elbow firmly.

"Come on, Rasim. Let's move."

"But—but how...you...?"

"Later," Kisia said. "When we're safely aboard the *Wafiya*."

"The *Wafiya*? But the crew...?"

Hassin flashed a smile toward him. "Mostly safe. Now come on, Rasim. We need to escape in the chaos."

A thud of relief slammed through Rasim so hard he could barely breathe. His whole body felt watery, and he couldn't quite get his legs moving. He knew he was crying again, but the tears spilled over a huge smile that wouldn't go away.

Everybody—or mostly everybody—was safe. Kisia and Desimi were here, somehow. Hassin was no longer in chains. Rasim didn't understand what had happened, but he didn't care. Somehow, almost magically from his perspective, they had survived. Things had gone right. He wanted to hug everyone. He wanted to sit down and cry. He wanted to throw up. He didn't know what to do with all of that, so he tried taking another step on his watery, wobbly legs, and this time, managed.

That was wonderful, too, and all of a sudden he was sure he could run. He could run forever, if he had to. If that's what it took to get away, that's exactly what he would do.

Lorens crouched beside Bayar, putting him a little below the small boy's height, and spoke in careful Shenryalan. Surprise crossed Bayar's face and he answered in the same language, then nodded. The prince turned away from him and Bayar scrambled up on his back to be carried. "I prefer horses," he said in Ilyaran, "but a Northern prince will do, under the circumstances."

The Ilyarans all laughed, big startled sounds. Lorens flashed a grin over his shoulder, then broke into a ground-eating trot that led them toward the water-logged gates. Kisia grabbed Rasim's hand and dragged him along, which was good, because his legs didn't work as well as he'd hoped, after all. Kisia's hand was so warm and *real* in his. Rasim thought maybe he hadn't really ever expected to see her again, and squeezed her fingers.

She gave him a bright-eyed smile that said she was as glad as he was, and Karluk, scurrying along at Rasim's side, breathed, "This is familiar."

Rasim gave a fast, high laugh. Truthfully, their exit

from the arena a few nights earlier had been orderly and sedate, compared to the madness around them now. The bewitched water didn't simply drop its passengers at the gate. It carried them into the streets and out of sight. Rasim suddenly imagined the water carrying them straight home, and wondered how the house slaves would react to their masters being deposited rudely in the gardens. Would they help them, or seize their opportunity to escape?

At a glance, many were clearly taking the chance to throw off their chains. The streets were filled with slaves clutching children or partners, as they ran away to anywhere but where they were. Some had found ways to cast off their collars, while others still wore them, and many, of course, couldn't escape the tattooed thorns that weighed around their shoulders. But there was a sense of jubilance amongst them that hadn't been present a few nights earlier. Then, uncertainty had tamped the hope. Now, after the second witchery-based rebellion in a handful of days, those who were running seemed to have the strength of conviction with them. They moved as though they had a real chance for freedom. Rasim understood how they felt: jubilant, amazed, disbelieving, excited—it all seemed to fill him, making it hard to breathe. Or maybe that was just the running, but he thought it was both, maybe. He wondered suddenly how many of the escaped slaves might turn toward Ilyara, once they escaped Moran's valley. Ilyara could well seem like the only safe place on the continent for those who had once worn slave chains.

Violence broke out in places. As Kisia pulled him along, Rasim caught glimpses of water-walls shooting up between antagonists, protecting former masters as well as former slaves. Occasionally, when the surprise of a watery interference wasn't enough to slow them, whole streams would open up, sweeping the opponents out of one another's reaches. "Where's all the water coming from?"

Kisia flashed Rasim another smile as they darted down a dry street. "Prince Lorens bought three stone witches. They opened up fissures to the water table without breaking the city apart. It worked, but the river is way down." Somewhere behind them, an explosion rocked the streets, throwing them all forward. Kisia lost her grip on him, and Rasim fell. He flipped onto his backside, trying to see what had happened while trying to get up.

Desimi appeared and hauled him to his feet. "You can look at the wreckage later. Run."

"I don't want any wreckage!"

The exasperation on Desimi's face made him seem forty, not thirteen. He didn't answer other than to push Rasim along. They hurried down another street, and suddenly seemed to be at the leading edge of chaos and change. People here weren't panicked yet, or fighting one another. They were shouting and pointing, curiosity clear in their voices, but the worst of the rebellion hadn't reached them. Faced with half a dozen foreigners running full bore down the street, the Moranese fell back in surprise. Someone would buy them drinks in exchange for hearing that story, later,

Rasim thought wildly. Assuming there was anywhere left in Moran to buy a drink, by morning. He hoped he wouldn't be there to find out. He was getting a stitch in his side, but tried to breathe around it. Lorens was carrying somebody else, and not complaining about it. Rasim could manage running with a stitch in his side. Besides, it wasn't too much farther to the docks. He told himself that with every step, and was grateful for a few minutes of relatively empty streets to run through.

So was Kisia, who said, "Maybe we'll make it," on short breaths. Desimi, who seemed less winded than either Kisia or Rasim, snorted. "Sure. Just as long as we don't have to run straight to the docks where the entire Moranese guard will be waiting for us. Oh, *wait...*"

Karluk looked at them both as if they were—well, journeymen, Rasim thought, or worse, apprentices. He laughed, which made Karluk include him in the next glance of adult exasperation, which he then shared with Hassin. To Rasim's delight, Hassin only shrugged and smiled, not taking the Skymaster's side of things. Karluk glanced at Lorens for support, but the prince had surged ahead, moving surprisingly fast for a man with someone on his back.

For a moment it felt like Kisia was right, and they would make it to the docks easily. Rasim caught a glimpse of the beggar woman he'd seen that morning— had it only been that morning?—who was now perched on a half-wall, gaping openly at the water and people in the streets. "We're almost there. Can we help her—?"

Karluk barked, "We can't help everyone, boy!"

Rasim, suddenly flushed with anger, came to a

complete stop in the middle of the street. "What if I'd said that about your family?"

"Then you'd be dead now, boy," Karluk said through his teeth. "Now run."

Rasim thrust a finger toward the beggar woman. "Tell her! Tell her if she wants to come to Ilyara, to come with us now!"

"For Siliaria's sake, just do it," Desimi muttered. "He'll stay here all day if you don't."

Karluk, his lip curled, snapped words at the beggar woman, who flinched. Then she drew her feet up under herself even more tightly, staring at the sky witch with suspicion. Karluk threw his hands open at Rasim, as if freeing himself from all further responsibility, and broke into a run again. Rasim cast the woman one more glance, then ran on with his friends, down the street he'd traveled earlier, around the corner that led to the docks.

And ran, as Desimi had predicted, into an army of city guard who stood calf-deep in river water with spears and swords at the ready. Desimi shot a look at Rasim and muttered something under his breath, then, without slowing his run, lifted his hands.

Witchery surged. Water yanked the legs out from under the gathered guards. They fell backwards in coordinated rows, the water pulling them just far enough apart that they didn't land on one another's weapons. Divots formed in the water over their faces, allowing them to breathe, but struggle as they might, they couldn't rise. Desimi said only one, strained word: "*Run!*"

Dozens of the guards were swept to the side, clearing a path straight to the *Wafiya*. Lorens was already halfway up the gangplank with Bayar. Kisia grabbed Rasim's hand, pulling him along, and Sesin dragged Karluk with her. Hassin and Desimi took up the back, with Desimi concentrating on keeping his witchery in place as Hassin guided him through the fallen soldiers. Lorens put Bayar down as soon as they reached the deck, but the Shenryalan boy's golden skin paled as it rocked beneath him. "We are not a sea-faring people."

"Get below," Kisia ordered. Bayar looked around, baffled. Rasim started to point him the right direction, but Sesin released Karluk and seized Rasim's head.

"Sorry, this is probably going to feel awful," she told him almost cheerfully. "And you'll—"

"Wait!"

Sesin froze. "What?"

Rasim collapsed toward her with a hug, burying his face in her shoulder for a few seconds. Sesin caught her breath, then returned the hug just as hard, whispering, "We made it," against his neck. A shudder ran through Rasim, bringing him near to tears again, before he pulled back and gave her his best smile. It wasn't very good, but it was the best he could do, and Sesin's seemed to match. "Right," she said roughly, "that was a good idea. And I'm sorry about this. You'll probably have to pee when I'm done. Kisia, get him water!"

"Wha—?" Witchery rushed through him before he even finished the word, twisting his stomach and his blood. It felt like he was being wrung dry from the inside. It didn't quite hurt, but pain might have been better, because Sesin was right. It felt *awful.* She released him and he lurched to the *Wafiya*'s rail to vomit over its side. When he was done he hung there, unable to stand. Kisia ran over with a water skin and held it for him while he drank while Sesin said, "Well, I thought it would make him pee," to her.

A glad cry erupted behind the healer's apprentice as Karluk's family burst out from below decks and flung themselves into his arms. They fell in a heap on the deck, laughing and crying. Bayar, finally seeing which way 'below' was, edged through a number of sea witches who were standing around on deck beaming at Karluk and his family.

Rasim crushed his eyes shut and blinked hard a few times. His head was spinning, like it was still being wrung out, and the water churned unpleasantly in his stomach, but it seemed like there *were* a lot of people on board. Most of them had their attention on the city, and—he could feel it now—they were working witchery.

The awareness that he could feel their magic sent his stomach into an uproar again and he flipped over to be sick a second time. Kisia stood up, shouting orders, which was ridiculous. She was a journeyman, and if Nasira wasn't here, then Hassin should be giving orders. The crew seemed to be listening, though. Sails rose and the ship began to have the air of being prepared to sail. Footsteps thumped on the gangplank and Rasim rolled his head to see Desimi and Hassin racing on board. Of course. Hassin *hadn't* been there.

Kisia still wasn't the person who should have been giving orders, but then, she'd been giving them in the arena, too. It felt as if something important had happened with Kisia in his absence, something that gave her more authority than expected. Part of Rasim desperately wanted to know what. The rest of him figured those questions could wait until later.

He clutched the rails and pulled himself to sitting again, trying to see what was going on, trying to make sense of the chaos. Lorens was helping to cast off, his earlier experience on the *Wafiya* now proving worthwhile. Sesin crouched to offer Rasim water again, and when he tried to wave it away, shook her head fiercely. "We've got to get the heartbreak out of your system as fast as we can. The whole crew has been working together to do this, but Desimi's been doing the heavy lifting and he's exhausted. We need you. Drink more."

"Sesi, my sea witchery is gone. Mostly gone, anyway. I only have as much as I used to, before Siliaria."

"You still think she *gave* you the power," Sesin said incredulously. "That's nonsense. Drink." She squirted water into his mouth and spoke as he coughed and swallowed it. "You always had the power, Rasim. Kisia's sure of it. She thinks maybe you were never a natural sea witch, so you really struggled with it, but that when you started using other witchery, it started breaking down the limits of your seamastery. But you always had it. And you still do. I just have to get the heartbreak out of you. Drink!"

Rasim drank, unwilling to argue about either the

water or his erratic sea witchery. "What happened after they took me to the arena? How did Kisia and Desimi get here? Why is Kisia in charge?" The water was staying down a little better this time, and he took another drink.

Anguish twisted Sesin's face and she forgot her part of the story to say, "Are you all right, Rasim? When they took you away…."

"I'll be fine." Rasim wasn't really sure about that, but he wanted to understand more than he wanted to count his own woes. "What happened?"

"Well, obviously it all went horribly wrong when they took you to the arena, but the captain had to pretend it was all right, and she made deals to sell some of us, but I thought of making everybody eat a palmful of salt as soon as they could after they were given mindkiller, so we were all sicking it up and mostly not under its control. We've all been carrying salt with us, in our pouches, with Siliaria."

"That was a good idea." Water surged in Rasim's belly and he threw up again, then sank to the deck, panting. "Kisia and Desimi…?"

A brief, bright smile flittered across Sesin's face. "They were in Hongrunn's sewers when the attack happened. When they realized our people were being taken, they swam out and stowed away on the slavers' ship. They're still arguing over whose idea it was, but they agree that they did it because they knew you would take any chance you had to, to rescue your crewmates, so they knew you'd come to Moran and that they'd find you here. And then they thought Nasira had betrayed us all and they stormed the *Wafiya* and nearly arrested her the first night we were in harbor." Sesin's eyes widened at the memory. "It took a *lot* of explaining to talk Kisia down. Do you feel better yet?"

"No." He did, though, and this time reached for the water himself, drinking with more enthusiasm. "What do you need me to do?"

"We don't have any skymasters until we stop for Arrat and his journeymen, so we're going to need a very strong river current." Sesin shut her mouth so fast it made a popping sound as Rasim gave her a rueful smile. "Oh. We do have a skymaster. We have two!"

"One Skymaster," Rasim disagreed, still smiling crookedly. "One apprentice."

"I fought you in the arena," Karluk said unexpectedly. He crouched beside them, Zyterna's fingertips resting on his shoulder, as if she was afraid he might disappear if she released him. "You're more than an apprentice. Healer, I've been given heartbreak, too. I'll submit to that unpleasantry, but I'm not as young as Rasim. I may not recover as quickly."

"How long do we wait for the captain?" Desimi asked from the ship's bow, his voice tight. "I can't hold them much longer."

"Sorry," Sesin said to Karluk. "This is going to feel awful." A moment later, the Skymaster was vomiting over the ship's side, with his children exclaiming gleefully over the sound and contents as it hit the water below. Rasim pulled himself to his feet and wobbled toward Desimi, whose face was ashy with exhausted concentration.

"Hand it over," Rasim said quietly. "I've got it now."

"You sure?" Desimi's voice was strained. "If any of this gets dropped, people are going to die. And I've been trying really hard not to let people die."

A stupid grin etched itself across Rasim's face. "I noticed. Thank you."

"Don't think anything of it," Desimi grated. "I just didn't want to have to look at your disappointed face for the rest of the voyage. Ready?"

"When you are." He'd barely finished speaking when the full weight of Desimi's witchery settled on him, and the other boy tipped backward in a faint.

CHAPTER TWENTY-FOUR

I t was one thing, Rasim decided immediately, to work a massive piece of witchery. It was something else entirely to take over someone else's. He sat abruptly, the weight of Desimi's working too great to stand under. A wobble ran through the magic. Pools of air buckled and splashed water into soldiers' faces, and the streams depositing Moranese masters around the city stumbled and dropped some of them. A dozen crew members picked up the slack, pursuing the goal of subduing Moran without hurting anyone, but Sesin hadn't been wrong: Desimi had been doing most of the heavy lifting, leaving finesse to the others. Rasim was already sweating. "Can't hold it long. Too much. Too fast." He didn't even know if anyone would hear him.

Sesin appeared beside him, checking on Desimi. "You don't have to. Just a few minutes, Rasim. Long enough for your skymaster to get his witchery under control. Then we can bring the water back to the river and—" She glanced away, as if confirming something before continuing. "And then we'll manage the currents. Desimi's all right. Just hold on." She disappeared again, leaving Rasim to dig his nails into the ship's deck and concentrate on holding the witchery until his head pounded with it.

The worst part was that there was some kind of disturbance in the magic, something running counter-current to its flow. He supposed it was Ilyaran slaves under orders from their masters and heading for the docks to stop the *Wafiya* from escaping. It felt like a ship's keel through the magic: a wide, sharp slice disrupting everything it touched. Rasim grabbed at the edges of the witchery left in its wake, trying to hold it together, but it was...

It was like trying to hold water. Rasim almost laughed at how obvious that was, but that was what it felt like. He struggled to hold on, but the power leaked away just like water would, leaving puddles that he couldn't collect again. He knew he was chanting, "I can't, I can't, I can't," through his teeth, but every repetition made him hold on a little longer, like all he wanted to do was prove himself wrong.

The counter-current wasn't just cutting through his witchery anymore. It was collecting the water he'd left behind, shaping it into a force of its own. It was going to slam into them and sink the *Wafiya*, at the rate it was picking up speed. Rasim struggled to his feet, hanging onto the railing and trying to focus on the world as well as the magic. He couldn't: he could barely see beyond the river bank. Everything past it was a blur of witchery and exhaustion and, he feared, the remnants of the heartbreak drug. "Sesi. Sesi. Kisia?"

Kisia was suddenly at his side, working her shoulders under his arm to help hold him up. He felt better instantly, just because of her presence. Just because she was *alive*. "Ship's almost ready to sail, Rasim," she said. "Just another minute."

"No. Too late. Cast off. Shield us." He couldn't think of how to shield the ship, and he didn't know if his broken gasps were even enough to communicate the problem. Or that there *was* a problem. "Hurry."

Kisia whirled away from him, bellowing, "Captain! Cast off! Rasim says to cast off!" In the dizziness that followed her support disappearing, Rasim wondered how Nasira had gotten back without him noticing. But it was Hassin who relayed Kisia's order as his own. Of course. He was the first mate, and with Nasira off-ship, he was captain. Kisia had apparently relinquished her own inexplicable position of command.

The wedge he fought had collected half the water in Moran now. There would be fighting in the streets. There would be soldiers at the docks. Rasim's thoughts were fuzzy, ideas coming to him without connecting to one another. It felt like a long time before he understood why he was worried about those things. When the onslaught of power he was trying to hold the line against hit, it wouldn't go to the trouble of saving the guards who were pinned down just beyond the ship's bow. Rasim spread his feet wide, bracing himself as best he could, and roared with the effort as he swept his hands apart, scattering the pinned soldiers to a safe distance before letting go of the witchery that held them.

No: letting go of *all* of it. He couldn't maintain the water in the streets while he'd moved the soldiers, and all at once, the whole city was flooded. Then the attack he'd been holding at bay came on full bore, a vast wall of water sweeping around the corner he'd come around himself, not very long ago. The ship lurched and Rasim fell forward, clutching feebly at the railing to stay upright. Above him, the sails billowed, filled with wind that hadn't existed seconds earlier. He caught a glimpse of the blonde Northern prince helping to reel the rope before a shout announced the anchor was up.

No current in the world could have moved the *Wafiya* the way it moved then. The river itself, shallow as it had become, surged and lifted the ship from its berth. Rasim's grip wasn't enough to hold him in place, and he fell backward as the river rolled backward, taking the *Wafiya* into its depths. At the same moment, the wedge of rolling water hit the river with a roar.

It crashed along the walled bank, hundreds of feet at a time, filling the river channel with a massive, ship-shaking splash. The water level leaped up in one huge surge, sweeping up and over the other bank—the other bank, Rasim realized, hadn't even been *touched* by the antics on the arena side of the river—and then back down again to rock back across the river. The *Wafiya* pitched and rolled, never in danger of foundering, but the ships still berthed in the docks shuddered and twisted and lurched, some of them submerging under the unexpected waves. Those would be salvageable with a little effort, Rasim thought.

A wedge of water still rolled toward them. Rasim lifted his gaze, trying to gather himself to break it up, and instead saw Nasira al Ilialio gliding serenely along its leading edge like an avatar of the sea goddess herself. A heartbeat later, the foaming wave deposited the captain on deck so neatly that not one drop of water touched the wood. Nasira, striding easily from the water to the captain's deck, called, "Set sail for the Northern Sea," with such casual calm that laughter rolled through the crew.

"Captain on deck, you heard her orders!" Hassin called over the laughter, and the *Wafiya* was under sail long before the tumultuous waters settled. There was almost no protest from shore: the western side of the city was in turmoil and those on the eastern side stood agape along the shore. A few fiery arrows were shot at them, but rivulets of water leaped up and seized them long before they threatened the ship. Rasim got to his feet again, staring woozily at the western city, where smoke arose in places and where fighting was visible and audible in the streets.

Somehow a woman's voice carried above all the noise, shouting something Rasim couldn't understand. Karluk's head turned, though, and he shouted incomprehensibly to Hassin, who shot a look toward shore and then at Rasim. With one quick shake of his head, he broke off from managing the ropes and sent a whirlpool of water skittering across the river's surface. The shouting woman's shouts suddenly turned to screams, and a few seconds later the beggar woman from Moran's streets was deposited, soaking wet and still shrieking, on the deck beside Rasim.

Nasira, from the captain's deck, looked down on her, then turned an expression so neutral that it demanded explanation upon Rasim. "I...invited her to come with us. To be free."

"Of course you did." Nasira's tone matched her expression perfectly. "Fine. She's your responsibility, Journeyman. Try to do a better job with her than you did with Missio."

Rasim, automatically, said, "Aye, Captain," before overwhelming bewilderment caught him and he blurted, "*Captain?*"

Nasira's gaze softened unexpectedly. "I'm sorry for what happened to that big Northerner, lad. We had to change our whole plan when you got hauled off to the arena, and then improvise again after you broke out. We had almost no time to plot before they came for me, and once I was under arrest I couldn't let anything risk what we'd discussed. I couldn't see how to keep our plan going without stopping you from enacting yours. I wish it hadn't cost as much as it did."

Nasira turned away, leaving Rasim to gape at her as Kisia came back to him, twisting her hands in front of her stomach. Rasim transferred his stare to her, then wordlessly grabbed her into a hug and didn't let go for a long time as tears leaked from his eyes. Kisia hugged him back as hard, her face buried in his shoulder until she finally mumbled, "C'mon below. There's food and

Sesin says you need more to drink. We've got a long way to go before we're safe."

"*You're* safe. How..." Rasim's voice broke and he hugged her again, even harder than before. "Sesin said you stowed away?"

Kisia shivered in his arms, then pulled back a step so she could see him as she spoke. "We spent two nights clinging to the bottom of the slavers' ship like barnacles. I wouldn't have made it without Desimi. I still don't feel like I've warmed up. It was better once we were able to crawl on board. Our people knew we were there and kept us hidden, and when we got near Moran we slipped off the ship to try and figure out what to do. Then we saw the *Wafiya* coming in under the slaver flag and watched Nasira sell you, so we made a plan to take the ship back from her and...well, you know the rest."

Rasim gave a hard laugh. "I don't think I know the half of it. Where's Bayar?"

"Bayar? The beautiful Shenryalan boy? Is that his name? He's below."

"Beautiful?"

Kisia blushed. "Well, he is!"

"I know. I just..." Rasim felt vaguely offended somehow, as if Kisia wasn't supposed to notice how handsome the Shenryalan boy was. Which was ridiculous. Rasim noticed pretty girls, after all. Of course Kisia would notice a pretty boy. Frowning uncomfortably, he followed her toward the stairs, then hesitated and looked back at the beggar woman he'd invited on board. He needed Karluk to translate, but Karluk was still guiding the winds that were helping to race the *Wafiya* downstream. Well, at least he'd learned a few words in the arena. "Come with me? We..." He didn't know the words for *have food,* so he gestured, pretending to feed himself.

The woman, with a mixture of suspicion and resignation—she had, after all, chosen to get on the ship—followed them. At the bottom of the stairs, Sesin flew across the hold and hugged him again, almost as hard as Kisia had, then let go with a breathless smile. "I wanted to do that when I wasn't about to make you throw up. I'm glad you're all right. Who is this?"

"This is..." Rasim turned to the woman, then touched his own chest. "Rasim." He pointed at Kisia and Sesin, saying their names, then pointed at the woman. "What's your name?"

"Nikki." The woman spoke with defiance, like she expected them to take her name away.

Rasim almost smiled at the thought, then considered how Karluk's masters had given him a different name, and responded, "Nikki," with more solemnity than he'd expected to. "It's nice to meet you. I'm glad you came with us. You're hungry?" He made the eating gesture again and Nikki nodded warily. "The galley is this way."

Bayar was there already, his head cushioned on his arms as he sat at a table. Beside him lay an untouched bowl of thick chowder and a hunk of bread. The ship's cook frowned at him from the other end of the galley, and started dishing up more food when Rasim and the others came in. "He won't eat."

"No? Bayar, aren't you hungr—" Rasim broke off to stare at the cook with surprise, then let out a shout and vaulted the table to catch the man in a hug. "Drissin! Drissin! You're alive!"

Drissin staggered back, laughing. "Aye, I am. Alive and free, thanks to the *Wafiya*'s crew. I never thought I'd take another free breath when the *Sinaz* went down."

"How? What happened?" Rasim clutched Drissin's arms, grinning so hard his face hurt. Drissin was in his forties, a thin witch whose scraggly beard had been shorn away, just as his Seamaster's braid had been. Rasim knew him by sight, but not well enough to hug him so enthusiastically. At least, not unless he'd survived both a shipwreck and slavery and ended up, through Siliaria's grace, cooking on the *Wafiya*.

Drissin's delight faded into seriousness. "Only a dozen of us survived the serpent attack, and only nine of us made it as far as Moran. None of us thought we'd see freedom again."

"Did we get you all?"

Quick as it had gone, Drissin's smile returned. "Aye, and a few more besides. Turned the city upside down, too, didn't you? Now eat, lad. And see if you can make that one eat." He nodded at Bayar, and began ladling up soup for the others.

Rasim sat beside Bayar, who looked up as he did so. His color was decidedly bad, a sickly green tinge wreaking havoc with his usual golden tones, but he smiled weakly. "Rasim. I was afraid for you, when your big friend fell over. Are you well?"

"I think I'm better than you are. Sesin, I think he's storm-sick. Can you help him?"

"Storm-sick," Kisia said with a laugh as she sat down. "We're not even on the open water yet!"

"Remember poor Milu?" The Stonemaster journeyman had gotten sick just stepping on the *Wafiya*, and not even Seamaster Usia's healing skills had been enough to help him stay well as they'd sailed north. "Usia," Rasim blurted. "Where's Master Usia?"

Kisia gave a short shake of her head. "No one knows." Her tone was so grim that a weight settled in Rasim's stomach, but Kisia threw off the worry with visible effort and added, "He's a master healer. I'm sure he'll be fine. And anyway, Milu is a stone witch. Nobody expects them to be able to sail. Here." Kisia pushed her chowder and bread toward Nikki, who had already finished what she'd been given. The beggar woman looked sharply at each of them, as if fearing the extra food was as in much danger of being snatched away as her name. She began to eat again, still hastily, when Rasim nodded encouragement.

Sesin waggled her fingers at Bayar. "May I?"

"Please." The Shenryalan boy groaned quietly as Sesin worked to sooth the water sloshing in his ears. Rasim felt the whisper of witchery and, heartened, began to eat eagerly. He was exhausted, but his magic was returning, and the *Wafiya's* crew was free. Everything was going to be all right.

A shudder ran through the ship, and Nasira called for all hands on deck.

CHAPTER TWENTY-FIVE

"They're rallying," Hassin reported as Rasim ran on deck. The western side of the river was still in chaos, but on the east, troops were gathering with Ilyaran slaves front and center.

"How many of us do they *have*?" Rasim asked in dismay. There were at least three or four dozen Ilyaran slaves on the eastern bank, and there had been considerably more than that on the western side of the city and in the arena.

Hassin gave a grim shrug. "Matisi had a whole ship's crew to sell, and witches leaving Ilyara to travel don't always come back. Some die, some settle elsewhere, and some..."

Some were enslaved. Rasim's thoughts hung momentarily on those who settled elsewhere, then lurched onward. Moran had enough, at least. They had enough Ilyaran slaves to stop the *Wafiya*'s escape, because they didn't really need numbers. All they needed was power. Rasim reached for his witchery, wanting to do his part to protect the ship, and his eyes crossed with exhaustion. He crushed them shut, cursing. If he couldn't reach his magic, there had to be something else he could do, something he could think of—

He whipped around, searching for Sesin. "Can you do anything from here? Can you clear the mindkiller?"

"They're too far. It's easiest if I touch them—"

"Can you show me how?"

Sesin stared at him a moment. "No. Not fast enough, anyway. But I can teach Kisia. She already understands—" She spun, shouting for Kisia. Rasim's eyebrows drew down in brief offense. If Kisia, who hadn't been a witch for a year yet, could do it, then why couldn't he?

"Because she's the one who'll squeeze a man's heart with the water in his blood," Desimi said from beside him, although Rasim was sure he hadn't spoken aloud. He startled, half glaring first at Desimi, then at the hold door the bigger boy had appeared from. Then relief swept him and he gave Desimi a quick, hard hug. Desimi muttered and shoved him away, obviously not entirely displeased. "Good to see you too, Sunburn."

"Worst nickname ever," Rasim breathed. "You look awful, Desi."

The big journeyman did, too: the red undertones to his skin were bleached from exhaustion and left him a shade closer to Rasim's own lighter brown. "Thanks. If the captain hadn't said all hands..."

"She probably didn't mean all hands who were

verging on fainting after lifting a river out of its bed," Rasim pointed out.

"You should talk. You're about the color of a bottom fish."

"So are you. That was amazing sea witchery, Desimi."

"I had a lot to live up to. Look." Desimi leaned on the hold door, clearly unable to do more than that. Rasim, who had barely enough strength to stand himself, sympathized. But he looked where Desimi pointed, and saw Sesin and Kisia in spirited discussions. Without warning, they dove over the ship's side. Hassin and several others ran to flank them. In a moment there were a dozen witches in the water, swimming forward at a ferocious rate, like dolphins. Lorens flung himself against the ship's rail, gaping, and Desimi's voice shot up. "What are they *doing*?"

"They only have to clear the sea witches of the mindkiller," Rasim whispered. His head hurt suddenly, as if he'd taken an unnoticed blow. "If they can clear them and teach a few more how to purge it, then those ones can start freeing the others."

"They're going to get *killed*!"

"Yeah. They might. But if they don't try we're all going to go down with the ship." Rasim swayed, help- less, as the *Wafiya* plunged and wrenched in waters normally too calm to be noticed. The crew were doing their best to keep it level, but storms, at least, had a certain terrible predictability. Dozens of enslaved witches all pulling in different directions made unex- pected pits in the water, leaving the crew unable to guess where trouble might strike next. "Hassin and the others will keep them safe."

Hassin *had* to, Rasim thought. *Had* to, because Rasim couldn't do anything. He kept trying: his hands kept lifting, and he kept trying to command the water, but his ability ended at his fingertips. He could *feel* all the power being used, and knew he wasn't numbed to it again. He was just too tired. Taking up Desimi's working so quickly after getting the heartbreak out of his system had simply been more than he could handle. He needed time to recover.

Desimi growled. "Is this what it used to feel like to be you all the time?"

Rasim glanced at him to see that he, too, was fumbling and failing with his witchery. "Pretty much, yes."

"No wonder you had to be clever. This is—"

"Frustrating," Rasim said with a faint smile. "At least it's only temporary."

"Unless we all die here!"

"I've gotten out of worse."

Desimi gave him a side-eyed glare that Rasim shrugged off with nonchalance he didn't feel. He wasn't certain he *had* gotten out of worse, but it wouldn't help to say that. He'd gotten out of just-about-as-bad, at least, including being chained in an arena on the verge of losing his head. A shipload of witches could get them out of this.

He whispered, "Probably," under his breath, then straightened with hope. "Look, they reached the first of them—what?!"

Desimi burst out laughing as Kisia and Sesin, powered by witchery, leaped gracefully from the water, grabbed two enslaved witches each, and simply pulled them off the thick seawalls and into the river. The soldiers holding their chains let go in alarm, effectively setting them free, but the freedom was endangered as arrows rained into the water. Blood rose and Desimi's laughter cut off. Rasim's stomach twisted and his body went cold, but after a few seconds another of the crew leaped out of the water with the stricken witch and deposited him on the *Wafiya*'s deck. One of the slaves, with an arrow in his shoulder.

Rasim blushed with shame at his relief. He shouldn't be glad someone else had been struck by an arrow instead of his crewmates. The ship pitched again, sending the slave rolling. Rasim and Desimi both scrambled for him, and together heaved the stricken man out of the crew's way. He was tall but thin, with shoulders that said his slenderness was from a lack of food, rather than a naturally slim build. His eyes and teeth were clenched shut, but he hadn't screamed when he'd been thrown. Rasim was impressed.

"Help me roll him onto his side," Desimi ordered. "Let me see how the arrow...it's a clean shot, all the way through. Rasim, can you break—no, of course you can't, you're about as strong as a drink of water."

"Hey!"

"Am I wrong? You're all right," Desimi informed the man. "What's your name?"

"...Cindu?" The man spoke as if he barely remembered his name.

Desimi flashed an unexpected and reassuring smile. "A stonemaster, eh? Well, Cindu, in a minute our healer is going to come get this arrow out of you—" In the middle of his sentence, he snapped the fletchings off the arrow and shoved the whole thing through Cindu's shoulder, freeing it.

Cindu did scream that time, which didn't surprise Rasim. Rasim *also* screamed, or at least shouted in horror, but Desimi was already packing clean cloth against Cindu's shoulder. "Sorry," he said without any real remorse. "Our healer is one of the ones who grabbed you, so she can't help right now, and you'll be more comfortable lying down below with that thing out of your shoulder. Rasim, can you help him down the stairs?" Desimi finished tying off the makeshift bandage with a few quick, efficient knots, and looked expectantly at Rasim.

Rasim, bemused, helped Cindu up, taking most of the man's weight to help him toward the hold door. At it, he looked back at Desimi, who was winding more stretches of cloth into place. "What are you going to do?"

"Help the injured," Desimi said as if he always did that sort of thing. "Get him comfortable and get back up here. I think they're going to need us." Even as he spoke, another witch was tossed onto the deck. Prince Lorens ran to help Desimi, and Rasim had a brief glimpse of fighting on shore before the *Wafiya* dipped and sent him stumbling down the stairs with Cindu.

The stone witch was sweating with pain as they hit the deck below. "This is the flagship," he whispered hoarsely. His Ilyaran was accented, like he'd almost forgotten how to speak it. "The *Wafiya*? Queen Anaish has sent it? And we're free? I'm free?"

Rasim breathed, "Gods," and got Cindu to his feet, guiding him to the berths. "It's the flagship, aye, but Anaish died years ago. It's her nephew Taishm on the throne now, and...we kind of sent ourselves. Lie down. Rest. You're free, yes, and we'll be clear of the city soon and you'll be safe. We all will be." He offered the most encouraging smile he could as he helped Cindu into a hammock, then spun and ran for the deck again.

There were fewer Ilyaran slaves on the river bank now, and more arrows and slings being used. Most of the arrows were going into the water, trying to pierce the swimming witches. Rasim saw fast, short currents zip around the witches to catch arrows and whisk them away. Spears hit the water with more force, and of the witches who had been brought to the *Wafiya*'s deck, two were mildly injured with arrow strikes. A third lay with her fingers wrapped around the spear that had caught her in the belly. Desimi left her alone, rightfully judging her injury to be more than he could manage. If Sesin didn't get back to the ship soon, the woman would probably die.

It wasn't clear whether the free Ilyarans were winning or not. The *Wafiya* was farther down the river than it had been, but they had a long way to go to reach safety, and the Moranese guards were still gathering on the broad seawalls. The *Wafiya*'s crew might be over-whelmed by numbers before they escaped. A few brave Moranese had even gone into the water to try catching the raiding sea witches, although that wasn't going well for them. Those who remained on the river walls were faring better with their arrows and spears and slings. Rasim couldn't see Kisia in the water, and clenched with fear every time a weapon slashed the waves.

On the captain's deck, Nasira roared suddenly, an excess of sound that was coupled with a tremendous surge of river water. She was powerful, of course. Everyone who made captain in the guild was. Now she brought her strength to bear.

What she was doing started farther away than Rasim expected, far up-river, where it began to gather speed. When it boiled around the seawall-lined bends toward them, Rasim understood. The momentum of her enormous effort would wipe out the smaller magic being worked by the uncoordinated enslaved witches.

And it did, crashing into their power with the relentlessness of the tide. The *Wafiya*'s own witches, caught in the surge, surfaced with splutters of astonishment and raced to board the ship again. Kisia swung over the railing, soaking wet and unable to decide if she was offended or delighted. Sesin came aboard dragging a miserable-looking, chained Ilyaran with her, as did two or three of the others. Hassin arrived with two non-Ilyaran slaves, one of whom flung himself into Hassin's arms and kissed him as he realized his freedom was at hand. Hassin blinked, startled, and then gave him a quick embrace.

Nasira's witchery faded as quickly as it had come, but the ship had surged well ahead, and the crew kept it going. The captain's intent gaze gauged the upcoming shore, where the river's walls gradually changed to earth, and then, the distance they'd traveled. Rasim could all but see her gathering breath to announce they were safe. Pride flooded Rasim's chest. They had succeeded, and everyone had been careful to cause as little loss as life as possible. It was as good an outcome as he could have hoped for. He gathered his own breath to lead the cheers after Nasira spoke—

—and found himself holding that breath in surprise as, behind them, the thick river walls began to crumble.

For a few seconds it seemed as if an earthquake had caught the city, but only the eastern bank began to fall, at first. The walls disintegrated in chunks, breaking along mortar lines and then coming in bigger blocks that cast dust into the air. It happened almost impossibly fast, with a rumble that shook the city.

No: it did far more than *shake* the city. The eastern half of Moran began to slide toward the water, without the river walls to shore it up. Rasim gaped in horror as soldiers and slaves alike sank into stone-filled water and didn't rise again, and as houses began to chase after them. Huge swaths of land slipped and fell, until on the eastern side of the river there were houses hanging half off the ground, dangling above the water. A woman in one of the houses pulled a man to safety before they both stood at the edge of broken brick and wood, looking down in disbelief.

The *Wafiya*'s crew went into the water without orders, trying to save the bystanders who were being pulled down. They deposited dozens of people on shore with their witchery, and some, they brought to the *Wafiya*, just because it was closer. Sesin, already frantically trying to save the sailor who had been stabbed earlier, sobbed with her inability to help everyone.

Another rumble sounded, signalling disaster elsewhere. Rasim turned to see the western shore starting to collapse with equal speed and devastation. Only a few feet away from him, Cindu, the stone witch, leaned on the hold door with his injured shoulder, with a terrible smile of triumph etched across his features. He held his free arm outstretched, clutching and tearing with each gesture, and with each one, more of the city fell into the river. He sweated from effort, but his incredible power tore at Moran without remorse.

Rasim howled and tackled him, almost glad that Cindu landed on his injured shoulder. The stonemaster's witchery cut off, but his smile didn't fade. "I've waited *twenty-seven years* for the chance to do that. The river walls, so badly constructed, riddled with sewer holes...I always thought, if I had the chance, if I had my freedom—! And you softened the city up with your escape..." Even lying down, he stretched his uninjured arm out, clearly ready to call witchery again.

Rasim made a fist and clobbered him with all the strength he could muster. Cindu's eyes crossed and Rasim lurched to his feet, choking on sobs as he turned to Nasira. "He killed people, Captain. He killed all those people!"

"What would you have me do, Journeyman?" The captain's voice was strangely clear in the uproar. "Will I turn the ship back so we can help? Will I hand him over to the Moranese Council to do with as they please, not knowing if he might regain consciousness and finish the job before they're able to constrain him? Will I take him with us, and hope *we* aren't condemned by his actions?"

Rasim stared at her, disbelief pushing through his horror. "You can't...I can't decide that!"

"No," Nasira said, almost gently. "The decision isn't yours, in the end. But what *would* you have me do, Rasim? What would *you* have me do?"

Rasim turned a bleak gaze onto the flooding, debris-littered river. No one was fighting anymore. Everybody, Ilyarans and Moranese alike, were trying to get people to safety. But the *Wafiya* was pulling away from the city's center. A few moments longer and they would be safe.

Safe, not just from whatever condemnation Cindu had earned for them, but what they'd earned for themselves with their rebellion at the arena, and in the streets. They wouldn't be enslaved, if they went back. They would be put to death, all of them. Everything they had done would be for nothing. No one would have gained their freedom. Agnet would have died for no reason at all. Rasim's heart hurt at the idea.

But if they simply left, Moran would absolutely bring war to Ilyara. They might not—they *might* not—if they were given vengeance for the destruction of their city. If Nasira gave them Cindu. If she condemned him, and him alone, to certain death for what they had all done, and for the singular damage he specifically had wrought. Cindu's death might save the rest of them.

Uncertainty clutched Rasim. What Cindu had done was wrong, but...what had been done to *him* was wrong, too. He stared helplessly at the captain, paralyzed by uncertainty.

"Lorens." Nasira's voice was still overwhelmingly clear and soft, as if she and Rasim were the only two people in the world, but somehow the Northern prince heard her and came to her side. "Have you any of the heartbreak, Lorens?"

"I do." The prince's answer was no louder, but every bit as clear as Nasira's own.

The captain nodded. "Administer it to Cindu."

"Captain—" Rasim's voice broke and he fell silent, not even knowing what he wanted to say. Lorens took a small black leather pouch from a pocket, knelt beside Cindu, flipped him on his back, and tipped his head to pour a dusty drug between his lips. The half-conscious man swallowed, coughed, then turned onto his belly again, coughing harder and trying to spit the stuff out. Lorens caught him with a quick, fluid motion, and poured more of the drug into his palm. Then he clapped his hand over Cindu's open mouth, throwing the drug down his throat, and forced his jaw shut.

"This will go easier on you if you comply," Lorens growled. "Swallow."

Cindu, wild with fury, struggled, but eventually had to swallow the mouthful that Lorens had given him. Lorens studied him momentarily, then pulled him up with one fist and hit him much, much harder than Rasim could ever have hoped to. Cindu's eyes rolled back and he sagged into a more profound uncon-sciousness than before.

"Captain," Rasim said again, and this time Nasira looked at him. "Someone on board should take a dose of that heartbreak," Rasim whispered. "I'd do it, but it doesn't work on me. Or it didn't, until I took three doses...."

A glimmer of hurt resignation slid through Lorens's gaze. He stood, dusting himself off, then dangled the pouch from one hand. "You still don't quite trust me?"

Rasim responded with a tight, unhappy smile. "I want to. You keep helping. But you also keep being the one who is going to get away free and clear even if the rest of us don't."

"Kisia!" Nasira's voice cracked through the air, and suddenly Rasim realized that the ship was all but standing still in the raging, debris-filled river. Wind howled around them, terribly loud as it carried thick dust from the broken city, but all of that had disap-peared from Rasim's awareness as he'd spoken with the captain. Now that he noticed it again, the sound was overwhelming, and the fact that the ship wasn't moving through the current told him how much power Nasira was expending to keep them in place.

Kisia appeared from below-decks, her brown skin as pale as it could be, from tiredness. "Captain?"

"I have an unpleasant favor to ask, Journeyman. We need a volunteer to test Prince Lorens's heartbreak."

Kisia's gaze flickered to Rasim, and at his faint nod, returned to Nasira. "I volunteer, Captain."

Lorens sighed and offered Kisia the little black bag.

She opened it, taking a pinch of the drug, and glanced between the adults. "Is this enough?"

"That much won't last long," Lorens said, "but then, it doesn't need to, does it?"

"I guess not." Kisia made a face as she swallowed the pinch, then stood there a few seconds. "How long should it take to work? Oh." Dismay shot over her face. "Oh, no. Oh, that's...it's how I felt before I joined the guild, I guess, except it was normal then, and now it's wrong. I can't feel the water." She extended a hand, obviously trying to use witchery to reach for the frothing river surrounding them, and her eyes widened. "Oh, this is *awful*."

Nasira met Rasim's gaze, her eyebrows elevated as if to ask if he was satisfied. At his nod, she gestured, and a spiral of water rushed on deck to lift Cindu. "Skymaster...Karluk? Is that your name?"

"It is, Captain." Karluk joined them from beyond the companionway, looking pale but sure of himself.

"Skymaster," Nasira said very formally, "I'm sorry to ask so much of you so soon, but will you carry my message to Moran, as I carry this criminal to them?"

"Aye, Captain."

Rasim's stomach clenched again as Nasira spun Cindu off the deck, propelling him at enormous speed back toward the half-fallen city's center. Her words, amplified by Karluk, filled the whole valley as she called, "The destruction of your sea walls and the ruin of your city was not sanctioned by the Ilyaran Guilds. We return the witch responsible to you, to do with as is found appropriate, and we offer our assistance in rebuilding your city." She gestured briefly at Karluk, and the strange quality in the air that said his magic was in play suddenly faded before she added, "Not, however, right now."

A thin smile pulled at the Skymaster's mouth. "No, not right now. We had better run, right now."

Nasira's nod was almost a waver. The *Wafiya* shuddered, as if the immense power she used to both hold the ship in place and send Cindu back to the Moranese taxed her limits. She said, "Hassin," and the first mate was there, as everyone seemed to be there at no more than the murmur of their name. The whole crew was already helping Nasira hold the ship in place, but Hassin, now at Nasira's side, visibly took on more of the effort, while the captain used the last of her concentration to bring Cindu into the heart of the broken city.

The water wall she carried him with was nothing in comparison to the one they'd dragged over the side of the arena. It was narrow, wide enough only to carry one man, and tall enough to be seen over rooftops, so that the city's survivors would know that Ilyaran magic had, indeed, sent Cindu to Moranese justice.

He was awake by the time Nasira's witchery set him on the ground; Rasim could see, just barely, the shape of him standing in the rushing water, instead of lying in it. It didn't matter. There was nothing he could say, awake or not, that would change his fate.

There was nothing Rasim could say, either, and worse, he wasn't sure if he should have even tried. He pressed his hands over his face as the *Wafiya* began to pick up speed as the crew urged it along the litter-filled river. Cindu should pay for what he'd done to the Moranese city, but then, *someone* should pay for what had happened to Cindu. And no one's death would make anything better, not really. Rasim didn't know what he should think or feel. It was too complicated, too big, and far more than he'd ever wanted to be mixed up in.

An unbelievable roll of thunder shook the air. Rasim looked through his fingers toward the sky, expecting clouds as dark as night. But aside from the rising dust from the city, the sky seemed clear enough. Thunder rumbled again, so violently it seemed even the rapidly-sailing *Wafiya* rattled with it. Rasim lifted his face from his hands, then went cold.

The western shore of Moran was collapsing again. No, not the shore: the whole of the city. Dropping inward, falling at a terrible speed, as if the very stone below it had turned to water. The arena, which wasn't visible from the river, suddenly *became* visible, and as quickly, disappeared in a shattering explosion of dust and sound and power. The river poured into the increasing void, and sea witches yelled their concern as the water level dropped precipitously. Rasim felt the surge of their magic coming together, keeping the *Wafiya* float and racing forward so quickly that its hull shuddered with the speed.

Lorens rushed to the ship's side, staggering with the *Wafiya*'s dip and sway as it raced away from the falling city. He clutched at the rail, trying to keep his balance as his cry of dismay brought others in his wake. Within a few seconds, half the crew was crowded along the railing, watching the utter destruction of Moran.

Wooden houses came apart in splinters, not just on the western side of the river, now, but on both sides, as if the land beneath them simply clenched itself inward, retreating from the surface. Rubble poured through the streets, changing color as river water rushed over it. Everywhere Rasim looked, something terrible was happening: the ground surged or caved away, leaving juts of bedrock that pierced buildings, or grinding walls of rock that turned other structures to paste. He covered his face, then forced himself to look again, as if a city's destruction deserved witness.

Desimi was nearby suddenly, helping the crew keep the ship upright in the madness, and the old beggar woman came up from below and began to scream. The sound was almost lost in the cacophony of the dying city. Sesin was on her feet, tears pouring down her face as she cried, "What's happening? What's *happening?*"

"It's Cindu?" Rasim didn't know who he was asking. The gods, maybe, because there was no way any of his shipmates could answer. But neither could Rasim doubt that it *was* the stone witch, exercising his incredible power despite the heartbreak drug. Or—

Before he could finish the thought, the destruction stopped as quickly as it had started. Or, no: the active destruction came to an end. Rasim didn't know if he *felt* it, or only understood that it had changed, but suddenly there was no new stone witchery being worked, no new devastation being wrought. There didn't need to be anything new: the city kept sliding into the river, into the pits that had opened beneath it, into chaos and devastation. The magnificent houses that had stood along the bank were dust and torn wood now, and fires were beginning to glow orange on both sides of the riverbank.

Rasim's stomach twisted so hard he would have thrown up, if there was anything left in his system to purge. "He's dead." He sounded hollow, even to himself. "Cindu is dead. Somebody killed him, to stop...that." He didn't think his voice carried beyond Nasira and Kisia and Karluk, who still stood near him. The rest of the crew remained pressed at the rails, or scrambled to keep the *Wafiya* rushing forward as the river tried to fill the holes and crevasses that had been opened for it.

The sound of wreckage wouldn't stop. It still rumbled and tore and shattered and slammed the earth and the sky alike, as nature took over where witchery had stopped. It would be hours, maybe days, before Cindu's efforts stopped affecting Moran.

"By the gods," Nasira whispered in horror. "How did he...did the heartbreak not work on him?" She turned a bewildered, almost angry look on Rasim, who shook his head desperately beneath the crushing sound of the city's death.

"I don't know why it didn't work on me at first! I thought maybe it was Missio's drug, but then I thought maybe it's because I can use more than one kind of witchery, and then I thought maybe mindkiller and heartbreak cancel each other out, or maybe—" He faltered. "I don't know!"

"He was really strong, like you are, Rasim," Kisia

whispered. "He pulled down half the seawalls as soon as he was free. Maybe heartbreak just doesn't work on incredibly strong witches without a huge dose. It's not like anybody's ever given Guildmaster Isidri any, have they? What do we *do*?"

Nasira's derisive bark answered the first question, and her nostrils flared, cords standing out in her throat as she met Karluk's eyes as if searching for an answer to the second question.

Or not quite like searching for one, maybe. It was, Rasim thought, like Kisia looking to him to make sure she should take the heartbreak. She had known what she planned to do, then. She had only wanted to be sure someone else agreed with her before acting. That seemed to be the kind of glance Nasira and Karluk shared now, before the captain gave one short, unhappy nod and looked at Rasim. "I want you and that quick-thinking mind of yours belowdecks before I have to be grateful for your wisdom in this particular case, Journeyman. We have to get home," she added grimly. "Ilyara needs to be warned that Moran is coming for blood."

"I am sorry." Bayar, his golden skin still pale from the rough waters, appeared in the causeway door. He looked very small there, framed by the darkness below, but his expression was implacable as he spoke once more in flawless Ilyaran. "I understand the urgency of your return to Ilyara, but I strongly believe that it would be in all of our best interests if you brought me home, first."

Nasira's gaze landed on Rasim like this was his

fault, but then she rolled her attention back to the Shenryalan boy. "And why is that, young man?"

"Because," Bayar replied calmly, "I am the crown prince of the largest Shenryalan tribe, and it appears that in the Moranese, your people and mine have a common enemy."

For a few seconds everyone stared at Bayar. Then Nasira spun toward Rasim, pointing accusingly at him. He threw his hands up in protest. "I didn't know! How could I know? This isn't my fault!"

"It's not," Bayar agreed, almost smiling. "I have told no one until now. Not even Agnet." The trace of a smile faded, and pain lanced through Rasim's heart.

Nasira was still snapping her gaze between the two young men, black eyes furious with indignation that there was no one to blame. Then, much as Rasim had done, the captain herself threw her hands in the air, yelling, "Fine! By Siliaria's tears and tongue and teeth, *fine*! Set sail for the Northern bloody Sea, and *nobody surprise me again before we get there*!"

With that, the captain stomped belowdecks, and after an exchange of glances, the *Wafiya*'s crew set sail northward.

CONTINUED IN

SUNMASTER, Book IV of the Guildmaster Saga!

ACKNOWLEDGMENTS

All hail Sharon Corbet, Mighty Finder Of Typos, and also Rachel Gollub and Bruce-who-has-a-surname-but-I-can't-remember-it-right-now-sorry, who are also Mighty Finders of Typos but perhaps not quite as many as Sharon. You early proofreaders help more than you can possibly know, and I thank you from the bottom of my heart.

My editor KB Spangler has made what was a good book into a much better one. You're a star.

Cover artist Aleksandar Sortirovski has created an absolutely beautiful piece of art for this book, and I am so, so happy with it. Cover designer Tara O'Shea has improved upon my attempts, and I wiggle with glee, thusly: *wiggle*!

And finally, of course, all my love and thanks to my family: to Ted for agreeing me getting an out-of-house office during the pandemic was a good idea, for my dad, who babysits, and for my son, who is now just about the same age my eldest nibling was when I thought I would *finish* this series. If I take much longer with the last book, this is gonna turn into a whole generational thing, but I'll try to do better than that. <3

ABOUT THE AUTHOR

CE Murphy began writing around age six, when she submitted three poems to a school publication. The teacher producing the magazine selected (inevitably) the one she thought was by far the worst, but also told her–a six year old kid–to keep writing, which she has.

She has also held the usual grab-bag of jobs usually seen in an authorial biography, including public library volunteer (at ages 9 and 10; it's clear she was doomed to a career involving books), archival assistant, cannery worker, and web designer. Writing books is better.

She was born and raised in Alaska, and now lives with her family in her ancestral homeland of Ireland.

You can find her online at CatieMurphy.com.